Sex with Strangers
A Black Lace erotic short-story collection

Look out for other themed Black Lace short-story collections

Already Published: *Sex in the Office, Sex on Holiday, Sex in Uniform, Sex in the Kitchen, Sex on the Move, Sex and Music, Sex and Shopping, Sex in Public*

Published August 07: *Black Lace – Paranormal Erotica* (short-stories and fantasies)

Sex with Strangers

A Black Lace erotic short-story collection

Edited by Lindsay Gordon

Black Lace stories contain sexual fantasies.
In real life, always practise safe sex.

This edition published in 2007 by
Black Lace
Thames Wharf Studios
Rainville Road
London W6 9HA

Mind the Gap	© Mae Nixon
The Art of Fucking	© Nikki Magennis
Lust for Glory	© Mathilde Madden
A Stranger, and Yet Not	© Teresa Noelle Roberts
Barely Grasped Pictures	© Olivia Knight
Behind the Masque	© Sophie Mouette
A Whole New City	© Nikki Magennis
The Highest Bidder	© Sarah J. Husch
Wet Walls	© Kristina Lloyd
Perks of the Job	© Jan Bolton
Reflections	© Maddie Mackeown
Stag Hunt	© Elizabeth Coldwell
Vacation	© A. D. R. Forte
Fish	© Stella Black

Typeset by SetSystems Limited, Saffron Walden, Essex

Printed and bound by Mackays of Chatham PLC

The paper used in this book is a natural, recyclable product made
from wood grown in sustainable forests. The manufacturing process
conforms to the regulations of the country of origin.

ISBN 978 0 352 34105 1

Contents

Newsletter

Want to write short stories for Black Lace?

Please read the following. And keep checking our website for information on future editions.

- Your short story should be 4,000–6,000 words long and not published anywhere in the world – websites excepted.
- Thematically, it should be written with the Black Lace guidelines in mind.
- Ideally there should be a 'sting in the tale' and an element of dramatic tension, with oodles of erotic build-up.
- The story should be about more than 'some people having sex' – we want great characterisation too.
- Keep the explicit anatomical stuff to an absolute minimum.

We are obliged to select stories that are technically faultless and vibrant and original – as well as fitting in with the tone of the series: upbeat, dynamic, accent on pleasure etc. Our anthologies are a flagship for the series. We pride ourselves on selecting only the best-written erotica from the UK and USA. The key words are: diversity, surprises and faultless writing.

Competition rules will apply to short stories: you will hear back from us about your story *only* if it has been successful. We cannot give individual feedback on

short stories as we receive far too many for this to be possible.

For future collections check the Black Lace website.

If you want to find out more about Black Lace, check our website, where you will find our author guidelines and more information about short stories. It's at www.black-lace-books.com

Alternatively, send a large SAE with a first-class British stamp to:

Black Lace Guidelines
Virgin Books Ltd
Thames Wharf Studios
Rainville Road
London W6 9HA

Mind the Gap Mae Nixon

If I hadn't worked late that night and if I hadn't wasted
five minutes going through my bag in the ticket hall
looking for my Oyster card, I'd never have caught that
particular train.

Looking back it's hard to believe it was all the result
of nothing more significant than chance and circum-
stance. But it's often like that, isn't it? We like to think
we're in control of our own destinies but sometimes it
just depends on being in the right place at the right time.

I'd got my job that way; I'd sent out literally hundreds
of CVs after I graduated but it was walking into an
employment agency to register at precisely the same
moment as a new company had phoned asking for a
trainee that had finally got me off the dole.

And I'd only taken business studies in the first place
because my A levels weren't quite good enough for me
to do the course I'd planned. But the funny thing was,
I'd loved it. It turned out to be what I was born to do
and I'd never have known it if I'd done better in my
exams. Was it luck or fate? I'll never know but it's funny
how chance often leads us somewhere we seem destined
to go. And that's exactly how I feel about that night.
Utterly random, yet utterly magical.

The brightly lit tunnels and escalators were eerie and
empty. The clip-clop of my heels echoed as I walked. I
heard the whoosh of a train arriving and I ran down the
steps to the platform as the doors began to close. I
jumped on, just managing to squeeze through the gap
in time.

As the doors slammed shut I realised I hadn't even checked that it was a District Line train and, for all I knew, I'd be ending up in Heathrow or Uxbridge. I looked up at the display and saw the familiar list of stations. I heaved a sigh of relief and sat down.

The carriage looked like a twenty-first century version of the *Mary Celeste*. The seats were littered with abandoned newspapers and food wrappings – detritus of the day. As I looked around I noticed another passenger sitting at the far end of the compartment. A young man in a raincoat, his laptop bag on the seat beside him. He was sprawled back in his seat with his arms folded and his eyes closed.

I'd assumed I was alone on the train. I didn't like travelling late at night; everyone knew there were muggings and worse on the Tube after dark. For a moment I considered moving into the next compartment. But the man seemed harmless enough. Just another office worker on the way home after working late.

We stopped at a station but nobody got on. My travelling companion never stirred. He just sat there, lying back in his seat, seemingly asleep. I wondered how he could sleep through all that juddering and rattling.

As I looked at him lying there I gradually realised that he was actually rather handsome. Short dark hair, masculine jaw and just the hint of a five o'clock shadow. And I'd always had a thing for men in suits. They seemed so archetypically male, designed to emphasise a manly figure and cut to create that illusion even if nature hasn't made him that way.

But nature had done a good job on my fellow traveller and his broad shoulders owed nothing to padding. He'd loosened the knot of his tie and undone his top button as if the formality of the day was an unwelcome restriction. But rather than ruining the effect of the suit, somehow it had made him look all the more masculine, bringing a rough edge to the formality of his appearance.

I was staring, I knew, taking advantage of his closed eyes to drink in every detail. His lips were unusually full for a man, softening what might otherwise have been a harshly masculine face. And his expression seemed gentle and somehow vulnerable.

The effect reminded me of Clive Owen, my favourite actor, who somehow manages to embody a dangerous combination of strength and sensitivity that I've never been able to resist. I've sat through several terrible movies just because Clive was in them, and no matter how dire the script or how slow the plot he's always guaranteed to make my nipples harden and my knickers grow damp.

As I sat there looking at the young man I realised he was having exactly the same effect on me. My heart had begun to beat a little faster and there was a watery shiver of excitement sliding up my spine.

I found myself wondering what he'd look like naked. Were his shoulders as muscular and broad as they seemed? Would his chest be hairy or smooth and was there a six-pack hiding beneath his shirt, hard and sculpted?

I bet his thighs were strong and thick like a rugby player's. I was just thinking about what might lie between those thighs when his eyes snapped open and he looked at me. I felt instantly guilty, like a voyeur caught in the act, but before I even had time to look away he smiled at me. His eyes were chocolate dark and his teeth were even and white. He held my gaze for several long seconds, then his eyelids closed again and I realised I'd been holding my breath.

The train shuddered to a halt and the lights went out. My heart seemed to lurch in my chest. Though I used the Tube regularly I'd never quite conquered my claustrophobia. Being trapped on a train in the dark was the sort of thing I had nightmares about.

It would be over in a few minutes, I told myself, and then I'd be all right. I'd probably even feel foolish for having been so scared. I forced myself to breath deeply, ignoring the sound of blood pounding in my ears.

I couldn't see a thing. I don't think I'd ever been in such a dark place. Outside, even if there were no street-lamps or buildings nearby, there was light from the stars and the moon and after a few minutes you could make out shapes. But down here it was inky black and terrifying.

My heart was thumping and I felt my composure slipping.

'Are you all right? Only you're breathing like a steam train. Try to calm down. I think I've got a pen torch in my bag, I'll see if I can find it.'

I almost leapt out of my skin when I heard the young man's voice and even though his words were reassuring, somehow they made me feel more imprisoned and helpless. I wasn't just trapped, I was trapped with a total stranger.

'I . . . I'm claustrophobic.' I felt ridiculous and ashamed saying it out loud. This sort of thing happened on the underground everyday and I felt childish and melodramatic.

'I understand. Try to stay calm. Let me find that torch.' I heard the rasp of Velcro ripping and then the sound of him rummaging through his bag. 'Here it is.' He turned it on and I could see his face and upper body illuminated from below like a Halloween mask. For a moment I was terrified, then I realised that his face bore an expression of concern and anxiety. He got up and walked down the carriage towards me, pointing the torch's tiny beam at the floor to illuminate a path.

He sat down beside me, plonking his laptop bag down

on the seat. We sat silently for several moments. He held the torch in one hand, pointing it up at the carriage's roof. We sat in the cocoon of dim light.

It had grown hot since the train had stopped and I was growing sweaty and uncomfortable under my clothes. The front of my hair was sticking to my face. The damp sooty smell of the tunnels seeped into the train. I could hear my breathing. It seemed to exist outside of me like the tangible embodiment of my terror.

'Here, you take the torch.' He held it out and I took it. 'I know it's scary but it can't last long. We're quite safe.'

'But how do you know that? Maybe there's been a terrorist attack up ahead and we'll be stuck here for hours. Or maybe it's a city-wide power cut like they had a couple of years ago. It could be anything.'

'Might be a power cut, I agree, but I doubt if it's anything more sinister. I mean, they'd do that in rush hour wouldn't they? Maximum disruption.'

'If you're trying to reassure me you're not doing a very good job.' I felt sick and light-headed.

'Sorry ... But you must try and calm down. Hopefully it won't last long, but we might be here for a while.'

'And you don't want to be stuck with a hysterical woman?'

'No, no, you've got me wrong. You're obviously very distressed. I'm concerned about you.' He was sitting directly beside me, our thighs touching. I held the torch in both hands, a talisman of comfort.

'I feel such a fool. I know it's just a phobia but it doesn't seem to make any difference knowing it's all in my head.'

'There's no need to feel foolish. With me it's spiders. I could sit here in the dark for days but if a spider scuttled across the floor I'd fall to pieces.' He shrugged his shoulders and smiled at me as if embarrassed by his vulnerability.

'Spiders?' I smiled back at him.

'Last week I saw an enormous one at the office and I jumped up onto my desk like a girl. I felt such an idiot. It's a silly phobia I know – they're harmless anyway and you can tread on a spider and problem solved – but I can't help it.'

'It's hard to believe a big macho bloke like you is scared of something so tiny. You look as though you're not frightened of anything.'

He shrugged again. It was a gesture I was already beginning to find charming.

'Well, now you know my secret.' He leant close and whispered. I could feel his warm breath on my face and I just caught a hint of his aftershave. In spite of my anxiety, under my dress my nipples peaked.

'I'd have been at home now if I'd caught my usual train. We've got a very important presentation in the morning so the whole office stayed late. Talk about bad luck.' I was rambling and I knew it, but anything was better than sitting there in terrified silence.

'Me too. We've got a big case on at the moment. I'm a lawyer. I've been working on it for months and it finally comes to court tomorrow. Otherwise I'd have been curled up in bed hours ago.'

The thought of him curled up in bed – even if it wasn't mine – set off another bout of palpitations and this time it wasn't caused by anxiety. Close up he was even more handsome. Even by the weak light from the torch I could see that his skin was smooth and even and had a sort of golden tint to it. His eyes were dark and sparkling and his lips always seemed to be on the edge of a smile.

I couldn't help staring but the funny thing was he didn't seem to mind. He just looked back at me, his big brown eyes examining my face like an explorer taking a claim. You could get lost in his eyes; they seemed to hint at depth and sensitivity and a deep seam of wickedness which was as inviting as it was terrifying. And all the time he was smiling to himself. His full lips were berry dark and shone slightly in the torchlight.

My nipples were rigid and painful and the hairs on the back of my neck were erect and tingling. I was still scared, but it seemed to be fading into the background, overshadowed by the more powerful sensations of arousal.

'Where do you work?' I sensed he'd asked me the first thing that had come into his head, just so he could go on looking at me.

'Collins and Read. It's an advertising agency.' My voice sounded dreamy and far away. I gazed into his eyes.

He laughed. 'Almost as disreputable as my profession.'

The torch went out, plunging us back into total darkness.

'Oh no!' My terror came rushing back, crashing over me like a flood. I felt his hand on my arm, reassuring me.

'It's probably just the batteries. I think I've got some spares in the front pocket of my bag, let me look.'

I heard Velcro rip and the sound of his hand sliding against the fabric as he felt around for the batteries. I took some deep breaths, trying to calm myself. After all, I was in no more danger than I had been a moment ago before the light had gone out.

'Here, I've found them. Give me the torch.'

I handed it over and listened to him fiddling with it, trying to interpret the sounds. I heard the discarded batteries hitting the floor and then metal tapping against metal as he tried to insert the new ones.

'Hurry up, please.' The final word came out in a sibilant rush.

'I can't work out which way they go in. It won't work unless you put them in the right way round. It's fiddly.' Something clattered noisily to the floor. 'Shit!'

'Don't tell me that was the new batteries.'

'One of them anyway, sorry.'

'Maybe I can find it.' I started to bend down but he caught my arm, preventing me.

'Don't bother, it could be anywhere and even if you find it you'll never be able to tell it from the spent ones.'

I sat back in my seat, defeated. 'I felt safe with the light on. I know it didn't really make any difference, but it didn't seem quite so frightening.'

'I understand. But you said yourself it was an illusion. We're perfectly safe and, anyway –' he fumbled for my hand '– I won't let anything happen to you.'

His skin was warm and smooth. His hand was much bigger than mine. Something about their relative sizes made me feel safe and protected.

'Thanks.' I leant against him, pressing my upper arm against his. It was an unconscious gesture, seeking comfort, and it never crossed my mind that it could be misinterpreted. I felt him dip his head and heard him inhaling. He was sniffing my hair.

My heart thumped so hard I was sure he must be able to hear it.

'You smell as beautiful as you look.' He nuzzled his face against my hair.

'You can't see me, how do you know I'm beautiful?' Goose pimples rose on my skin. I was tingling all over.

'I took a good look at you before the lights went out. Just like you did. I caught you looking, remember.' His mouth was close to my ear. I could feel his hot breath on my neck.

'At least the darkness is covering my blushes.' I turned my face towards his.

'I wish I could see that.' He laid his hand on my cheek and brushed the tip of his thumb along my lower lip.

'What are you doing?'

'Finding your lips.' He bent his head and kissed me. His mouth was hot and soft and hungry. Air rushed out of his nostrils, like dragon's breath. I reached out in the dark, running my hands over his raincoat trying to locate the landmarks of his body. I slid one hand between his arm and torso and pulled him close.

My nipples were rigid. My crotch felt hot and liquid. I could feel his heart beating against my chest. His body was hard and muscular and comforting. His big hands slid up and down my spine, making me tingle.

Unable to see, every sensation seemed magnified and intense. The slightest brush of his fingertips elicited a wave of shivery tingles which started at the nape of my neck and slid all the way to my toes.

I could smell soap and deodorant and the individual components of his aftershave: citrus, a woody note and musk. I could smell fabric conditioner on his clothes. Cutting through all that, was the unmistakable scent that was all his own. Earthy, masculine and irresistible.

He stopped kissing me and slid his mouth down my face and onto my neck. I felt his hot wet tongue trailing along my throat. Instantly, goose pimples rose and my nipples prickled with pleasure. I tilted back my head, allowing him access.

I felt his hands at the front of my dress, fumbling for an opening. His clumsy fingers moved between my breasts. I covered his hand with mine and noticed that his was trembling.

'There are buttons all the way down the front, let me.' I undid the buttons, practically ripping them open. One of them pinged off and I heard it hitting the floor. I fiddled with my bra. It was the only one I owned that opened at the front and I couldn't help thinking how fortunate it was that I'd chosen to wear it today.

I took his hand and gently laid it on my bare breast. He let out a soft sigh of appreciation and his fingers instantly found my nipple. It tingled and came to life as he rolled it between finger and thumb. I moaned.

The seat creaked as he moved to take my nipple in his mouth. I gasped at the sudden hot wet intimacy of it. I could smell his hair now: shampoo and hair gel and an undertone of hot skin. I found the back of his head with fumbling fingers and pulled him closer.

He began to nibble, stretching my excited nipple with his teeth, and I arched my back. I could hear blood pounding in my ears. Between my legs I was hot and tight. My skin was alive with pleasure, tingling and sensitive.

He sat up and used both hands to find my face. I could still feel the ghost of his mouth on my nipple. We kissed. His breathing was noisy and erratic. His stubble scratched my lips. His hot breath warmed my skin. Tension throbbed in my belly. My crotch ached.

He ran his hand down the front of my body. He moved it down between my breasts. He cupped the curve of my belly, then slid it down over my crotch. I opened my legs and he stroked the length of my pussy with the tips of his fingers. I sighed. Even through the crotch of my knickers the sensation was intense and incredible. My legs began to tremble.

'Help me to take them off. Stand up.' His voice was urgent and hoarse.

We both stood up and he squatted in front of me and pulled at my knickers. He slid them down my legs.

'If I lift my foot, you should be able to get one side off over my shoe.'

He fiddled with them in the dark until my foot was

free. 'Good, now the other foot.' It took him several seconds to get them off. 'Now sit down on the edge of the seat and open your legs.'

I did as he asked, putting my bottom right at the edge of the seat and using my hands to support myself. I spread my legs, feeling absolutely wanton even though he couldn't see. I felt his fingers on my thighs and instantly my nipples began to tingle. I was uncomfortably hot now. My hair clung to my nape. Sweat prickled in my armpits.

His fingers found my pussy. He ran one fingertip along its length, agonisingly slowly.

'That's so good.' My voice was practically a whisper. I let out a long slow moan as his fingers stroked my lips.

'No hair ... Lovely.' He pulled my lips apart.

'I'm glad you like it.'

I felt his breath on my pussy and, a second later, his mouth. It felt unbelievably hot and as soft as velvet. I was tingling all over. My nipples were hard and prickling with pleasure. Flurries of delicious shivers slid up and down my spine like ghostly fingertips.

He covered my clit with his mouth and flicked it with his tongue. Robbed of my sight, all my other senses were operating in hyperdrive. I could feel tiny differences in pressure as he used different parts of his tongue. The tip felt fluttery and gentle and the flat of his tongue felt strong and powerful. Every tingle and throb seemed intense and overwhelming.

I reached down and laced my fingers through his hair. I rocked my hips, rubbing my crotch against his face. I could hear him panting, feel his fiery breath on my skin. My thigh muscles were quivering. My breathing was noisy and shallow. Tension throbbed in my belly. My crotch was tight with excitement.

I felt a fingertip at my opening. He dabbled it in the

pooled moisture then slid it inside. I gasped as it entered me, slipping past excited nerve endings and muscles. My clit tingled.

He found my G-spot and I practically hit the roof. My arousal cranked up a gear. I was gasping and panting now. Sweat trickled down my body. My chest heaved.

He pressed his fingertip hard against the sensitive spot. My body jolted. I moaned – a long, single note of pleasure and arousal. He sucked on my clit and did it again. The reaction was identical. My crotch burnt with pleasure and sensitivity. Tension built.

His mouth moved away and he began to get up. My hands slid off his head as he got to his feet. I heard clothes rustling and a zip being pulled down, then the seat creaking and shifting as he sat down beside me.

'Straddle my lap. Sit astride me.' His arousal was unmistakable. I reached out, feeling for his erection in the dark. I felt naked hairy thighs, strong and muscular, then slid my hand across to his crotch. He gasped when I touched him and I felt his body shudder.

I gripped the base of his penis, wrapping my fist round it. I could feel the blood and gristle, hard and pumping. It felt thick and hot and silky. I slid my hand along its length, pulling his foreskin once over the helmet and back. I ran my thumb across the swollen glans, spreading the slick pre-come. He moaned.

I wondered what it looked like. Was the tip purple? Was the skin taut and shiny? Were his thighs as muscular and hard as they felt? I bent my head and lapped up the slippery liquid gathered at its eye, tasting the salt. I swallowed him to the root.

My scalp was tingling, like someone touching my hair. My erect nipples burnt. A fist of excitement and tension pulled at the base of my belly.

My nose was buried in his fragrant pubes, my nostrils

filled with his intoxicating man smell. My chin pressed against his balls. I reached down and stroked them, rolling them in their sac. I felt his thighs tremble and he let out a deep guttural moan.

I sat up and clambered over the seat, feeling my way with my hands. He caught my arms and supported me while I got into position. I climbed astride him, my knees either side of his thighs. He scooted forwards and sat on the edge of the seat and I manoeuvred my bottom, positioning myself.

I felt his mouth on my throat and I bent my head to kiss his hair. I reached between us and found his erection. I slid it up and down the length of my wet pussy then held it in place while I lowered my hips.

A tear of sweat trickled down my spine. Wet hair clung to my face. My heart was pounding. I was rigid with anticipation and excitement.

He slid into me millimetre by delicious millimetre. He felt hot and hard and thick, stretching and opening me. My crotch tingled. My skin was alive with pleasure.

I felt his hands sliding under my dress and over my hips. He cupped a buttock in each hand and began to rock his hips. I wrapped my arms round his shoulders and tilted my pelvis, meeting his thrusts. His breath snorted noisily between taut lips. Every so often he'd dip his head and kiss me, nibbling and licking wherever his mouth made contact.

He moved inside me like a piston. I could feel his thigh muscles, taut and hard as he moved. I was wound up with tension. Fire burnt in my belly. My nipples ached.

I moved my hips backwards and forwards, rubbing my clit against his scratchy pubes. He moved inside me, stretching and filling me. The seat underneath my knees was rough and itchy. I gripped handfuls of his raincoat as I held on. I could feel the excitement building towards a peak. I was moaning constantly, panting and sobbing as our bodies moved.

He picked up speed and I matched his rhythm. I ground my crotch against his, exciting my clit, building towards orgasm. His fingers dug into my buttocks, his arm muscles taut and rigid.

He was groaning and panting, animal grunts of pleasure and excitement. I could feel his hair damp against my neck. My nipples rubbed against his clothes, making them tingle.

I reached for his face with one hand and lowered my head to kiss him. He tilted back his head and our lips found each other. His mouth was like soft wet velvet, his lips yielding and hot.

Our hips pumped. My clit rubbed against his pubes. His thighs beneath mine were damp and slippery. My hair fell in my eyes.

I was sobbing and moaning as excitement built. I was close to the edge, riding the luscious, tantalising knife-edge between arousal and release. I rocked my hips, intensifying the friction.

His strokes grew shorter. His fingers dug into me as he pulled me onto him. His groans grew louder and more urgent. His thighs were rigid and trembling. I pressed my body up against his and matched his rhythm.

He gave a final short jab of his hips and I felt him twitch and dance inside me. It was all that was needed to tip me over the edge. I rotated my hips, grinding myself against his crotch.

The tension focused and burst. Sensation overwhelmed me, knocking the breath out of me and making me tremble. Pleasure pumped round my body from the roots of my hair down to my toenails. My muscles were taut and quivering. I was tingling all over.

We clung to each other, gasping and panting. His heart pounded against mine. He was rigid inside me. I moaned and sobbed. Tears ran down my face.

'I can feel you coming for me. Your muscles are gripping me,' he whispered into my ear.

My pulse was racing. My body trembled and shook. Wave after wave of pleasure crashed over me like the tide coming in. I pumped my hips, grinding my crotch against his. He was hot and hard inside me, his thighs muscles taut and straining. The sound of our excited breathing seemed to exist like a separate entity, underlining the excitement.

He held on and rode it out with me, pulling me onto him with his strong hands. It kept on coming, peak after peak. I was breathless and trembling, sweaty and exhausted. I arched my back and howled into the darkness.

When it was over we didn't move. Neither of us spoke. I lay with my head on his shoulder and listened to his breathing return to normal. One hand stroked my hair, the other moved up and down my naked back.

I felt him soften inside me and slither out and I moaned in disappointment. He laughed softly. I sat up and found his face with both hands. I bent my head and kissed him, pressing my body up against his. He wrapped his arms around me tight, as if he never wanted to let me go. I stroked his face as I kissed him, running my fingers over every curve and feature.

'Thank you,' I said finally. 'I'm not scared of the dark any more.' I climbed off his lap and fumbled to fasten the buttons on my dress. I heard him stand up and the rustle of clothing as he pulled up his trousers and zipped up. When he'd finished he sat back down beside me and reached out for my hand.

We sat silently, hand in hand. I leant up against him and rested my head on his shoulder. I must have drifted off for a moment because when the lights flickered back on it woke me up with a jolt. I blinked in the light and shielded my eyes with my hand. A moment later the tannoy clicked on. A voice apologised for the delay, calling it a 'technical fault' and assuring us it was now resolved. The train began to move.

'At last.' I turned to him and smiled.

'I'm sorry for getting carried away. I hope you don't regret it.'

'Of course I don't. How could you think that?'

'I'm glad. Neither do I. But there is something I do regret, now I think of it.' He reached out a hand and brushed my hair off my face.

'What's that?'

'Never getting to see you naked.'

I still don't know why I did it. It was absolutely out of character and something I'd never even have contemplated before that moment. I got to my feet and stood in front of him. I looked into his eyes and slowly began to undo the buttons on my dress.

My fingers were clumsy and disobedient and it took me far longer than usual. He gazed up at me, his beautiful eyes glowing. When I'd finally got them all undone I pushed my dress wide open and unfastened my bra, exposing my breasts. My heart was pounding. I could hardly breathe.

'You're as beautiful as I imagined.' He stood up and pulled off his tie, stuffing it into his raincoat pocket.

The short hairs on my nape instantly became erect when he said that, as his words elicited a wave of shivery tingles over my scalp and face.

He fiddled with his shirt buttons with trembling fingers. When his shirt was undone, he pulled the tails out of his trousers and pushed it open. His chest was sprinkled with dark hairs and his belly was every bit as sculpted and hard as I'd imagined. A trail of hair ran down from his navel and disappeared under his waist-band, leading down to paradise.

My nipples stiffened and my crotch seemed to soften. He undid the button at the top of his fly and lowered the zip. He slid his trousers and underwear down over his hips, slipping in a hand to free himself. He pushed everything down to his knees then straightened up.

His thighs were big and muscular. His cock was thick and already growing hard again. He reached down and slid his foreskin back, exposing the tip. I could see his chest rising and falling as he breathed. His cheeks were flushed. His lips were dark and plump, half smiling. His eyes were glistening and intense. My crotch ached.

We saw lights in the distance and we both hurriedly began to dress. I did up my bra and had only just managed to button my dress when we pulled into Hammersmith station.

'This is my stop.' He fumbled with his shirt buttons. 'I've got to go.' He gripped the front of my coat and pulled me towards him for a kiss. I closed my eyes and wrapped my arms round him. I could feel the bulge of his crotch pressing into me. 'I've got to go.' He got off the train and stood on the platform looking at me.

As the doors closed he reached into his pocket and pulled out my knickers. He brought them to his face and inhaled. The train began to move and I stood there looking back at the platform long after he'd slipped out of sight.

Almost as soon as he'd disappeared from sight I realised I'd forgotten to ask for his phone number. I didn't even know his name.

For a long time afterwards I'd hang around at work longer than necessary waiting for that particular train in the hope of bumping into him again, but it never happened.

It had been almost perfect, when I thought about it. The way sex only ever is in books or fantasies: exciting, loving, hungry and abandoned. Without complications or consequences.

As time went on the memory of it seemed to get somehow transformed and idealised. Like a dream that was perfect, slightly unreal and could never be recaptured.

If it hadn't been for the torn button on my dress and the missing knickers I could almost believe it had never happened. I wondered if he'd hung around in the station hoping to see me again. Or if he kept my knickers in his bedside drawer and took them out from time to time, holding them to his face to drink in my scent. I hoped he did.

Funny thing was, I was never scared after that. Even if the lights went out or the train stopped in the middle of a tunnel all I had to do was close my eyes and remember sitting astride him in the dark, our bodies moving as one and the sound of our breathing filling the train.

I never saw him again but the funny thing was, after a while, I didn't mind. It was part of what made it so special. Two souls coming together at a particular moment in time, sharing something exquisite and unrepeatable and then moving on.

The Art of Fucking
Nikki Magennis

My flatmate couldn't even imagine the desert that was my sex life. She leant back in her chair, swinging her long tanned legs. Sandy's body always seemed to fall beautifully into place – wherever she was, the room would arrange itself round her. She looked like Botticelli's Venus, only with more lipstick.

If Sandy was a classic Italian painting, I was an abstract expressionist mess. As we sat in the sun-filled kitchen, sharing tea and our Sunday hangovers, I compared the two of us.

Not a good idea. My short fingernails were rimmed with dark-blue paint, a perpetual stain which never seemed to scrub off my hands. Sandy's were shining and polished, and just long enough to suggest they'd been raking over a man's back all night long.

They had. The night before, Sandy had scored.

'An absolute raging beast,' she said. 'He fucked like a tornado. I mean howling and screaming all the way.'

In fact, I'd heard the howls of the raging beast and the rattling of Sandy's headboard in the small hours. I'd covered my head with a pillow and tried to block it out. Just another loud reminder of how different Sandy's life was from mine.

I'd lain awake for a few hours, wondering how the hell I'd ended up where I was.

I'd just moved in with Sandy after splitting up with my live-in boyfriend, and was still adjusting to life in a shared flat. Sandy's wild lifestyle and messy habits intimidated me, so I spent most of my time in my studio. It was a dingy building in the wrong end of town; a quiet, cold ten feet square space where I wrestled with my own obsession – painting.

It was a difficult beast, and fickle too. I needed a truckload of expensive and potentially lethal poisonous materials, plenty of uninterrupted solitude and the right kind of light.

North light. You need a flat even light that doesn't splash itself over the canvas or turn orange at the end of the day. A steady source that is never brash and never surprising. It felt like my life was lived in a constant north light. The smells of turpentine, linseed oil and white spirit surrounded me. After a day in the studio I'd be giddy with fumes, the colours of the street outside on the way home would shock me. Nothing I painted could ever compete with the noise and the huge blast of electric reality that confronted me when I stepped out into King Street. I painted big canvases, used strong colours, threw daring shapes into the compositions. It never quite clicked. My life was all about reflecting what I saw, trying to show the huge terror and beauty of the world. But I always felt like I was watching from the sidelines, painting half-hearted pictures of a life not fully lived.

Sandy, by contrast, lived in the eye of a beautiful storm. I'd been amazed at how fast she tore through men. She bedded whichever passing guy caught her fancy, discarded them afterwards like used tissues, moved on to the next one. And I? I was still stuck in the melancholy aftermath of heartbreak, still attached to my ex, unsure of how to change or of exactly what I needed. Knowing I needed something.

'A good fuck', was Sandy's opinion. Inevitably, for a woman who relished every juicy, sticky detail of a one-night stand, her answer to all life's problems was a good fuck. Now, I was a little naïve when it came to loveless encounters. I guess I was a romantic at heart – I liked the slow build-up, the shy smiles and late-night conversations. I liked to feel it was meaningful before I fell into bed with someone. Steady, gradual. Sex like the north light, no surprises and no brief flashes. The smell of love in the air before I joined my body with a man's. I didn't know if I could sleep with someone I didn't love, though it made me feel old-fashioned to say it.

'But who says it's not love?' Sandy threw her hands in the air like she was tossing my morals aside. 'There's a hundred kinds of love out there, honey, a different one for every person you meet. Why not try tasting a little sample of what's possible? A mouthful of fun? An adventure, even. God knows, you could use a little excitement.'

Monday I trooped to the studio as usual, to face the current work in progress. I uncovered the palette. Limited to three colours at the moment – raw umber, Prussian blue, a little squeeze of scarlet. I was working on an interior, a picture of a kitchen. Just a table and chairs, a window, the angles of the walls. Simple, quiet, shadowy. The kind of room you could sit in and be alone with your thoughts. I was working up the background, layering washes of thin paint over each other until the colours merged into a muddy neutral depth. Deepening the shadows. I plugged in my Walkman – I like to listen to something dark while I'm working. Mazzy Star played some haunting guitar chords, and I dipped my brush into the turps. Softened the bristles, rubbed at the squeeze of blue paint till it melted into a liquid pool. Approached the easel and faced the canvas, hand poised over it, ready to make a mark. I saw where the colour needed deepening, and started work.

And then I was joined, hand moving with eye, locked into a space where no one could touch me. Wordless, nothing but the light and the colour and the resinous smells of the studio, music washing straight into me, suffusing me with steel guitar and a voice singing songs I knew so well I didn't even listen to the words. Painting an imagined room, losing myself in a place that didn't exist.

The hand fell on my shoulder like a thunderclap. I jumped so high I knocked the edge of the turps tin with my hand and saw the splash of dirty blue water explode over the floor, the palette, my jeans. I looked up to meet the startled gaze of the guy who'd just touched me. In my ears, some old electro song was still playing, and I felt like I was still locked in the dream state with a stranger intruding rudely into my headspace. He had the grace to look upset – a pale face with blue eyes that were cracked with shock and concern. Delicate lips that were moving fast, forming words I couldn't hear.

'What?' I said, pulling the earphone away. The cold sound of real life rushed against my ear, mixed with the sound of the guy's apology.

'. . . so sorry, I didn't mean to scare you.' His voice was pleasantly rich, that warm woody tone that some Americans have. Sounded like a bass guitar, a good whisky, an autumn day. Sounded male.

'Am I late? I had a bit of trouble finding the place,' he continued, taking off his jacket and looking around for a chair to put it down. I was mildly confused by his actions, but still lost in that dizzy, detached space I get to when I'm painting, and mesmerised also by the sight of him. A tangle of tarry-black curls that was shockingly dark against his white skin. Those perfectly drawn lips, a full Cupid's bow as red as carmine that gave his face a

cruel, tender beauty. His cheekbones sat high and proud.
And the lines of his body – I could see even under the
loose-fit trousers and shirt that he had a sculpted body.
The way he moved. The way he stood, jacket in hand,
letting the clothes hang from his bones with a silent
confidence that suggested that underneath he was hard
and perfect.

'Uh, are we working in here?' he asked, looking a
little confused by my silence. I stared back, trying to
figure it out. His lovely blue eyes narrowed.

'Jo?'

Then it clicked. 'Joe' worked next door. Big photo-
realist charcoals. Young men, mostly. He hired models
from time to time, had the poor bastards pose in the icy
studio space for a tenner an hour. This guy was a stray.
I opened my mouth, to laugh, to tell him his mistake. To
point him in the direction of Joe's space.

Instead, I surprised myself. Perhaps the fumes had
overcome me.

'Yeah.' I nodded. 'We're working in here.'

And that little white lie, I realised afterwards, was where
I crossed the line. I'd stolen Joe's model. I was telling a
stranger to strip for me. Strangely calm, but with a heart
that was hammering like a drum, I watched as he
moved across the space.

Remembering life-drawing etiquette, I shook myself
pulled the curtain across the doorway, and ducked outside for a moment, It's fine to stare at the model while
you're drawing them, but modesty forbids you watch
them undress.

I left a chink. Enough to see my borrowed model
unbutton his shirt and quickly, casually remove it. Skin
like marble, firm and smooth. The form of him, the
curves and the tense swell of his muscles. His low-
slung trousers showed a pair of sharp hip bones, and I

swallowed as he reached down to pop the button, unzip. He pulled down trousers and shorts in one movement, revealing the graceful legs of a dancer and the dark mess of his pubic hair. In the centre nested his long soft cock and the dusky-rose sac of his balls. I couldn't take my eyes off him. Watched his cock swing gently as he piled his clothes on the floor and stood waiting. Hugging himself, rubbing his arms to try and warm himself.

The studio temperature usually hovered around ten degrees – a fucking icebox no matter how warm it was outside.

Clearing my throat, I walked back in and started ferreting around for a sketchbook, a stick of charcoal.

'How do you want me?'

His question could have been entirely innocent, but as I looked at him standing there hugging himself, calmly displaying his full-frontal cock and balls, I thought I saw a faint spark in his expression. The slightest curl of his lip.

'*It only takes eye contact.*' I remembered Sandy's lesson on how to tumble a man.

'*A little smile. That's all. Then it's just a matter of finding out how to cross the distance between you and touch them.*'

Well, I couldn't just march up and grab him. No matter how strokable that gorgeous body looked, I had a charade to keep up.

'Uh, standing, is that OK? One hand on your shoulder, your weight on the right foot. Yeah, that's it.'

I couldn't help it, the way he looked. I couldn't resist recreating the pose of David, the classic stance. A tilt to the hips, the suggestion of vulnerability despite the strength of the body. I was playing with him. But he seemed willing to go along with it. He shifted and relaxed into the pose. He turned his face and showed the sweep of his neck. I could bite into that, I thought, imagining the smell of him – aftershave and soap and the sweet tang of male sweat.

I drew him slowly, pulling the charcoal over the paper like I was stroking the contours of his flesh. Smudging the lines with my finger, I had the sense of running my fingertip along his arm, across his abdomen, down his hipbone. His body hair was sparsely scattered – little tufts under his arms, a trail from his belly button spreading out over his groin. I worked deeper with the charcoal, enjoying the chance to ogle his cock. Keeping my face poker straight. Drinking in his beauty.

The Renaissance artists believed the study of the male form was the highest of arts. As I drew my model's beautiful form, I felt inclined to agree.

I was so absorbed by the task, it was only after half an hour that I noticed the shake in his legs.

'Oh Christ, sorry. Do you want a break?' I said.

He relaxed immediately, shaking his limbs out and slapping at his leg. 'Circulation's gone,' he said, rubbing vigorously.

The sound was like charcoal scribbling over paper, and it made me want to feel his hands on my body with the same friction.

'Pins and needles,' he said. 'Fuckin' cold in here, too.'

'I don't really notice it any more,' I said.

'No, you're totally absorbed. Can I have a look?'

I blushed. I actually blushed. Showing someone how you see them naked is a tricky moment. Still, I couldn't refuse. I stepped back, and let him walk round to see the sketches on the easel. Now we were close. The gap between us, as Sandy described it, was very small. I stood as still as I could. My hands were black with charcoal dust.

He nodded, and looked at me thoughtfully, like he was appraising me. 'Beautiful drawing. You have a mark –' He reached up to rub at my cheek. Let his thumb push down to my mouth. Held my chin and tilted my face up. Leant over, brought his face closer to mine, his eyes glittering and his mouth open, hot breath on my skin.

The distance reduced to zero and his mouth was on me, wet lips covering mine in a warm shock. All of a sudden the cold tension of the studio was flooded with sensation – the quiet northern light was eclipsed by the movement of this man against me, his hot human aliveness crashing into my world, encircling me, gripping me in those naked marble-smooth arms. Everything was dark, but dark in the way of flesh, with a heartbeat and a pulse and the vivid animal sounds filling my ears.

I didn't pull away, and I didn't miss the smell of love in the air. Instead, I felt the delicious surprise of an unfamiliar man kissing me, and the want and the need to feel him closer yet. Michelangelo always said the sculpture was already in the stone, and he just had to work out how to find it. When the model kissed me, it felt like he'd found a new image of me, of what I could be. Like he'd dug out the long-forgotten, reckless girl I used to be from where she was buried deep in the cold hard rock and brought me back to life.

His prick was stiffening, pressing against my leg, while he slid his tongue into my mouth and we tasted each other.

'*A mouthful of fun,*' Sandy had said.

I'd never been so hungry in my life. I knelt.

The wood planks of the studio floor were hard under my knees as I took hold of the guy's hips and pulled him towards me. I buried my face in his pubic hair, letting it scratch against my mouth. His cock bobbed against my cheek and I nuzzled at it, feeling the smoothness and the heat of what I'd been longing for for months. I'd spent a half-hour looking at his body, trying to recreate it on paper, but drawing his beauty was nowhere near close enough to this. Touching him, taking him in my mouth, sucking on him. Tasting the bittersweet honey of his pre-cum as his cock swelled and grew rock hard.

Fuck drawing, I thought. It doesn't get to the heart of the matter. I realised just how flat a picture can be, as his hands tangled in my hair and I pulled at his ass, sticking a fingertip into his hole and feeling the corresponding spasm in his cock. This wasn't static, everything was in motion, stimulating all my senses at once, and we were sinking inside each other, intertwining, pushing and pulling at each other. He was tumbling down to kneel in front of me and his hands were burrowing into my clothes, seeking out the pockets of heat, the dark and wet spots that connected straight to my brain. His fingers ran into my knickers, slid quickly between my thighs and into my pussy. A slight resistance, before he found the groove and the moisture of my pussy and dived into it. Two fingers, three, jammed inside me, opening me up, wriggling in there with a funny little shock before I felt the rhythm of it, the to and fro rocking that made me feel like my body was caught in a tide. Waves ebbing and flowing, he was imitating the beat of sex that would sink into me and pull me under.

I couldn't even get my jeans off before he was pushing me over, holding his cock to guide it in and nudging at my slit.

'Stop, stop, wait,' I said, remembering one of Sandy's rules. 'We should use a condom.'

He nodded, breathless and beyond speaking now, then leapt up nimbly to find his jeans and check the pockets. He sprinted back to where I lay with a foil square in his hand.

'You brought one to work?' I couldn't quite believe it. Was I the only person in Glasgow who didn't anticipate a casual fuck at lunchtime?

My model grinned, biting at the foil to rip it open. He had a wicked smile. 'Boy scout motto. Always "Be Prepared". You never know who you'll bump into.'

I wasn't in any position to argue, so I gave in and just marvelled at the sight of him, cock in hand, unrolling the rubber down his length and checking to see it was on tight. I lay back.

But he wasn't ready. The pause seemed to have given him an idea. 'How about we even the score a little?'

'How d'you mean?'

'You've spent half an hour staring at every inch of my naked ass. But I haven't even had a peek. I feel like I hardly know you.'

I laughed. It was a little one-sided – a fully clothed artist taking advantage of her new employee.

Even so, I felt strangely shy as I struggled out of my jeans and sweatshirt. Untying my shoelaces, I could feel his eyes on me, curious and searching. My skin seemed fragile, tender – as if it had never been exposed to daylight before. I was struck forcefully with the realisation of what I was doing – getting naked and amorous with a total stranger. I unhooked my bra and forced myself to resist the desire to cover my breasts. I slipped out of my panties and sat back while he looked at me.

The awareness of his gaze on my body had an unexpected effect. Even as my cheeks reddened with shame, I felt my spine arch, my hips rock a little. I was leaning back and enjoying this display, presenting my naked breasts to this man like a glamour model. My inner voice screamed '*Crazy*', but my body was opening to his attention. Then it dawned on me. I was showing off.

Why the hell not? What did I have to lose? I didn't even know this guy's name, and he'd probably disappear into the anonymous city in an hour or so. We were just having a brief taste of each other. A little adventure.

Suddenly reckless, I spread my legs for him in invitation. I was acting lewd, shocking myself, and I hadn't felt so damn alive in months. He swept down to join me, to kiss me again with those perfectly pretty lips and press the length of his body over mine. When his cock nudged at my slit and then entered me, it felt like I'd discovered the fast way to make a new friend. I don't mean that glibly either – he was moving in me so softly and so intensely I felt I was suddenly close to him, not just interlocked physically, but discovering him in a way that hours of late-night conversations and shy dates just wouldn't do. How else do you know a man, I thought, as his cock – long and thin and hard – filled me. I could feel him going deep and grinding against my pubic bone.

The quality of his love-making was as much part of him as his conversation – light and rapid, eager and somehow tender. He cradled my head with one hand to kiss me, lifting my mouth towards his. The kindness of strangers, I thought. He fucked me with easy strokes, and the rhythm I'd felt earlier – his hand inside me, darting against the inside of my cunt – was repeated with his hips. His kisses were playful and interspersed with little bites. As his hand roved down to stroke my body, he tweaked my nipples and gripped handfuls of flesh. He wormed his hand in between us, flicked at my clit, latched onto it and started frigging me in time with his fucking.

My body was opening up to him, hungry for the thump and bang of his hips against mine and eager to absorb his cock as deep as I could. We rolled on the floor, collecting broken bits of charcoal on our flesh and slipping on a pool of turpentine or oil or something, and the two of us kept sucking at each other, licking and thrusting and not giving a fuck how dirty and cold and uncomfortable our situation was. I had his hand hard against my clit now, and he was fucking me less playfully, driving into me with more emphatic pushes, pulling back as if he was taking a big in-breath, running his cock back into me with the urgency of approaching orgasm. I was jarred against the floor, hit hard by his body every time he pushed into me, feeling the magical tingling buzz in my cunt that meant I was going to come too, all over his hand and with him stuck deep and hard inside me all the way to the hilt. The whole of my body, inside and out, was alive and screaming for release, every part of me fucking back and forth, rubbing up against him, feeling him in and on and around me as he thrust with big heavy hip-jerks. It hit, hard.

He jolted against me one last time.

And cried out, and spilt himself inside me, and finally made my orgasm explode like a black starburst. Deep in my brain the inverse of colour swept through me, blanked out my mind, swallowed colour and transmuted it into pure burning, animal sensation.

Our bodies dissolved together and shook, hands slipping over each other, clutching hard, grunts and moans falling from our mouths involuntarily.

Perhaps I had lost my mind. I rolled around on the floor, feeling the last sweet stings of orgasm shoot through me, making me shiver as I held onto the guy.

I felt the sweat cool on my body almost instantly, the hard floor and the scratches on my ass and back from whatever the hell mess we'd just been lying on. The sudden emptiness as he pulled out of me, leaving my pussy tender, free-falling. The cold air rushing at my body, reality hardening the edges of the moment. Him sitting back and the unfamiliarity of his face reasserting itself. Looking shockingly strange. I didn't know him.

The distance between us was suddenly as great as it

was when he'd first entered the studio – two strangers in daylight, trying to breathe normally.

There was an awkward moment when it came to paying him – and when I had to admit I'd nicked him from Joe's life-drawing session. But we laughed it off and, as he took his leave with a curiously chaste little kiss, I felt a sudden pang of affection for him. Not that we'd be repeating the encounter – that was pretty clear. After you've fucked someone on your studio floor without asking their name first, you'd be hard put to go through the whole rigmarole of dating and flirtation.

It was a short and sweet encounter, nothing more. But my heart felt somehow lighter that evening as I walked home with the rolled-up sketches under my arm and an aching body. I would pin up the pictures of my 'David' on my bedroom wall to remind me of my studio adventure. To show myself that beauty can turn up in unexpected places and that life tastes sweeter when you take the odd risk. I walked across town and for the first time in a year felt like I was plugged in to life. Part of the whole colourful, terrifying, electric game; like the switch my heart had been flicked to 'on' again.

In the swarming, messy crowds of rush hour I saw the young guys and the rough-at-the-edges guys, dark and light and moving fast around me. A thousand possibilities for a little buzz, a little smile, a little warmth. A thousand gaps that weren't that hard to cross if you took the chance.

As Sandy says: 'There are a hundred kinds of love out there.'

Now I intend to taste as many as I can – one mouthful at a time.

Lust for Glory
Mathilde Madden

Tuesday nights mean only one thing to Gracie, William, Mark and me: *Lust*.

Oops. Actually, that's a bit of a Freudian one – not *Lust*, *Lost*.

Lost, the TV show, that is. Every Tuesday Gracie, Mark and William pile round my place and we all watch the show. And even though we don't always follow the plot all that closely, it always, always seems to hold our attention. Mark, Gracie and William are all super hot for Doctor Jack, whereas I, not being one to follow the herd, am torn between Sawyer and Sayid. Although, I say I'm torn, but really, why choose?

We have a strict rule during *Lost* nights: no talking during *Lost*. It's complicated enough without unnecessary distractions. Not that we're that into the plot, as I said. But rules are rules and even random lustful comments have to be stored up for the ad breaks. So, because of that, tonight I've made sure that we are all sitting on the sofa with our g and ts a good twenty minutes before the show's start time, because I have something wanted to talk about: Lust.

Really, this time. Except, actually, his name is James.

James. A friend of William and Mark's. A very very lovely friend indeed. I'd met James in the pub with Mark and William about two weeks ago and I hadn't been able to think of much else since. I was smitten.

The three of us had met up in the pub – without Gracie – for a post mortem on a highly significant event. Mark and William had, after months of bribery, corruption and general skulduggery, managed to get themselves a pair of invites to a very special party. A big dirty gay party. One of the biggest and most notorious ones anywhere, held in some big fancy house somewhere on the South Downs.

I was, being something of a fan of Mark and William's nefarious activities, desperate for the lowdown. I wasn't disappointed. When they described events to me, well, 'party' seemed to be a rather tame word for the event in question. Orgy would have been a little more appropriate. And, big nutso gay orgy where loads of oiled-up men writhed around, under, over and in and out of each other would probably have really hit the nail on the head.

Nice.

Naturally, I pumped them both mercilessly for a full and frank account. When they gave me the description I craved, room by room, one thing fascinated me more than any other. Sure, I loved hearing about the orgy rooms and the dungeon and the sex swing and the go-go boys. But none of those things were as endlessly fascinating to me as the glory hole.

'So, it's like, just a hole? Like, in a wall,' I said.

'Um, well –' William pouted and screwed up his face with the supreme effort of remembering it just right '– it's more like a big box. In this case. I think sometimes it is a hole in a wall. Well, it can be all sorts of things, but at the party it was a big box, about five-foot square with a hole in it, like the size of this.' He held up his thumbs and forefingers, touching the tips to make a circle.

'And you just stick your . . .'

'You just stick your dick in it,' Mark said with a laugh.

'And someone inside...'

'Someone inside sucks it.' Mark again.

'What if they, um, what if they don't want to suck it?'

William looked at me like 'does not compute'. 'Well, the person inside, see, they're kind of in there because they *do* want to, so that doesn't really come up.'

I sighed. Fuck, but that was horny. Something about the idea of the glory hole just seemed to embody everything I found so compelling about dirty anonymous sex. The idea that men just stuck their cocks into this hole not knowing or caring who was inside to service them, spoke to a dark place inside me. And even more vividly arousing – perhaps because I don't have the required piece of anatomy to be the one sticking myself into the hole – was the thought of being the person inside, anonymously taking whatever was offered.

And then, before I really felt like the subject was exhausted, Mark shouted, 'Ooh, there's James. Hey, James.'

And this blond head at the bar turned around and, I swear, I heard birds singing. (And I don't just mean Kylie and Danni on the jukebox.)

James took my breath away. In that moment – with the boys' salacious talk of glory holes still buzzing in the dirty part of my brain – he had it all. Beautiful, witty (OK, I found that out a bit later), single and, as Mark and William couldn't wait to point out, gay. Or in Mark's later words, 'So gay. Gay, gay, gay, gay, gay, gay, gay! Get it? Gay!'

Usually, I don't hold by those kinds of aphorism; the type of things about all the handsome men being gay or gay men taking better care of themselves. That stuff. I reckon all that is just made up to make women feel bad. And, me, I'm not that big a fan of feeling bad. Not when there are so many other great ways to feel. However, it was very true that James was both handsome and gay.

Very handsome and very gay. ('Gay, gay, gay, gay, gay, gay, gay!', in fact, let us not forget.) And I wanted him nasty bad.

William and Mark – I should point out – I didn't want. Still don't want. Even though there really would have been no problem there, because William and Mark weren't so much gay as sexually gluttonous. A pair of dirtier boys I had never yet met. Sometimes I thought that Mark was probably properly bi, and William was mostly gay but open to opportunity, but I never really figured it out. Needless to say though, our combined dirtiness (dirty to the power of three) was probably the cement that held our friendship together. But we never took all the frisson and flirting into the bedroom. There was a line. An unwritten rule. It never quite went that far. Although, actually I'm pretty sure it spilt over into the bedroom between Mark and William, but not between me and either of them. (Well, OK, I'd snogged them both. Separately. But what girl hasn't snogged her gay(ish) male mates? Just as an experiment.)

But I'd always insisted that Mark and William were just my fag bangles. Or maybe I was theirs. I never quite figured out how that term was meant to go.

But anyway, after two weeks of obsessing about delicious James, I decide enough is enough. Nothing ventured and all that. So making sure I've got a good ten minutes before *Lust*-I-mean-*Lost* starts I tell William and Mark and Gracie of my enduring passion.

'Angel,' William says, after I outline my angst, 'James is gay. Forget it.'

'But, but, but,' I say, stalling for time while I wait for something to appear in my brain. 'But he might be one of those gay guys who sleep with women.' *Rather like the two I'm looking at right now.*

'He isn't.'

'But he might want to sleep with a woman just once, just to check he doesn't like it.'

Mark shakes his head. 'If – and that's a giant-size "if" with flashing neon lights on the top – he did want to do that, he probably would have done it by now.'

'But he might just not have met the right woman yet.'

'I'll pretend I didn't hear that,' William says, raising his eyebrows so high they almost wrap around the back of his forehead.

I scrabble around for some chance I might get my way. 'But, well, couldn't I convert him? I hear you and your friends boasting about converting straight guys all the time. What's that joke? "What's the difference between a straight guy and a gay guy?", "About five pints of lager." Couldn't it work the other way? Can you turn gay boys straight with enough alcohol?'

'No,' William and Mark say, both at once and snappily fast.

'But couldn't I just suck his cock? I mean, what difference would it make?' I say hopefully, my James fantasies suddenly clashing with my glory hole fantasies and almost overloading my brain.

'What?' Again they both speak together. It's like they have become one consciousness.

'What difference would it make if I were a guy or a girl then? I have a mouth, right?' I insist.

'Babe,' says Mark, 'cock-sucking is an art, perfected by gay men over the millennia. There is no way you could suck cock as well as a gay guy.'

'Actually, I'm pretty good at sucking cock,' I say, because actually, I am. I enjoy it. Over the years I've made it my business to be good at it. I know some women don't like it, but I don't get that, what's not to like? What else has the same twisted conflicting rush of being empowered by being able to give such incredible pleasure while at the same time being used and degraded? It ticks all the boxes.

Mark gives me a yeah-right kind of look.

'He'd never even know the difference,' I say, quite softly.

William shakes his head. 'It doesn't work like that. I mean, you're not just talking about James getting his rocks off. You're talking about a person's political, social and sexual identity. You're talking about light years of repression.'

'Light years is a measure of distance, not time,' Mark points out, unhelpfully.

'But if he *thinks* I'm a guy, what difference does it make?'

And then Gracie, who has been very quiet throughout this debate says, 'It's starting,' and I have to shut up for ten whole minutes until the first ad break.

I don't get to set the conversational agenda to me, me, me in the first ad break because Gracie says, 'Do any of you lot want to earn some extra spending money this weekend?'

Gracie runs her own sort of company. Sort of. It's basically a catering company, but she likes to pretend they do events management and party planning as well. They don't. They reheat vol-au-vents and serve champagne. And it's not really even a proper company because Gracie's family are utterly loaded and the entire organisation is being propped up by the generous handouts her family keep giving her (supposedly to avoid paying inheritance tax).

I don't like working for Gracie at the weekend. For any number of reasons born of both laziness and class-warring principle, but she does pay pretty well and I've been a bit trigger happy on eBay lately – my last credit card bill was just a piece of paper with the words 'Oh my fucking God' written on it.

'Front of house?' I ask, because wafting around topping up champagne glasses is slightly better than unloading and reloading a dishwasher in an ancient kitchen.

Gracie winces. 'Front for Willy or Markie, back for you, Lou.'

'What? Why?'

'Um, well, it's kind of a men-only kind of party,' Gracie says and makes such a weird face that you would actually think she couldn't possibly conceive of why a group of men would want to have a private party with no women around. Her. Her who is sitting here next to Mark and William. William with his hand down the front of Mark's trousers – I swear he's giving him a little squeeze every time the good doctor appears on screen.

Then William says, 'Um, I don't think I can make this weekend, sorry.'

He and Mark exchanges glances. And then Mark says, 'No, nor can I.'

'Lou?' Gracie says to me. I'm still feeling a bit pissed off about having to be behind closed doors. It's a bit much that I have come off badly purely because of my gender twice in the space of half an hour. But I think of that credit card bill again and shrug my shoulders. 'Sure.'

In the next ad break Gracie goes to the loo and I say to William, 'This is going to be one of *those* parties, isn't it?'

'One of what parties?'

'One of those dirty parties. Like you told me about in the pub. The plushie orgies?'

'Oh.' William nods. 'Oh, yes.'

Mark says, 'Actually you do know "plushie" means

something very specific. You should watch you terminology there, girl.'

But I ignore Mark's sexual semantics lesson. 'So how come you're not going?' I ask both of them.

William gives me a look. 'Who says we're not going?' he says, with emphasis.

Then, when Gracie returns and *Lost* starts up again, I find I'm not really paying attention to the show any more, despite the delicious parade of prettiness dancing across the screen – and I don't mean Hawaii.

Four days later it's party time. Except not for me. The work on Saturday afternoon is hard. The house itself is stunning, a real country pile, all huge stone steps and crunchy gravel drive. Not that I'm seeing much of that. I'm strictly below stairs.

My job seems to be mostly washing up baking trays in a huge Belfast sink which screams whenever the taps are run and refuses to supply me with water any more than a few degrees above room temperature. That and running around fetching things.

It's hard to decide which is worst really.

At about six thirty the grumpier of the two chefs (not that the other one isn't grumpy) yells at me that we haven't got any fresh basil, and before I can respond that that is hardly my fault, Gracie appears and apologetically explains that a tray of fresh herbs seems to have gone missing and could I possibly run round to the front door of the house and find out if it got delivered there by mistake.

I nip out of the kitchen door and sprint around the side of the massive house. It's further than I would have thought possible. When I get there, there's about twenty cars parked on the drive, but no one around.

I look around hopefully, wondering if I will see a tray

of herbs that has been tucked neatly by the door, like the postman sometimes does with my eBay parcels if they won't fit the letterbox.

But nothing.

And then I notice the front door is actually just a little bit open. Which makes me think that maybe I could cut through the house and get back to the kitchen that way rather than go around the outside. Not very upstairs downstairs, I know, but I'm pretty eager for a sneaky peak at the dirty party set-up.

Inside the house isn't the riot of tapestries and old masters I might have imagined from its façade. It's kind of like an ordinary house really, only on a more massive and massively kinky scale. Just the entrance hall I am standing in contains a bank of man-sized cages, a set of stocks and a huge overflowing bowl of condoms.

As I walk through this den of iniquity I stop by the condom bowl. Something has caught my magpie eye. Right in the centre of it is a gold condom. Hardly the most spectacular thing in the room, but strangely compelling. It holds my gaze. And then I reach out and grab it.

But as I do that, I realise that there is the soft sound of conversation coming from the room on my left. I go over and peek through an ajar door into a gorgeous ballroom. And it's full of people. Men. Most of them naked, semi-naked or wearing various exotica. *Oh my God, the party has already started.* I stare around the entrance hall. Frozen. And then I hear it. Footsteps. Someone is coming up the steps outside, any minute now they're going to be coming in the front door. I don't know what to do. I dart behind the bank of cages and leg it up the imposing staircase behind me.

I try to make my way back to the kitchens as best as I can, keeping a look out in case I bump into any party guests. But the upstairs part of the house seems deserted. Maybe the party hasn't really begun properly yet. I still manage to take a few wrong turnings though. Get lost. Get double lost. Try to retrace my steps. Fail. Double back again and find I am utterly, well, lost. Real life being lost – nothing like as fun as the TV show. I can't even find my way back to the front entrance. Desperate, I head up another flight of stairs.

But being further upstairs doesn't seem to be proving any better for finding my way out. Damn my retarded sense of direction. I just seem to be winding my way deeper into the house.

Here the party-in-waiting becomes something rather darker than the almost light-hearted bondage fun downstairs. Upstairs, most rooms are dark, in half-light or freakily strobe lit. The background music has changed from twinkly classical to throbbing German industrial.

I glance into a medium-sized room, which is mostly empty. All it contains is a heavy red velvet curtain, through which peeks a large wooden box, with a hole in it. A really very large wooden box with a rather small hole in it. Of course, I know exactly what it is. And I know I shouldn't, but I can't resist a closer look.

But before I get even halfway across the room towards it, a voice behind me says, 'Excuse me.' And I turn around to find if not the last person I would have expected, certainly a double-take-worthy coincidence.

'William?'

'Lou. Hey.'

'Um . . . I got lost,' I say, feeling a bit awkward. 'What are you doing here?'

'Well, I kind of told you I might be here.'

'Yeah, but what are you doing *here*? Shouldn't you be downstairs?'

And then William starts to look shiftily at the box,

and I follow his gaze with one of those dawning revelation feelings. 'Oh.' I point across the room. 'You're meant to be in *there*.'

But before I can say anything else, a tinny tune strikes up from somewhere in William's pocket. 'Woah,' he says. 'Girl, interrupted.' And fishes in the pocket of his tight, tight jeans for a phone that is playing the theme to *Bewitched*. 'Yep. Mark, hey dude,' he twitters into it.

I look over at the box while he's talking. Thinking about what he told me about the glory hole. Feeling myself get buzzy and wet with the filthy idea of it.

And I suppose I'm lost in all of that, which means I don't notice the way things have changed in William's voice. The way most of his phone conversation is being punctuated by angry and frustrated swearing. 'Fuck!' says William. And then again, 'Fuck!' as he hangs up the phone.

'Something wrong?'

'That stupid fairy Mark's only gone and locked himself out. I'm going to have to drive back to Brighton with my keys and sort it.'

'What? Isn't Mark here?'

'No, he's revising. He's got an exam in the morning. Hence me having to go and let him back in. All his notes are in the flat.'

'But didn't you tell him you were kind of busy?' I tip my head towards the box, which is making its presence felt like a third person in the room.

'Yeah, but, oh God. What can I do? Look, it'll only take three-quarters of an hour, max. I'll just find someone else to take my place for a bit. James is downstairs maybe he would –'

'James is downstairs!'

'Yeah.' William blinks at me, like he's thinking, why is that surprising?

I'm still holding the little gold foil packet in my hand.

I rub my fingers across it like a lucky charm. 'I'll do it,' I say.

At first William looks at me like I've just said something in a foreign language. 'You? You can't.'

'Why not? No one'll know. Go on, William, you can sneak out. No one'll even know it wasn't you in there all night.'

William puffs out his slim chest. 'Oh, you still reckon you can suck cock as well as a gay boy, do you?'

'Sure. How hard can it be?' I say, turning to walk over to the box, not looking back at William, just hoping he'll follow me.

'You are such a dirty bitch,' he says, appearing right at my shoulder, and my heart leaps.

I don't reply. I push aside the heavy velvet curtain that the box protrudes from. And once we are 'backstage' I see exactly how it works.

The box has no back to it. So it's more like a sort of cubbyhole. Inside it is a small firm cushion for the person inside the box to kneel on. And if a person were kneeling on that cushion, facing the wooden wall of the box, the small hole would be at about face height. In fact, to be really strictly accurate, it would be at mouth height.

Still not speaking, feeling the tension in the air, I drop onto my knees. Oh God, the buzz hits me straight away.

I look over my shoulder at William. He has an odd expression on his face. 'Are you really OK with this?' I ask, not really knowing what I'll say if he tells me he isn't.

'I don't know,' he says, biting his bottom lip. 'It's just, it's not very ethical, is it?'

'I guess not. But then, when did you last worry about ethics when it came to sex? I mean, you're always joking about getting straight guys drunk and shagging them.'

'Yeah, but that's just a fantasy, Lou. I don't actually do it.'

'You don't?'

'No!'

'Oh.' I look at William for quite a long time then, so long I actually start to worry about Mark and his revision timetable. 'Are you really not OK with this?'

William seems to have a change of heart then, because he sort of micro-smirks and then says, 'Nah, not really. Well, except that I'm worried that after this everyone will think I can't suck cock for toffee. Do you want the cuffs?'

'What!' I sort of splutter, because that really blindsided me. 'Cuffs?'

'Yes, uh, some people like to be, uh . . .' William's voice kind of drains away along with the colour in his face.

It's weird. William and I are really close. Tight. I'm closer to William than I am to Mark. I could tell William anything, despite his occasional screams of 'Ooh, you breeders!' Which is a bit rich really seeing as how William is all for a bit of heterosexual action when he can get it. Really, he reserves that squeal for when I tell him about something a little too risqué even for him. I've always been the slightly more adventurous one out of the three of us, which, I think, he sees as upsetting the natural order of things. But, see me kneeling in a glory-hole box at a gay orgy right now for details of my spirit of sexual derring-do.

However, despite all of that, all that sexual camaraderie, this is maybe a bit too far. That line I talked about – the one that stops us all sleeping together. It's here too. Drawn across the sand. The idea of William putting the cuffs on me. A bit too much. But I really want them. So I have to screw up every ounce of my sexual courage to say, 'Actually, yes. That would be good.'

While I kneel in the box, my knees quite comfortable

on the soft padding and my lips just a breath away from the ominous hole, William straps my wrists together behind my back with something that feels firm and restrictive and comfortable all at once. I can't help sighing while he does it. It feels so good. So right.

I'm not really very with it when William says, 'OK, Lou, I've really got to go now. Mark, etc.'

'Yeah, um, before you do though, I need a favour.'

'*Another* one?'

'Yeah, look, take the condom that's in my pocket. I want you to give it to James.'

'To James, why?'

'Just do it.'

William is actually quite well behaved as he roots around in the pocket of my jeans for the condom while my hands are tied. When he snags it and leaves, with a gentle goodbye of a finger trailing on my shoulder, my heart is banging like a drum and my clit is throbbing in perfect time with it.

My lips suddenly feel dry. I lick them in anticipation. Then I wait.

For quite while nothing actually happens. I listen to the faint thrum of the Rammstein playing in the hall and wonder if anyone will actually come and use the box, feeling faintly disappointed that I'm not much of an attraction.

After, I guess, five minutes though, I hear sounds in the room outside and without any warning I feel the unmistakable soft force of a rubber-coated cock pressing against my suddenly dry lips. I open my mouth and suck.

God, it feels amazing. Hard to explain. The anonymity. The bondage. And the fact that the room on the other side of the wooden wall is now full of people. That unique mix of power and subjugation is like a head rush. I use every wile I have. Every last trick of lips and teeth. When my mystery man comes, he groans loudly and falls against the wood so hard it shakes.

One down.

There's another hard cock jutting through the hole before I even draw breath.

I open up my mouth again for the next one, cutely jacketed in bright blue and, as I do so, I tug a little at the restraints holding my hands behind my back. God, it turns me on not to be able to use my hands while I'm being used like this. It makes everything so much more arousing.

My clit is burning as I let the new cock force its way inside and jerk roughly in my mouth. This guy is much more forceful. He doesn't let me play artful games, but thrusts hard through the hole. In and out. Fucking my mouth. I hold still and let him. Squirming with pleasure when I hear a distinct and masterful snarl.

Three follows, then four, then five. My wrists get sore, and my jaw starts to ache, and my cunt gets wetter and wetter.

I've just finished number six, when I start to wonder where the hell William has got to. I can't see my watch so I don't know how long I've been here. There's a part of me that's worried, but a bigger part that, despite my aching neck and jaw, kind of hopes he never comes back.

And then – lucky number seven – in through the hole comes what I've been waiting for. And I'm going for gold.

I pause for a moment to look at it. It's beautiful. The last part of James that I get to study in depth is every bit as pleasing to behold as the rest of him. It's so big and thick. I never knew I was a size queen, but James doesn't disappoint on that score. He's going to be more than a mouthful.

He's also got this little kink in his cock. It bends over to the left. It's nice. It's quirky. Makes it more real – him not being dildo straight and perfect. It doesn't hurt that the whole thing is clad in golden rubber either. I pause maybe a moment too long looking at its golden glory, because there's a knock on the wooden wall above my head.

James. I open my mouth and suck.

James's big hard cock is filling my mouth, thrusting hard, mercilessly using me. I can hear some faint groaning coming from the other side of the wall. *Him.* Too faint to recognise, but it's got to be him. I'm so wet, my clit feels like it's burning. I tug at the restraints that hold my wrist, both frustrated and fiercely aroused by not being able to touch myself. As James keeps on going, holding out for longer than anyone else has tonight under my cock-sucking prowess, I squeeze my thighs together. Over and over, setting up a strong pulsing rhythm. I squirm around on the cushion, ignoring the protests from my sore knees and find a way to get the pressure on my clit just right, even without my hands. I concentrate on the way James is forcing his way right down my throat, the way my lips are stretching around him, going numb. The way he has no idea that it is me, William's friend, so quickly dismissed, that is making him feel this intense pleasure.

James starts to move faster, jerking like he's not in control. I suck as hard as I can, using my tongue to massage the underside of his shaft. I squeeze my thighs harder together. Twist a little. Feel the pressure just right and there it is. James is spasming hotly under his rubber sleeve and I'm coming so hard I don't know which way is up.

I don't know if I could have taken another cock after that. So thank God that the hole goes dark for a minute or two after James withdraws.

And then I hear a sound behind me, and look over my shoulder to see William, reaching over to unfasten my wrists.

'Bloody hell, William, you've been ages.'

'I've been less than an hour.'

'Well, it seemed like longer.' I pull my arms free, struggling to move, not knowing what part of me to massage first. I scarcely even get my wits together before William practically yanks me out of the box, through a side door behind the curtain and directs me down a flight of stairs to the kitchen.

Gracie looks up as I walk in, tottering gingerly like I am eighty years old. 'I'm not even going to ask,' she says as I collapse into a chair. 'But if you think you're getting paid for today . . .'

I'm not listening.

A couple of hours later I try to make amends to Gracie. My body feels rather more alive after two gin and tonics and about a hundred vol-au-vents. My jaw actually does still work, despite early reports of it completely seizing up. Flaky pastry has brought it back to life. Eventually I struggle over to the pre-war dishwasher and start loading champagne glasses in and out, all the time feeling hot flares at the memory of James and his spectacular cock in my mouth. *Oh yeah.*

At about 1 a.m. this guy called Sebastian, apparently the host of the party although it's the first I've seen of him, appears in the kitchen to slather us with congratulations. Either it's gone extremely well or he is extremely pissed – possibly both. Sebastian invites Gracie, me, the chefs and Gracie's other galley slaves up to the hall for a final drink. I raise my eyebrows at Gracie because of the whole no-women thing, and she just mimes 'too much to drink' with an invisible glass to her lips.

In the hall, I approach William, who almost jumps out of his skin. 'Hey, Lou, what you doing up here?'

'Heh. We've been allowed above stairs. Where's James?'

'Um.' Suddenly William looks awfully shifty.

'Has he gone home?'

'Uh, yeah. That's it, yeah, he's gone home. Busy day tomorrow or something.' Which would be perfectly plausible if it weren't for the look on William's face.

But I don't worry about that too much. 'Oh, right. Did he say anything about my blow job? Best ever, right?'

But before William can answer me, someone appears at his shoulder. Someone who changes everything.

'Hey, Lou,' says Mark.

William glares. 'Mark.'

'Mark. What are you doing here? I thought you were at home, revising?' Two and two are rapidly making four in my head.

'Um ... Oh,' says Mark, reddening a bit.

'But you're not, are you?' I say to Mark, then turn to William. 'So you didn't have to go and let him into his flat, did you?'

'Uh.'

'Did you?'

'No.' William looks at his shoes. But he's smirking.

'So, what? You set me up. Why?' And then something else dawns on me as I cast around the room. 'James was never even here, was he? I thought it was weird. I thought he didn't seem the type.'

Mark and William look bashfully at me. Then Mark says, 'He *was* here.'

I shake my head. 'Don't lie.'

'It's true,' says William. 'He was, but he's gone now.' They're both smirking. I honestly don't know if they're lying or not.

'OK, well, was it him then? Was he the one with the gold condom on?'

William reaches out and touches my shoulder. 'Well, honey,' he says gently, 'the fact is, you *thought* it was him. So really, what difference does it make?'

A Stranger, and Yet Not
Teresa Noelle Roberts

I stopped pacing long enough to glance at the clock. They'd be home soon, my boyfriend Gary and his friend Matt.

His best friend from high school, whom I'd been hearing about for ages, but had never met because he'd been teaching in Japan until recently.

The stranger I was about to fuck.

In the eighteen or so months Gary and I have been together, we've spent a lot of time talking about fantasies – and playing them out whenever we can. I've dressed up like a cat-girl and a naughty nun for him. He's played pirate for me. I've taken one of those strippercise classes and then performed for him. They wouldn't let him take the strippercise class, but he gamely bumped and grinded for me anyway, and I stuffed dollar bills in his underwear. We had a threesome with a bi girlfriend of ours – Gary's fantasy, but I liked it as much as he did. (Unfortunately for us, she met Ms Right shortly afterwards and became happily monogamous.) I've fucked Gary in the ass with a strapon. He's fucked me in the ass with what the good Lord gave him.

But a few favourite fantasies haven't seemed practical as anything other than hot whispers in the dark. I'd be glad to try the sex-under-a-waterfall fantasy if we ever find the right waterfall, but it's going to require a tropical vacation. The mad-scientist one requires a few too many props, and ideally a lovely demented assistant (see the 'my adventurous bi friend fell in love and is having all her adventures with someone else now' whine, above). And Gary's willing to let me dress him in women's clothes, but he's six foot three and craggy featured, with a beard we're both rather fond of, so the dream of transforming my lover into a girl for a night of clubbing and semi-public teasing isn't going to happen.

And then there was my faceless stranger.

Ever since I was a young teenager, full of hormones and not sure what to do about them, I've masturbated to fantasies about being made love to by a stranger.

No, being fucked by a stranger.

No, that's still not right – being taken by a stranger. It's not a rape fantasy, because I'm all kinds of willing and excited, but there's an element of being overwhelmed, by him and by lust, of him making sure I'm too swept away by sensation to have second thoughts or ask silly questions such as, 'Who the hell are you and why don't you have a face?'

Now, Gary could see why that fantasy was hot for me, could see it well enough that we both had fun with him playing a masked man. No matter how hard he tried to act like a mysterious stranger, though, Gary's familiar body, familiar touch, familiar voice would always break through the illusion. Definitely a fun sexy game – and he looked damn good in that mask – but not quite the fantasy. Yet actually finding a stranger wouldn't do for a whole number of reasons: diseases, psycho-killer potential, the general sordidness of either putting an ad in the personals section of the alternative paper or having Gary walk up to someone in a club and saying, 'You look like a likely candidate. Want to fuck my girlfriend?'

Then Matt let Gary know he was coming back to the

States for an extended visit between semesters, said he hoped he could swing a visit, finally get to meet me, etc.

And Gary remembered that Matt was, among his other sterling qualities, an amiable pervert. Loved sex, loved women, loved erotic adventures, the kookier the better. (When I say, 'Gary remembered that . . .' etc., what I really mean is 'Matt was telling Gary about his recently ended relationship with a neighbour in Tokyo, who liked dressing up like a schoolgirl and pretending he was a tentacled monster, and it dawned on Gary that . . .')

So Gary made a suggestion, and Matt accepted – eagerly, if Gary was to be believed – once he figured out that a) Gary was serious and b) so was I.

Fantasy-fulfilment problem solved.

Matt was a stranger to me, but not to Gary. They trusted each other implicitly. Back in the day, they'd dated some of the same women, though not at the same time, and Gary had gotten a pretty good idea of Matt's good and bad qualities. The bad quality, from most girls' point of view, was that he was pretty much incapable of monogamy – but at least he was always honest about it. All to the good on our end. The good qualities, apparently, included being Captain Condom. The boy played hard and wild, but he played safe.

I wasn't going into this completely blind. At Gary's insistence, I'd been reading the blog Matt kept of his life in Japan, getting a good feeling for a guy who was adventurous, observant, smart and witty – just the kind of guy I'd expect Gary's best friend to be. He cared about his students, enjoyed watching the neighbourhood cats bask in the sun, had gotten friendly with the elderly artist next door (as well as with Tentacle/Schoolgirl Woman, but he didn't go into those details in the blog, just mentioned occasional dates and the eventual amicable break-up). I'd seen a few of the emails and IMs that had gone back and forth, setting the visit, and the fantasy, up, although not enough to give away all the details of their 'evil' plan. He seemed like a good guy, a fun guy.

An imaginative guy, if the emails were any indication.

Yum.

But I still hadn't talked to Matt directly. Still didn't know what he looked like, other than Gary's assurance that I wouldn't need to put a bag over his head.

A stranger, but a stranger I could trust with my body. And with my heart, because let's face it, part of the reason we hadn't wanted to take out a personal ad or try some other way to find a random playmate was the potential for things to get strange emotionally, even if the guy was perfectly decent. I can't claim I've always been in love with the people I've slept with, but there's always been friendship. At least Matt and I were connected through Gary. Vicarious friendship, or whatever you want to call it, made it less scary, but my brain kept saying it still should have scared me.

The rest of me didn't want to listen to my brain, at least not right now. I was apprehensive about whether it would go smoothly, whether it would be fun for everyone or one of those awkward abortive experiments, but that felt more like social anxiety, only a little worse than I'd be jittering about making a good impression on Gary's best friend under more usual circumstances – with all my clothes on, for example.

Instead of being anxious, my heart was racing with excitement, my cunt was dripping with anticipation and my nipples were so hard they ached. I'd expected, as Gary left to collect Matt at the airport, that by this time I'd be half-tempted to put my clothes back on (my fantasies always began with the stranger clothed and me naked – maybe my hindbrain couldn't figure out the taking-off-clothes-in-front-of-a-stranger part – and so

Gary suggested I start out naked for this), run out the back door, grab my car and head for the hills. Instead, I was half-tempted to grab my favourite vibrator and get started on my own, just to keep from going out of my skin with need.

I don't think I could have bolted, even if I'd been sure I wanted to.

One fantasy I've never had is the whole master/slave thing, from either end of the equation. A little spanky goodness, sure, but all in fun, and with tonight's spankee just as likely to be the spanker next time – not the deep stuff where it's about giving over your will to another person on a more serious level.

Yet as I paced naked through our house, quivering with arousal and excitement, I felt oddly submissive and oddly happy about it. My fate had passed utterly out of my hands and into those of Gary and Matt, and I was pretty much fine with that. I imagined it was how a BDSM slave might feel, waiting to fulfil some scary-yet-hot whim of her master's, knowing the decision was all out of her hands, that her only choice was to trust in her lover.

No, the analogy didn't really hold. For one thing, I could back out – no shame, no harm, no foul, not even a safe word needed. (They show up and find me dressed, we pretend it was never discussed and go get dinner, end of story.) For another, although Gary and Matt had worked out the scenario, they were spinning out my desire, my fantasy. I was the one who had the real power here, even though I'd given over control of the details to the guys.

And that was hot all by itself, without any BDSM component – that Gary loved me that much and, hell, that Matt was that turned on by the idea of playing with me.

The phone jangled, startling me out of my thoughts.

The guys had just turned onto our street. They'd be at the house in just a few minutes. 'Matt says to say he's as hard as rock,' Gary said. Before he hung up, he added softly, 'I love you.'

I went upstairs, into the bedroom. As we'd agreed, I slipped on the blindfold.

Soft leather lined with padded silk, it smelt warm and alive, caressed my skin as it settled into place. My faceless stranger really would be faceless until it was all over – or at least until my curiosity got the better of me. The darkness settling over me was warm and somehow comforting, as if this wouldn't really count (unless, of course, I wanted it to) if I couldn't see Matt's face, Matt's body, Matt's hands on my skin.

We'd experimented with blindfolds enough that I wasn't surprised my other senses felt instantly sharpened by the deprivation. The air shivered against my skin. I could smell the smoky musk of my arousal, and under it the soft fresh scent of the rose soap I'd used in my morning shower.

And, of course, sound was heightened. I swore I could hear the cat purring downstairs in the den, children playing in the neighbour's yard. My own breathing sounded crazily loud and harsh, like my grandma on a day when her asthma was bad.

I sat down on the edge of the bed and waited. Let my fingers stray between my legs, not so much trying to make myself come as marvelling over how wet I was, how eagerly my pussy sucked in first one finger, then two.

The smell of my juices grew stronger, drowned out the soap, drowned out just about everything.

Would Matt finger me like this, pumping in and out as I was doing to myself? Or would he just throw me back and dive in cock first, not bothering with preliminaries because I was already soaked, hot, ready for a stranger's hard cock to stretch me, fill me, fuck me?

I clenched around my own fingers – not quite an orgasm, but close – at the thought, and the sensation took me so strongly that, even with my hearing heightened, I almost missed the sound of the front door opening, of two men pouring in the door.

I froze, fingers still in my cunt, straining to listen.

'Karen's upstairs,' Gary's familiar, comfortable voice said. 'Second door on the left. First one's the bathroom.'

'Thanks, man.' A deep voice, both rumbly and silky, sort of James Earl Jones without the Darth Vader effects. The kind of voice that could turn a woman inside out by reading the phone book.

'I'll be in here.' I imagined Gary gesture towards the den. It would be just like him to play World of Warcraft while Matt was fucking me – he wouldn't want to leave the house in case of Unspecified Horrible Weirdness, but he'd want some distraction. Also a nice twisted bit of symbolism, since one way the guys had kept in touch while Matt was in Japan was by playing that damn online game together at strange hours.

Then Gary raised his voice to a pitch I would have heard even if I'd dozed off waiting for them. 'Have a great time with Matt, Karen. I love you.'

Something in the tone of his voice, a combination of lust and tenderness and a curious kind of pride in me – like he was a kid showing off a neat new toy, I thought – just about melted me. (Yeah, maybe I had more sub in me than I thought, because I'm sure my rational, nonhorny self wouldn't have liked the favourite toy comparison one bit, but under the circumstances it just made me melt like butter in the hot sun.)

Footsteps on the stairs.

I realised my fingers were still inside me and pulled

them out in a frenzy of embarrassment. Gary had seen me playing with myself plenty of times and that was always fun, but having a stranger see me was different. Humiliating. Living proof that I was a bit of a slut.

Then again, it wasn't like he could have any illusions that I was shy and uptight, and it was a compliment to him, and to the fantasy, that I couldn't wait. I left my fingers circling my clit, not really with intent, just keeping warm for him.

I thought I had a little more time, but he bypassed the bathroom. I heard him walk a few steps into the room, heard an appreciative whistle. I looked up instinctively, even though I couldn't see anything. My hand froze, hovering a fraction of an inch off my throbbing clit.

Suddenly my heart was pounding fit to shatter my ribs, and I was choking on panic. What had I gotten myself into?

'Damn,' he said in that voice of silk and gravel, 'you're even hotter than your pictures. Gary is a lucky bastard. Nothing like a pretty girl playing with herself. No, please don't stop.'

Matt's sexy voice ran over my skin, caressing me from a distance, soothing me. Between that and the momentary distraction of wondering if Gary had sent him *those* pictures, I let the panic go, went on stroking myself as if in a dream.

Despite nerves, despite distraction, I could feel an orgasm coming on.

I'd never fantasised about this, about the idea of beating off under a stranger's gaze, but my pussy was twitching, and I was squirming under my own touch, and I was embarrassed to realise I was moaning and mewling.

A soft shush of cloth hitting the floor.

'I've been looking in your window,' he said, moving towards me. 'A burglar, maybe, planning to break in, steal your stuff and leave, but instead I've been watching you playing with yourself, getting so hot and bothered you didn't even notice me. But now you have. You see me opening the window, coming towards the bed, my cock out just like it is. I don't want to hurt you, don't even want to rob you any more. Just want to fuck you senseless.'

Gary had obviously told him one version of my fantasy in detail – The Well-Hung and Welcome Intruder, an oldie but a goodie.

'Yes,' I whispered. And then, 'I'm gonna –'

'Not without me you don't,' Matt growled, and it was simultaneously so sexy and so menacing that it almost finished bringing me off, even though I had moved my hands out of the way.

The sound of movement.

Hands on my thighs, hands squarer and, I thought, a little smaller than Gary's, but hard and strong.

A warm tongue, flicking where my fingers had been.

Hands flailing, I grabbed him, one hand brushing the top of his head in passing.

Shaved head. Hot silky skin. Shoulders like a god's, or at least they seemed that way to me.

And a tongue that definitely knew its way to a woman's hot spots. He licked me like I was ice cream and he'd spent the past year on a diet.

My world exploded.

I arched, clawed at his shoulders. I screamed like a wounded panther (not that I know what a wounded panther sounds like, but it seems like it would be loud and ragged and startling even to the panther, and that about describes the noise I made).

And he didn't stop. Just kept licking, kept making me come, while he somehow scooted me further back onto the bed.

Eventually, I pushed him away, spent, making 'gkk-

gkk-gkk' sounds, needing a breather – but not a long one.

I heard the welcome sound of a condom packet being torn open.

A few more glorious licks, lighter. Definitely pleasurable, but not trying to wring another orgasm out of me immediately.

Then he kissed his way up my body. And by 'kissed' I don't mean a few light brushes with his lips on the way to a place where he could get his cock into me. He licked, kissed and nibbled, covering every inch, getting his teeth involved sometimes as if he wanted to take away a chunk as a souvenir, and it felt good enough that I'd have let him. One leg was between my thighs, rubbing, grinding, keeping me wet and open even if I wasn't coming right at the moment. The leg was hairy – with my eyes useless, I noticed that kind of detail more – and hard and strong feeling.

He felt solid overall, not as tall as Gary but broader – not fat, but built differently from Gary's lean, rangy runner's body. His ass, when I grabbed for it, was rock hard under my hands. Not a small peach of a butt, but big and solid like the rest of him. Big and solid and glorious, like the cock brushing against me, making me crazy with need. I wanted it inside me, fucking me hard, splitting me open, but I didn't beg for it because at the same time I didn't want him to stop what he was doing.

Especially when he reached my nipples.

Licking, suckling, biting down so red spirals of pleasure edging on pain gyred through me. I arched against him, ground my mound – my throbbing, oversensitive, almost sore mound – against his leg, getting pleasure but not the release I'd hoped for. Matt cupped his hands around my breasts, pushed them together, worked his tongue-and-tooth magic on the valley between them.

Damn. Gary didn't do that. No one I'd been with had done that, at least not with such dedication, such focus. I'd always thought most of the nerves in my breasts were centred in my nipples. Not so, apparently.

Finally he had had enough of that and moved up, taking a good bite at my shoulder on the way.

He positioned himself, the head of his cock nudging against my slit. 'Don't need to ask if you're ready for me,' he purred. 'You're soaked.' He rubbed himself against me. He felt huge to my overheated senses, as if the head of his sheathed cock was the size of an orange.

I mewled, squirmed, tried to push him in. He chuckled, the laugh rumbling through his whole body and mine. It vibrated my nipples, my clit.

'Please,' I managed to say. 'Hard.'

And then Matt was pushing into me, hard like I'd begged, and while he wasn't really as big as an orange – probably around Gary's size, maybe a hair bigger, meaning nice sized but not a stallion cock – he filled me well, filled me fast, filled me deep.

He rose onto his knees, grabbed my hips and pulled me towards him in a frenzy of motion.

In a choked, lust-filled voice, I heard him say, 'Gary. *Now.*'

A familiar weight settled onto the bed next to me, the weight of a body I knew as well as I knew my own. A familiar warm man's scent filled my nostrils. Familiar hands, gentle but eager, eased the blindfold off me. Light pressed against my closed eyelids. I wanted to see, wanted to see Gary above me, Matt in me, but the light seemed almost too intense after the long darkness and instead I kept my eyes closed, breathed in Gary's kiss, arched my back to press my breasts into the beloved hands that were running down my body.

A stranger was pounding into me, the man I loved was caressing me and my entire body was alive with pleasure. For once in my life I didn't want to start coming around a cock right away. I wanted to keep feeling all these distinct amazing sensations, not the glorious confusion of orgasm. Not just yet.

'Open your eyes, love,' Gary said. 'Look at the man who's fucking you.' It was a request, not a command, but I don't think there was any way I could have disobeyed.

I blinked in the light, found I was looking, by some instinct, at Gary rather than Matt. It was hard to tear my gaze away from Gary – his wide eyes, his hard cock, his expression of lust and amazement – but I did.

The few brain cells that could still think about anything other than fucking and getting fucked were astonished that Gary had never thought to mention that Matt was black.

Well, not so much black as a yummy reddish brown. He was bald, as I'd thought, and muscular in a squared-off way, and had one of those faces that was attractive without being handsome in any of the easily definable ways, features that individually didn't seem that gorgeous, but added up to something more than the sum of their parts. His eyes were screwed shut, his features distorted with effort and lust, his dark skin glazed with a thin film of sweat, and if I hadn't already been turned on more than any three women had a right to be, that image would have done it.

I looked from him to Gary, all long lines and a blond's peach-tinged pallor, and then back again.

'So lucky.' I wanted to say more than that, but I couldn't.

Not so much because I couldn't articulate, although I really couldn't, as because Gary shifted position at that second and teased at my lips with his cock.

I took a deep breath, drank in his scent of Camembert

and spice, took him into my mouth, and that did it. I wanted to suck him like no man had ever been sucked, show him just how much I loved him, how much I appreciated this gift, this beautiful stranger/friend he'd given me.

But I was too busy coming to put any art into it. All my muscles rippled around Matt, and I shouted out, pounded one fist into the mattress and the other into Matt's hard thigh. Gary was stroking himself, and I was licking and sucking as best I could around the shock waves passing through me.

As my body let up and I figured I could trust myself not to bite down, I shifted my hand, cupped Gary's balls, started focusing on the hard shaft in my mouth as well as the one in my pussy. I pressed into the spot just below his balls that always made him insane and was rewarded with his cock jerking in my mouth, his voice catching as he said, or tried to say, 'If you keep that up, I...'

'Do it,' Matt growled, and I wasn't sure which one of us he was talking to, but it really didn't matter. I suckled and swirled my tongue and played with that magic spot behind Gary's balls. Gary pinched my nipples hard. Matt's hips began to snap as he pounded into me in a way that made the earlier fierce fucking seem like he'd been holding back.

As come filled me at both ends, another wave of orgasm washed over me.

I think I may have actually blacked out for a few seconds. In any case, the next time I was coherent enough to notice much of anything other than aftershocks, I was snuggled up next to Gary, who was murmuring words of love into my hair.

Matt was sitting next to me, one dark hand on my hip. 'Hi,' I said, because it dawned on me that I never actually had. 'I'm Karen Steele. Have we been introduced?' I grinned as best I could with my melted muscles.

He laughed nervously. It was a very odd effect, hearing a nervous titter echoing inside that basso rumble. 'Hi, pretty lady,' he said. 'Matt LeComte. And I look forward to actually talking to you ... over the pizza I'm about to go pick up. Mind if I take your car, dude?'

I felt rather than saw Gary nod.

Matt pressed a kiss on my forehead, gathered up his clothes and walked away. At the door, he turned back briefly, smiling. 'Don't take this wrong, guys. It's all good. It's just that I could eat Italy right now, never mind a pizza, and I bet I'm not the only one. And besides, I think you two need a little alone time.'

I didn't see Matt leave. I was too busy pressing myself against Gary, nuzzling him, kissing him as if he'd been away for six months.

Reacquainting myself, after the pleasures of the strange, with the pleasures of the familiar and much loved.

Barely Grasped Pictures
Olivia Knight

When she's on holiday, she play-acts herself (unless, of course, she's in Spain with other English people around, in which case she pretends to be French). Floating into seaside coffee shops in a long summer dress, dark glasses and a floppy hat, she can pretend to be the sort of person who floats into seaside coffee shops in a long summer dress, dark glasses and a floppy hat. She enacts being a character who buys long drinks with mint in them and condensation sparkling on the sides, and watches how the light from the water dances on the walls of the sort of arty sparse café that a person like her frequents. Because she is transient here, she can be what she seems. The moment is perfect because it is frozen.

Forget that there is another place where, choiceless as a child, she must arrive every day by nine o'clock, uniformed in what is appropriate, and stay there, humdrum and appropriate and known as 'the one who...', until half-five or six, and even then follow the deeply grooved rut of the office worker to commute home, sometimes via the supermarket, fix supper, eat, relax, wash, get to bed at a suitable time, sleep. Repeat whether or not desired. Forget the people who know her sources, habits, limits of her knowledge and workaday pigeonhole in life. Here, she is the tip of her iceberg – cool, remote, unfathomable. A disaster waiting to happen.

One slim foot has half-escaped its sandal, which dangles from her toes; the artless childishness belies her creamy composed smile. Her bag, hanging from the back of the chair, is a smudge of straw. Her hair, fluffed up by sea air, froths out beneath her hat in fuzzy curls. Can she feel the eyes watching her?

He stepped in and she came alive. It was barely perceptible – her shades hid the sparkle of interest in her eyes. One hand rearranged a curl by her ear, almost absent-mindedly, and drifted back down to her glass. Once there, it was awkward and the fingers stretched out to twiddle the straw between the ice cubes – as one does, as anyone does, quite naturally. Her face was angled towards the panorama of sea through the French windows, through the door by which he stood hesitantly.

He'd seen her here every day this week and her presence, like a cloud of perfume, was spoiling his favourite haunt. He could no longer saunter to the bar, knowing her eyes were in the room. He could no longer sit at a table and lose himself in a book and a cloud of cigarette smoke, with his spine tied to hers by invisible string. This was *his* coffee shop, where *he* could be a recluse, and all week he'd only been able to orbit her. Now, standing within the range of her gaze, even his hands were shy and made to hide themselves in the pockets of the jacket he'd forgotten he wasn't wearing. Day by day, her skin was turning to pale gold, though he never saw her lying on the beach, steaming and sweating under the sun, like the other tourists. She wore three long dresses, by turns: a white one that whispered at her ankles (could he but be that hem, to kiss those ankles), a pale-blue one that knotted together at the back, exposing her angular shoulders, and a pale-pink silk one with cream and maroon flowers softly splotched across it. Luggage restrictions, of course.

He knew what she was, that she would leave and he could have his coffee shop back, that her presence here would evaporate like the early spring morning mist the tourists never saw, and he would be left clutching at air, yearning for a woman whose name he didn't know. But he *did* know her – he knew she was only pretending to be what she was. He saw it in the consciously elegant curl of her spine when she sat, the way her foot trembled to feel the sandal dangled but let it hang nonetheless. He had to speak to her.

He'd spoken to her already, of course. Every night when the cold salt air blew in across his room carrying the babble of voices and thrumming of music from late-night bars, when the orange lights of the boulevard bounced up onto his ceiling, his body lay in bed and his mind drifted through the streets with her. When he climbed the metal stairs to his concrete box of a room, her ghost trailed behind him. When he opened the door on his almost-empty room, she saw what he did: not the poverty of furniture and unswept floor gritty with sand, but the moonlit breakers rushing towards them framed by the long window. Lying alone, he turned to her imaginary face and let his hand be the soft brushing of her lips against his. Then his hand became hers, small and sweet as it cautiously explored beneath the covers, and the pillow was her body against his, and he made her cry out many times before he let himself be buried completely, no holding back, in the clasping warmth of ... his fist. She always vanished when he came, so that he was left alone in bed again, gasping, holding only his own faded pillow and wilting cock, and feeling a little desolate and just a little ashamed. Only then, could he sleep.

'You have ruined my coffee shop with your beauty.'

'Can I buy you a drink?'

'Since I saw you, I can't sleep without the fantasy of you coming repeatedly under my hands, my tongue, my cock.'

'Excuse me, I couldn't help but notice you . . .'

So far past the opening moments in his head, he couldn't think of an opening line, and walked to the bar rather than stand vacillating by the doorway. Never mind butterflies, his stomach was a lake of lava and ice: would he buy her a drink, would he approach her table, would he peel back the cool façade and pry into her elegant untouchability, through which her real thrumming life couldn't help but shine? Would he teach her to drop her dress and pretences onto the sunset sand?

She can feel his presence behind her, the admiring eye that completes her seeming. He's a blur in the background, daubed in and suggested at rather than exactly delineated – but then she too is not so precise and her edges blur into her surroundings. A suggestion of a white T-shirt and blue jeans, body leaning against the bar, head twisted over his shoulder to look at her. Her back is to him, but every aspect of her posture is angled for him: the tilt of her chin as she stares out, the brush of her hair against her bare back, the slow swing of her foot, the restless mashing of ice cubes. His eyes burn her skin and lift her breasts. She knows she is a dream, right now, and wants to play out the dream to be it better. He is the permission she needs to be beautiful. So she stays where she is rather than moving out into the world of sunlight and water and holidaymaking that is only refracted into this scene.

They stayed in their places while the sun drew its reflections off the water and behind the mountain, turning the sea view into three bands of dark blue, pale pink and pale blue. They lingered over their separate drinks while the bartender walked around the near-empty café, lighting the candles, preparing for the crowds that came out with the stars. She walked to the bar with her empty glass and he glanced towards her, away at the wall and down at the bar where her wrist rested.

'We could just carry on getting quietly slaughtered,' she said shakily, 'or we could actually say something to each other.' Her vowels were neatly shaped, rounded, high in her mouth – all orderly Englishness. Her consonants ended quickly where his would linger.

'Um, how's about getting slaughtered together?' he said, before he could think – but it was OK, she was laughing, she was slipping onto the barstool next to him.

'Hi.' She gave him a smile she'd only ever given the mirror before, and felt the power of her eyelids over him.

She lies on his bed in the orange dark of his night-time dream place, at the hour when all souls weep, but they are smiling. Her arms are behind her head, a slight fuzz of hair beneath her armpits which she needn't hide because he's already licked them hungrily and buried his nose in the scent of her. Her breasts are pulled taut, at this angle, and her nipples still stand firm. Though his kisses have subsided, for now, the sea mist is clouding outside and cooling her skin. His duvet is half under her hips, half tumbled to the floor, and the faded pillow which played her part is squashed and folded beneath her head. Her hips are twisted at an angle, so that her waist dives into a deep curve and she can feel the swell of her hips as succinctly as if she's running her own hands up and down them. In the low light, her pale-gold skin is copper and sunset gold, her eyes are huge and black, her lips are knowingly parted. The bright flush still glows on her cheeks and breasts. He sits on the chair, smoking a cigarette and studying her through the feathers of smoke. In another place, in another world, she might be the sort of person who would complain about cigarette smoke – fully dressed, with her hair tied back and not squandered all over the pillow, she might object. Here, she can be the sort of person who doesn't care, who links this moment backwards in time to nineteenth-century Parisian flings, who can see his examining of her, reflectively smoking, in the light of philosophy, expressionism, art-house cinema. The light is right, for that. She is still floating on the things he has done to her, she can still feel the outlines of her pussy where he rubbed so frantically in and out of her while she screamed her voice ragged and gulped in lungfuls of his unfamiliar skin smell like sandalwood or cedar, hints of musk, a haunting bouquet of salt, Shiraz and sex. Just by looking at her lying there, one can know that this is what has happened. One can see: she has been well fucked and the person watching her will return to her side. She is clearly between bouts.

He stubbed his cigarette out, the rickety desk wobbling on the floorboards as he did, and sat down by her on the bed again. His hand ran over the tickling mass of her hair, tenderly.

'You're incredible,' he murmured, making it so with his words. They had talked, earlier, of things she'd forgotten she knew, or left behind for too long, or didn't even realise she knew. In the humming tension of their skin not touching, at the bar, they had used words instead of fingertips to play with each other and send frissons down their backs. He thought her glamorous and knowledgeable. She thought him more whole and true to himself than anyone she had ever met. Best it stayed that way.

* * *

They'd walked across the road, in a bubble of sexual tension and talk which removed them from the short-skirted tottering crowds and striding lads out to play for the night. In the consent of silence, they left the masses behind and their legs took them across the endlessly stretching beach.

'The bare and boundless sands stretch far away,' he said, and she didn't recognise it for the misquote he suspected it was. Instead, the rhythm of the lines carried them in acquiescence through the night. The bars fell behind them until even the music was just a thin trail hovering like a thread between the stars. The hotels dropped away, the houses became sparser and finally the beach ended by a piled-up wall of broken rock and boulders, long since tumbled down the slopes from the mountain to settle here. They stood still then, knowing they would kiss because they were alone by moonlight on a beach and had kept walking, further and further, to find this moment. His hand touched her waist, lightly. She slid towards its warmth and raised her face upwards. He bent and kissed her, pulling her slowly closer, as she returned the brushing of lips and hesitant darts of tongue. It didn't matter that she had never been the best of kissers: on his lips, she turned herself into an artist, playing with the space between them, letting her tongue slide across the edge of his mouth, pulling his lower lip into the embrace of her teeth.

She was the one who pulled her dress over her head and dropped it onto the sand, so she could be perfect in moonlight – even though she was the one who dressed under a towel in the gym, here she was fearless. And anyway, it's easy to be perfect in moonlight – daylight is harder. She had no bra on. Usually, she always did, but with that dress it was impossible to wear one, because the straps would show, and blah blah blah – who cares about why, who explains, who thinks the truth of the film is to be found in the projection room? She had no bra on, and he fell to his knees. With his arms raised to cup her loose free breasts, he kissed her stomach and trailed his tongue around her belly bar. His hands moulded the shape of her breasts, her back, her waist, her bottom, making her shapely; she rested her hands on his soft thick hair and looked up at the upside-down moon, crying softly with bliss as he held her panties aside and pushed the tip of his tongue down through her slit. Her legs bucked repeatedly, she could hardly stand, he guided her fall onto her dress and knelt between her legs, cradling her thighs as they fell apart, then drank and tasted.

New taste: sweet and sharp, like sour cream and seawater, with a whisper of bitter iron. It was as strange as the first time he tasted olives, or Brie, or mussels, and he licked again to learn it better, found that it sent him wild with lust and pushed his tongue in deeper to get more. He was French kissing her parted lips as if it were her mouth, forgetting to be Good At It in the maddening taste of her. He only emerged from his trance when she came, wailing softly.

Standing again, with her dress shaken free of sand and slipped back over her head, he kissed her and she smelt herself on his lips and chin. They were conspiratorial now, giggling at the sand and rocks and scrubby bushes which had borne witness to their secret. He held her close to the hard swelling that his jeans trapped against his thigh.

'Would it be forward to ask you back to mine?' he whispered into her flyaway hair.

She shuddered with still-subsiding bliss, chill and excitement. 'Yes, it would,' she said, low and soft, bright-eyed, 'but I'll come anyway.'

* * *

They had no patterns or ritual to follow when they walked into his room. His hand fluttered by the light switch and pulled away, without touching it. She was the empowered one, because she was the stranger in his place, and she could call the shots while he flickered on the edges not knowing whether to open wine or offer food or kiss her again, this time not just for the sake of a kiss but as a signal to recommence activities. She sat on his bed and pulled him to her so he could feel her hot breath on him through his jeans. He'd rearranged himself, surreptitiously, on the walk back and now the soft skin on the tip was pushing itself up, peeping above his waistband. Her tongue flickered across it, curious and judgemental – was this a taste she wanted in her mouth? She tasted around the glans, letting the strong red flesh of her tongue tip wiggle to find its way beneath that peeling-back sheath of skin, and her lips closed over it. When she unzipped him and pulled his jeans and underwear down, he sprang out, shuddering like a ruler. She clasped him in both hands and nuzzled him, breathing him in. The memory of the shape of her breasts was fresh; he wanted to see them again, in this light. While she crooned over his cock, hardening it still more against her cheek, his shaking fingers found the tie of her dress at her neck beneath the masses of uncontrollable hair. When he finally fumbled the knot loose, the dress fell to her waist and a vision of sweetly wanton womanhood looked up at him and smiled. They hardly knew what to do next – follow the imperatives of their bodies, yes, but how, in what order, should he break from the delicious clasp of her fingers to feel her nipples in his mouth? Without habit, they were carving each moment out of untouched time. But they grinned, and she drew her hand up and down him, delighted by the firm feel of it against her palm, discovering and making the length and breadth of it.

His jeans were around his ankles and she had to let him go to pull them off and then slide his T-shirt over his head, his arms raised like a child's, because unfortunately clothes don't simply 'fall away' – or at least, men's clothes don't. When she stood, her dress descended her hips and made a puddle of white fabric on his floor, next to his bed. Seeing that, more than seeing her near-nakedness, made him realise wildly that she was real, really there, ready to succumb to him – or him to her, or them to their images of each other, or to the images of themselves they gave each other. It didn't matter, they were all these people, and mostly bodies whose skin tremored with proximity and nostrils flared and tongues discovered. She raised her hips with her hands to let him remove her panties, and so he couldn't help but bury his mouth against her again.

He licked. She stretched out backwards, running her outstretched arms over the bobbled texture of a cheap much-washed unfamiliar sheet. Someone else's sheet, while the someone else dabbled his tongue in her and drew light wet lines up the sides of her lips. She moaned aloud, and the new sound of her own pleasure sent a thrill through her. He raised her hips with his hands, as she had, and wrote secrets on her clitoris with his tongue. *I want to penetrate you*, he patiently spelt out with tiny upstrokes, circlings and dashes of his tongue. He listened to the crooning whimpers, and licked in cursive. Her eyes wide open, unseen, stared at the streaking car lights across the half-lit wall and ceiling, how the shadows flowed across the room and leapt back into place. She didn't need to think of anything in this hiatus: no day-to-day responsibilities of home flitting through her head, no questions about where this was leading – that was unquestionable. Just the feeling of his tongue exploring her, just the burning gold of pleasure washing over her, just the feel of her arms swimming across his sheets and his fingers swimming in her flesh. He rocked against her in time to his fingers sheathing themselves, hypnotised with the sight of her clasping round them and the thought of pushing into her. Her breasts, flattened by gravity and pulled up by her outflung arms, were two low soft mounds, pale as beach sand, tipped with crisp nubs of pink. He had a vision of erotic ecstasy, and fulfilled it: he held himself above her and took one bright hard nub in his mouth while his hard cock-head touched her entrance. Her cry arched her breast into his mouth and rubbed his tip between her juicy lips. He nibbled and jabbed, trying to find the way into her sweetness, meeting wet succulent flesh everywhere but always slipping away – until there he was, there she was, a sweet tunnel waiting to be dug. He bit gently, folding her narrow shape into his arms, pushing slowly inwards, inwards, inwards. She felt his shaft forcing her warm walls to part for him, little shoves bringing him closer to the crowning centre deep inside her, and she let her body give itself up entirely. Spreadeagled, moaning, her head rocking back and forth, her pelvis rising against him, she was cool and ecstatic.

But the calm, remote little centre of her mind couldn't withstand him forever. He plunged into her deliriously and swung her over, dragging her legs off the bed – she knew her thighs slammed against the wooden frame, but it was lost in his repeated stabs deep inside her. Her legs raised to wrap around him backwards, he held her horizontal and shoved deeper. Her hands pressed flat against the wall to meet his strokes, her throat roughened with screams they barely heard. He fucked away the sort of person who floated into coffee shops hidden behind sunglasses, who folded elegantly into a chair, who toyed with a chic drink, and fucked into being the sort of person whose hair was damp with sweat, whose back shone slickly as she sat astride him and flung her arse up and down his length. Holding her against the cool wall, staggering on the uncertain ground of the mattress, he heaved his cock up through her, destroying the palely interesting face as he made her flush red and contort her features in spasmodic glee. The fascinating silence of her became squeals and guttural gasps. The foot from which her sandal had so coyly dangled was in his mouth, his lips wrapped around her toes, and his tongue found the embarrassing joy of the skin between them. His eyes were meeting hers as he sucked – there was no escaping his recognition. His hand fondled between her legs and prised her open to his gaze. Each time she came, he said only, 'You're not finished yet,' and forced yet more pleasure on her. She came riding him, she came squashed against the mattress, crushed to the wall, on her hands and knees, with his cock buried inside her, with his fingers deep, with both their fingers tangling together to twirl and dive, with his tongue whisking her swollen clitoris to another howling splashing collapse into joy. She hadn't known she could come so much. She was half off the bed, almost handstanding on the floor, when his plunging strokes spiralled out of control and he shagged her to the floor, and made her the sort of person who cried uncontrollably on the cold boards of a seaside room while her hungry, insatiable womb filled with his spunk.

She lay sprawled, naked and shameless, on his bed while he smoked. She drank sharp red wine poured from a five-litre box.

He stroked her hair and whispered, 'You're incredible.'

She shook her head sadly. 'If only you knew,' she said, *how boring and ordinary I really am*. All the time they'd talked, she'd hidden the true tedium of her reality away, letting fragments and sketches fill in the seeming of a much more interesting glamorous life, of a more entrancing her. And now he'd fucked away all possibility of pretence.

A single splash glitters in the light, the water flung up by the force of her body, now unseen beneath the smooth rolls. For an invisible moment, everything hangs: the elongated, shattered sheets of water; the sparkle of light on the smooth tense surface; the living person one can only imagine beneath, suspended in liquid.

Even though it was lovely beneath, even though sand rose like gold dust around her feet and strange little caverns were formed between the rocks, she swam to the surface to breathe. The tide had filled the rock pool to capacity, and was now turning. No more waves disturbed its surface, and the rocks held their cup of water a little higher than sea level, at least for now. Little by little, it would leak away, but the moment of the water being washed back and forth was perfect. She floated, buoyed up by the salt of long-since evaporated water, watching the dreaming sky and listening to the sound of the waves rushing back and forth against the barrier of rocks. *Shhh, shhh*, whispered the ocean as it cradled her.

She lay on the rocks by the side, their shallow hollows making room for her, while the sun dried her. Her hand dangled down towards the still water below. One tiny fish hovered by a pebble. After observing closely for several minutes, she realised the slight blurs on its sides were fins, flicking too fast to be seen by a casual glance. A cool breeze rolled over her still-damp skin and she was glad to be out of the water, in the air of the beating sun again. I wonder if you get cold? she thought to the fish.

Do you ever want to get out? ... No, I suppose you couldn't breathe then ...

The fish darted, spinning itself around, and in an instant was standing guard on the other side of the pebble, fins still fluttering, as intent as ever. Nothing else moved. Now why did you do that? For a brief vertiginous moment she felt herself inside the fish's mind, and reeled. She pulled away before she drowned in its aquatic thoughts and sat up, shading her eyes. There he came, walking down the thin yellow footpath which feet had barely eroded from the dry grass around it. From a distance, in shorts, a daypack slung over his bare chest, he wasn't the fearful figure who had stripped her bare last night.

He jumped confidently from boulder to boulder, slowing where black and green patches betrayed slime, and sat next to her. She looked down, but his shadow had scared the fish away.

'Hi.'

'Hi.'

They didn't have a repertoire to fill the meeting-moment – How was your day? How did this or that go? – or an established habit that dictated a kiss. Instead, he unzipped the daypack and pulled out wine, two glasses she recognised from his room, wrapped in a little blanket, a packet of crackers and some supermarket tubs of hummus, sundried tomatoes, olives: no sandwiches for lovers, so perhaps there was a repertoire to draw on after all.

'I thought you might be hungry,' he said, almost apologising.

Then they looked at each other. The skin on his neck was still as burnt red, gold brown as it had been in the dim alcohol haze of the coffee shop late at night. His chest still looked as sweet to the taste, its small nipples crinkled into tiny pebbles.

'You are so beautiful,' he whispered breathily. He reached out one hand to touch her sea-dreadlocked hair where it curled in her neck. 'I thought maybe you'd have run away before I got here.'

She shook her head, her throat shuttered with delight.

He leant forwards hesitantly. Despite everything they'd done the night before, he was unsure whether he had permission to kiss her. She met him halfway, their dry lips touching lightly, brushing back and forth. Their hearts and lungs stopped for that moment so they had to pull away just to breathe, just to let their blood continue flowing. He uncorked the wine and that was something to do, although eating was more awkward and embarrassing.

They lay on the blanket on the rock, side by side. In the swathes of goose-pimpled flesh around her bikini and his shorts, their skin touched warmly. Her head rested on the muscle where his arm met his chest. They had nothing to do but stare at the sky and exchange talk – not facts and personal details, but the flimsy soaring ideas that can pretend to be fully formed and so thrive and be born. He had become not just a stranger against whom she could reflect herself, but a person in contrast to whom she could explore herself. His hand ran lightly up and down her arm. The tide was receding, the rock pool sinking slowly, the tiny shadows of the granite lengthening. She told him about the fish, and he pulled her to him for a long slow kiss. He ran his hand up the ever-goldening side of her breast, brushing the sticky plastic tensile fabric of her bikini. Beneath it, her nipples rose. Just his hand, brushing back and forth over the mounded flesh, made her dream her way into the ocean and its everlasting textures of sand. Under the water, in the places where his exploratory hand took her, light was texture – the different depths of water, lit in pale grainy turquoise, aquamarine, cerulean and Prussian blue; the sandy floor rising in clouds and falling in drifts; the fragments of sparkling shell falling through the gloom...

She cried out as his fingers found her nipple. He was so slow and shy now.

'Yes, please, yes,' she whispered, as he peeled the bikini cup away and lowered his mouth.

He tasted sea salt and felt shell textures with his tongue. She moaned, feeling the flow of her body rise like the tide for him. Now he was a person – already known and barely grasped. Hands, behind which stood a fully fledged mind, a history, an identity and a myriad of thoughts, were sliding down her thighs while his mouth sucked at her. He found the curve of her waist, which made her stretch and elongate. He found the sensitive space just above her knee, inside her thigh, and moved to kiss it as her legs made way for him.

'I think we should move,' he said, raising his head from the honey of her flesh.

He guided her, over the boulders and shards of shattered rock, to the crescent of cove below and to the side. The sand was still damp from the receding water, and he spread the blanket out again. Now, they could see no paths or hillside or distant houses, just the overhang of cliff, the rock where they had been and the sea stretching out ahead of them.

He drew her bikini bottoms off slowly and bent his head again to that small patch of skin on the inside of her knee. His tongue brought alive skin she hadn't noticed since she was sixteen. All she could say, again and again, to his touches, was 'Yes'. His silky hair nudged her thighs apart as he kissed his way upwards. Her thighs were a country he mapped with traces of saliva, discovering that *here*, at this inch, she sank back into the pleasure, but *there*, just a quarter-inch further, she rose up and cried out softly. As patient as a teenager who doesn't dare believe he's allowed to do even as much as he's doing, he licked upwards.

When a new, deft dart of his tongue set off springs in her back, and her body leapt involuntarily forwards in shudders of joy, she saw the horizon of sea and sky, the sun making low pathways of gold. He held her wide open and delved. She wept. She clutched his hair in her hands while shimmers of sun gold scattered through her. His tongue tip found her clitoris, at last, and began to circle it lovingly. Once upon a time, far far away, she'd found it difficult to come from this. Now, there was no difficulty, because there was no trying – only grainy sand, which yielded to her clutching fingers, a setting sun, which painted her secret bliss across the ocean, and his tongue, which seemed to have found out all her secrets. Her sudden wails bounced this way and that around the cavern and floated off, across the water. She was left, basking in the glow of joy, her pussy still tantalisingly responsive, him still kneeling between her legs.

'Look!' he whispered.

On the rock where they had started making love, a woman stood, her pale skin catching the light of the dying sun.

'It's my dress,' she said with a giggle. It was identical – probably mass-produced in China, certainly distributed to and sold in branches all over England in tasteful displays of holiday fantasy, created for the illusion of places just like this. The same floating white hem skirted the woman's ankles, fluttered by sea breezes. Her face was hidden by a floppy hat and sunglasses, although the sun was now just shards of red scattered on the horizon. After all, it's the holiday look that counts. She was leaning far over the rock, as if peering at her own reflection in the water.

He turned to her again. He'd abandoned his shorts. Sometimes, when you're not looking, not thinking, even men's clothes melt away. His cock rose above her soft belly, firm and fresh and young. It said, let me bring you delight. So she reached her hand down and guided him slowly into the passages he'd made so wet and welcoming. As she helped him, her spine arched again, her legs lifted, spread further and wrapped around his hips to draw him closer. She felt him sliding in, no inch-by-inch forcing but a smooth, tight welcome. When he pressed his open mouth against hers, she met it gladly.

They rocked each other, in and out, back and forth, tender and ecstatic. She felt the whole column of him inside her, not just the jutting tip or grinding shaft, and made suckering starfish on his back with her hands. No postures, no angles, no posing, no impressing, no trying – just the rhythmic roll of unthinking perfect bliss inside each other. So he glided, she shuddered, it didn't matter if he came, if she came, or when they did, only the clasping ecstasy was all. She came, repeatedly, finding towers of coral peaks in their underwater world of sex, no orgasm final, just a constant well of clenching and shuddering around his flowing cock. She was herself, then. When she screamed, loud and clear and untrammelled through the night, he lost all words and rushed into her, blissfully, and so neither saw the waters break open, or saw the splash frozen in its moonlight moment, or how the surface rocked and settled and wasn't broken again, or knew what might have been. They lay in each other's arms forever, that night.

Behind the Masque
Sophie Mouette

This was it. Tonight. The biggest job of our short but so far quite illustrious career.

The Lucchese Star. Sixty carats of sapphire, as big as your fist. Makes your mouth water just looking at it. Makes you think of Caribbean seas, the summer you were ten, the eyes of the lover that got away.

Inside my turquoise doeskin gloves, my palms itched. They didn't sweat, not a drop; I wasn't nervous. It was all about the anticipation, baby. The lead-up. The foreplay.

George and I made a good team. I wouldn't go so far as to say he was the brawn and I was the brain, but it shook down kind of like that. He had the most amazing hands – steady, delicate. He knew exactly how, when and where to touch, to coax out the exact response he wanted. No safe, no security system, no alarm could resist his ministrations. Powerless beneath his touch.

Kind of like a woman.

Oh, yes, George could use those hands to work magic on me. Bring me to helpless, shuddering orgasms long into the night.

Problem was, when we were getting ready for a job, George eschewed sex. Distracted him, he said. Put him off his game. He needed to be focused.

Which left me more than a little on edge, if you know what I mean.

My outfit tonight didn't help that one bit. The

custom-made corset fitted me like a lover's hands, moulding against my waist, urging my breasts up to pillow enticingly. My hard nipples rubbed against my fine silk underdress just at the line of my corset. Teasing. Taunting.

George might have been the one to cajole the secrets from a coded alarm system, but I was the one who got us in place. He always said I could talk my way into, or out of, anything.

I glanced down at my enticingly displayed décolletage. I could talk the talk, but the girls helped, too.

I can't tell you the number of times I've been pulled over for speeding, only to drive away without a ticket. I can convince the proprietor of a swanky shop that I really did buy this item, but I lost the receipt, and I honestly do deserve a refund. I can charm the fur off a mountain lion, as they say.

Getting George and me invitations to this very swanky, very private reception at The Venetian was child's play.

Ah, The Venetian. An only-in-America fusion of Italian Renaissance decadent beauty, glittering luxury skyscraper and the edgy 24-hour liveliness for which Las Vegas was famous. A huge casino, an in-house wax museum and gondola rides along a faux canal. Talk about gaudy.

But tonight the gaudy was the sort a Venetian doge in his ornate ceremonial robes would have approved. The Venetian also housed the Vegas branch of the world-renowned Guggenheim Museum. Tonight, it played host to a grand Carnivale-themed charity ball, celebrating the opening of its latest exhibit 'Jewels of Venice'. Museum supporters, art lovers and high-society types were crowded into the hotel's largest ballroom, all dressed in top designers' quirky takes on Renaissance dress or some equally elaborate and fanciful get-up.

And masks.

Which would make our job – absconding with the Lucchese Star – that much easier.

Faking IDs is so much easier when you don't have to show your whole face. Masks weren't just requested, they were *required* for this soirée. My own was a confection of peacock feathers and pearls, made to match the dress I'd commissioned. Because I had to look the part of the filthy rich patron.

To go along with the masquerade, attendees were asked to pick personas to further 'disguise' themselves. We were announced as Count Giovanni Belli and his wife Francesca, and we swept in as if we owned the place. Give yourself a suitably impressive title and the bearing and outfits to go with it, and people will assume you should be on the guest list.

The ballroom looked like it belonged in another century, or possibly in another world. Women in boned and beaded gowns; men in velvet doublets and tights. People dressed as satyrs, nymphs, gods and goddesses, and other fantastic creatures as depicted in Renaissance art. People in ordinary evening dress (all right, *Vogue*'s very expensive idea of ordinary) but still sporting elaborate masks.

A silver-haired woman, tall and elegant in silver-embroidered black velvet with a severe silver mask blanking out her face, led an amazingly costumed anthropomorphic leopard on a leash. A couple I'd swear were Brad and Angelina, dressed like Bacchus and Artemis, chatted with a Renaissance lady whose emerald necklace made my fingers itch, even with the Lucchese Star almost in my grasp.

So close. So fucking close.

We'd timed our arrival for half an hour before the viewing, giving us time to mingle and become anonymous, part of the greater crowd. Afterwards, nobody would remember us; we hadn't stood out, looked or sounded different than anyone else there.

The whole purpose of this bash was to celebrate The Venetian Guggenheim's borrowing of the Lucchese Star from the Guggenheim in Venice. (Yeah. Don't think about that too hard.) Everyone here (well, everyone except us, obviously) had donated scads of money to help with the acquisition. As such, tonight we'd get to view it first, before it was put into the museum proper.

They announced the viewing and we filled our champagne glasses in anticipation. The door (looked like wood, but was lined with steel) opened, and we surged forwards. In a polite, societally appropriate kind of way, of course.

I didn't have to restrain my reaction, because everyone gasped and murmured at the sight of the Star. I kept just enough attention on myself (making unremarkable comments to those around me) so that no one would notice that George was stealing glances at the Star's prison of a display case, assessing whether the way it was set up deviated from our research.

All too soon, we were ushered back into the main ballroom. I spared a wistful glance over my shoulder.

Soon. Soon, baby.

I set down my untouched champagne (no mind-altering substances until *after* we were safely away) and nibbled a tidbit that involved beluga caviar, eyeing one that seemed to combine lobster and Kobe beef carpaccio. Definite perks to this gig.

George seemed cool and collected behind his full-face Harlequin mask, diamonded in rich tones of copper, gold and an emerald green which brought out the colour of his eyes. Typical. He contained all that sexual energy, internalised it, transformed it into single-minded intent.

Whereas my job was to exude as much sex appeal as humanly possible.

Just before we'd headed to the party, George had sent off the coding that would send dummy images (the ones I'd sweet-talked out of a museum staffer for a magazine article I said I was writing) to the security cameras and disable a few critical systems, just long enough for him to swipe the Star.

My job now was to distract the guard. I admired my abundant cleavage again, stroking the creamy flesh with a fingertip. I shouldn't have a problem with strategic flirting. Unless the male security guard I was expecting had traded shifts with the happily married female ex-Marine. In that case, I'd be faking a seizure and hoping for the best.

I flipped open the pocket watch cunningly disguised as a pendant. It was time.

I touched George on the arm, whispered in his ear as if I were about to head to the ladies' room.

Then I walked right past the ladies' room, headed down the service stairs to the casino level, and up another set that led up to the far side of the ballroom, into a deserted, blocked-off hallway.

The service entrance to the anteroom where the Lucchese Star was displayed was down that hallway.

A security guard was stationed at the hallway entrance. I made no move to evade him. Instead, I approached him, one hand extended, the other gracefully over my heart, calling attention to my cleavage.

'I'm so sorry,' I said, twisting my accent slightly to sound vaguely Southern. Men liked Southern. 'I think I've taken a wrong turn?'

'Looks like it, ma'am. This area is off-limits.' The guard wasn't the man I'd expected to see. My research into The Venetian's security personnel had prepped me for a fiftyish black man, not a well-built white guy in his mid-thirties.

Damn cute one, too. *Whuf.* Big brown eyes, wavy dark hair and the kind of chest I could all too easily imagine curling up on between rounds one and two of wild monkey sex.

Well, it was entirely possible they'd hired extra staff for this event. This fine hunk would be just as much fun to distract as the one I'd been expecting.

I touched the back of his hand, gently. 'Has a man come through here? With a red-headed showgirl type?'

Bingo. I'd picked the right ruse. The mix of concern, sympathy and, face it, curiosity, could only do me good.

He shook his head. ''Fraid not.' Slight, charming traces of Texas in his voice. 'Someone taking those "what happens in Vegas stays in Vegas" ads too seriously?'

I let my lower lip quiver, just for a second, before I squared my shoulders and composed myself. In a way that clearly implied my composure was all an act to hide my anguish.

'That would suggest the city is the problem.' I sighed. 'You know, when he keeps it discreet, it's one thing. But to leave me standing there alone – to sneak out of the ballroom and flaunt that he's going off to have his fun ... It's too dayamn much.' I faked an expression of surprise and embarrassment, knowing that most of it wouldn't show under my mask, but hoping it would be reflected in my eyes – eyes that glittered with the threat of spilling tears. 'I'm so sorry! I shouldn't be talking about this to a complete stranger.'

The big man – the name on his uniform was Joe – shrugged. 'Easier to talk to a stranger sometimes, and you must be as mad as a hornet.'

I'd been stepping a little closer while we talked, edging Security Joe away from the hallway entrance. I did a quick mental calculation of how much time had passed. George should be at the top of the un-alarmed back stairs, about to step into the hallway at my signal.

Time to step up the distraction level.

'Mad means both angry and crazy.' I stepped close enough to smell a combination of healthy man and inexpensive but not unpleasantly spicy cologne. 'I feel a bit of both. Humiliated. And yet ... it's his loss, right? If he can play at the game, why can't I?'

One step closer and I could feel the heat of Joe's body. I touched the peacock-feathered fan dangling from my wrist, triggering the communication to George.

'Ma'am? Are you sure...' the Texan politely protested even as he put his arms around me.

'Tonight, I'm Francesca,' I whispered, and kissed him.

Kissed him more thoroughly than I'd meant to.

I'd planned a little flirting, a little smooching, then dissolving into tears of guilt and jealousy. Most men haven't a clue what to do with a sobbing woman. The security guard would comfort me as best he could, helpless patting on the back and whatnot, and I'd make enough noise long enough for George to relieve the case of the Lucchese Star and get back into the stairway.

Change of plans. Ramp up the smooching instead.

Because despite Joe's protestations, he was getting into the smooching just fine.

His hands tightened on my corseted waist as I parted my lips, flicking my tongue out to touch the corner of his mouth. He pulled me closer, causing my breasts to pillow even more impressively out of the top of my bodice. Polyester may not be sexy, but there was this shocking sense of naughtiness at his uniform brushing against tender flesh that I don't normally expose in public.

All that barely suppressed sexual energy that had built up since we'd started planning this heist bubbled to the surface.

I reached up to stroke the chiselled planes of his face, urging him to deepen the kiss. When his tongue entered my mouth, I couldn't hold back a moan of pure pleasure.

'Francesca,' he murmured against my lips. 'An exotic name for an exotic lady.' He slid his hands up over the curve of my breasts and drew his finger along the line where fabric met flesh. My nipples tightened in response. 'But you're not that much of a lady, are you?'

I stiffened, fearing he'd seen through my ruse. But then he was coaxing my breasts free of the corset. First my nipples showed darkly through the semi-sheer silk, but he pulled the top of the chemise away. He brushed his thumbs against the needy buds, and I clutched his arms.

'More like a courtesan,' he said. 'Brazenly tempting men.' He increased the pressure, rolling my nipples between his fingers. A steady aching pulse started between my legs.

He kept up that maddening, rhythmic pressure while his lips languidly wandered around my neck, my ear lobes, my clavicle, the swell of my cleavage. By the time his mouth found one nipple, my hips were moving in time to the rhythm, thrusting forwards. He was leaning over me to kiss and lick and suckle, though, so I was humping empty air.

Until he stood and my mound connected with the impressive swelling in his uniform pants.

Oh! Well, then.

'What have we here?' I murmured. Unable to keep my hands off something like that – a hard cock is almost as enticing as a hot rock, and certainly more fun to play with – I pressed my palm against the bulge.

His hips jerked, and I felt his prick throb even through my gloves. My mouth watered.

Well, what better way to keep a man distracted? With a rustle of silk and brocade, I sank to my knees.

'Oh, sweet Jesus,' Joe said as I tugged his pants down. His cock sprang out. Long and slender, with a proud curve and darker mushroom head.

I started to peel off my gloves, but Joe's harsh whispered 'No' stopped me.

'Leave them on,' he urged, and who was I to argue?

He tasted as earthy as he looked. I took him full in my mouth, slicking him with saliva, and brought my hands up to encircle him while I sucked.

My pussy lips were getting just as slick. I could feel them rubbing together, my clit throbbing between them. As tempting as it was to fight one hand beneath the layers of skirt and fondle myself, I resisted. I *like* giving blow jobs, for one thing. And for another, I had to keep alert for any sounds of George, and make sure I kept Joe from noticing anything other than what I was doing to him.

From Joe's reactions, I was pretty sure he wouldn't have noticed a parade of elephants galumphing down the hall. His hands on my head, he urged me to increase the length of my oral strokes.

'Oh yeah, that's it,' he said, his voice rough with desire. 'Take me in. Suck me. Play with my balls.'

I was more than happy to comply, and moaned my agreement as I did.

'Oh, yeah, you like it when I give directions?' he asked. 'Naughty girl. That's it, suck me. Use your hands. The leather feels so good against me. Faster now.'

I increased the pressure and speed, feeling his balls contract up towards his body. He was close, and I wanted to bring him off. That feeling of power, of control.

He groaned something unintelligible, and came, twitching. I rocked back onto my heels, savouring his tang, feeling smug about the relaxed, slightly goofy, absolute content look on his face. OK, maybe George wouldn't be thrilled if he found out what I'd done, but it had certainly worked. With that as a distraction, there was no way the guard could have heard any very faint sounds that George might be making.

That George might still be making.

I'd taken my time, both for distraction value and because Joe had a yummy cock and a delightfully dirty mouth.

Where the hell was George? A delicate operation like this one might require more time than we'd anticipated.

Suddenly the corridor seemed tomblike, so silent (despite all the normal background sounds you get even in a quiet corridor in a busy hotel) that I fancied Joe could hear George breathing in the other room, let alone going through all the meticulous steps needed to snatch the Star.

I could go with Plan A, Part Two: tears, confusion, repentance.

But my slick pussy and throbbing clit had other suggestions for continuing the distraction.

And they sounded like a lot more fun. Never really enjoyed playing out the weeping-woman scenario, though it's killer effective. Ruins the mascara and all that.

I stood up, one graceful motion, swaying only a little in my high heels. (Yes, I do practise things like that. It pays to stay limber, and grace adds to the erotic-distraction factor when I need it.)

Pressed myself against Joe. Might be risking a few lingering drops of come on my brocade gown, but it wasn't as though I'd be wearing this a lot in the future. (Although George had dropped hints that once the job was done, he had some amusing uses in mind for the corset and the nearly sheer split-crotch silk drawers – both historically accurate and practical when you're dealing with sixteen acres of skirt – that went underneath everything.)

Kissed him, letting him taste himself on my lips.

Felt the silk drawers get even damper than they already were.

Moaned 'please' into his mouth and didn't have to act to get that tone of sheer brazen want. I was squirming with need.

'Please what? Tell me what you want, Francesca.' His big hands glided over the ample sensitive mounds of my cleavage, not quite touching my aching exposed nipples. I arched against him, tried to wiggle my nipples under his hands.

No good. He was onto me. 'You have to tell me what you want if you hope to get it.'

As he said that, he did pinch one of my nipples – unexpectedly and hard, jolting electricity through my body so once again all I could manage was 'Please.'

'Please what?' he repeated, toying with my nipples some more.

This was work. Supposed to be work, anyway. I was supposed to stay focused, even if the job was offering perks beyond amazing hors d'oeuvres. But dammit, my whole body was one giant ache, and I wasn't George, able to deflect my desire into something else.

I took a deep breath, found my brain just long enough to say, 'Please get me off. I don't care how. Just please make me come.'

He grinned, a cat who'd found not only cream, but a whole roast chicken and a catnip garden for dessert. Manoeuvred me around so I could lean against the wall – and a good thing too, since my knees were already shaky and I didn't think they'd be getting more stable any time soon. 'Lift up your skirts,' he ordered, his voice as rich and decadent as the best dark chocolate or a fine vintage Bordeaux.

I did, crumpling expensive silk and brocade as if it were cheap cotton. Almost drowning in fabric, I didn't have a good view of what he was doing. But oh, I felt it all right.

His leg roughly pushed mine farther apart. Coarse polyester brushed fine silk, taut wet skin. He ground against me for a few seconds, until I was sure my juices were leaving a stain on his uniform. Then he moved, and his fingers slipped into the slit in my drawers.

'You're soaked,' he breathed. 'Such a wanton naughty girl. And so hot.'

Fingers circled my clit, sending pleasure spiralling through me. I started making alley-cat sounds under my breath, and my world narrowed its focus to between my legs. Then he got his other hand involved, sliding two fingers into my dripping pussy, and began to pump.

I clutched at Joe's shoulders, held on tight, came like there was no tomorrow and no yesterday either, just a long mind-melting *now*.

When I could focus again, I could see that Joe was once again standing at attention. Or maybe he was one of those lucky guys who stayed hard even after he came if the situation were interesting enough.

A compliment in either case.

A very distracting compliment. I may have come, but it had been a long dry few months, and one orgasm, even a toe-curler like that one, was just enough to take the edge off my need. I was still throbbing, still open and ready.

I should save it for George, who'd be relaxed once the job was over, relaxed and full of all the sexual energy he'd been channelling elsewhere for so long.

But that didn't keep me from staring at Joe's renewed erection with the longing of a poor girl staring into Tiffany's display window. It looked hard as gemstones, but a lot warmer . . .

I realised what I was doing, mentally shook myself, opened my mouth to begin the next part of the act (flustered nerves and mild guilt). Before I could say anything, though, Joe took my arm. 'Want to be inside you,' he said, his voice husky and hypnotic. 'There's an electrical closet down the hall. Come on.' He tugged at me.

The jewel thief in me sang out gleefully. The only thing better than a distracted guard was an absent one.

The female-in-heat part of me made an inarticulate moan of surrender. I could imagine that cock sliding into me from behind, inch by glorious inch, and while I could imagine more scenic places to do it than an electrical niche – one of the now-empty exhibits, maybe, so I could be surrounded by things I'd like to steal given the chance – my pussy didn't much care at this point.

But the part of me that did the strategic thinking glitched. On one hand, maybe Joe was just killing time at a job he didn't care about and willing to risk a priceless but anonymous-to-him gem to get some hot sex. (A trait I liked in a man I was duping, especially, as in this case, if it meant I also got the hot sex.)

On the other hand, it seemed almost too convenient, and that made me curious and a little nervous. Not much in our line of work was convenient.

Play the part. I was supposed to have given big bucks to get the Lucchese Star to this country. I'd be at least a little concerned about it. 'Aren't you supposed to be guarding . . .' I gestured towards the door.

Joe shrugged. 'This place is so wired, alarms will squawk all over the building if an unauthorised person so much as breathes in there. They hired some high-priced security firm on top of what we already have for the casino and they rigged a bunch of stuff – I don't understand half of what they've got set up, but that thing's guarding itself. We're just back-up.'

'Well, that's a weight off my mind.'

And it was. Joe was a slacker – a really hot slacker – relying on a high-tech security system to do his job for him.

Which it would have if I hadn't scrambled half of it and George wasn't dismantling the rest even as Joe and I played. Well, at least Joe would get his hot sex before he got fired without references, poor gorgeous bastard.

He ran his hands over my still bare breasts, sending shudders through my body, making me forget any qualms I had, including the ones involving George coming to find me and hearing strange noises coming out of the closet.

OK, a little bit of me thought it might serve him right. I was crazy about George, I really was, but a woman can only handle so much chastity – especially when the person she wants to be unchaste with is right there in bed with her, but not interested.

The closet was as unglamorous as you'd imagine: criss-crossed with wires, unventilated, humming with various mechanical noises. It smelt like dust and electricity, and it was barely big enough for the two of us.

And at that point, I didn't care. No time to worry about atmosphere. The only nicety we took the time to bother with was a few rough but sweet kisses, the kind where you try to devour the other as if you'd never get a chance to touch again, which in this case was true.

When he turned me around so I could support myself against the wall, the cold grey-green breaker cabinet I found myself leaning against brought goosebumps to my heated skin.

The good kind of goosebumps that added to my arousal.

I briefly considered flipping a few breakers while Joe was figuring out what to do with my layers of skirt – create some confusion to cover George's retreat, and all that – but then Joe's cock nudged against my heated pussy.

And after its long hunger, my pussy took control of the situation. Just sucked that magnificent cock in, I swear, because I don't remember any transition between that teasing tap and hot crazy full-on fucking. Joe's hard cock pistoned inside me, stroking all those long-neglected spots that even the best toy can't hit the way the real thing does. One of his hands cupped my breasts, fingers scissoring and stroking the nipple, the other infiltrated under my skirts to circle my clit through wet silk.

I pushed back, met each hard stroke with force of my own. No time for subtlety or tenderness. This was an unabashed quickie and I didn't care. Wanted it that way. Wanted to push myself over the edge and take him with me, here, surrounded by the drone of the hotel's inner workings.

Besides, we had to be fast. George should be done by now, and Joe was deserting his post. I couldn't speak for him, but the edge of danger just made me hotter, made my inner walls clench around him, made me wild and made him wild along with me.

If I weren't an endorphin junkie, I'd still be creating security systems, not cracking them. I like risky business, and this job was pushing thrill buttons I hadn't even known I had.

Joe's fingers found just the right rhythm on my clit, and his cock pounded into me, and I rolled my hips like a jazz dancer.

And then I thought something must have happened to the electrical system because everything went black, then exploded around us.

I didn't see stars as I came. Not exactly. I saw the Lucchese Star, all sixty spectacular carats of it, cloned fifty times and dancing behind my eyelids.

Strong arms circled me. 'That's my good bad Francesca. Feel a little happier now?'

'God, yes.'

Another wicked grin from my talented security guard. 'Sometimes getting a little yourself is the best revenge.'

Oh yeah. I was supposed to be playing a part here, wasn't I?

In a small voice laden with fake confusion, I whispered, 'I guess so. It was fun, anyway.'

Deep breath. Satiated but somewhat uneasy smile. Sudden concern with smoothing out my skirts and repairing my lipstick, my hands trembling.

We managed to pull ourselves together and get out of the closet and just in time.

'There you are!' George hurried up to us, his hair a little mussed and his Harlequin mask the tiniest bit askew. 'I've been looking all over for you. That poor girl – she was feeling sick, so I helped her find the hotel doctor – and when I got back, you were gone.'

Nicely played, with hints of both concern and guilt in his voice. Then he narrowed his eyes at Joe. 'Who's this?'

'I went looking for you, and got lost, honey,' I said meekly. 'He was just giving me directions . . . back to the ballroom.'

Joe clapped George on the back. The gesture was hard enough to make George stumble forwards a step, and Joe caught him. 'You've gotta keep a better eye on your lovely lady,' he said, sounding all amiable and between-us-boys. 'You don't want her to slip away.'

'Yeah,' George said, staring at him funny. I caught my breath, worried that he'd figured out what we'd done. But all he said was, 'Yeah, I'll do that.'

We were an hour into the desert, headed towards LA, when my cellphone chimed to let me know I had a text message.

I take it your partner hasn't noticed I lifted his
phone. Means he hasn't noticed something else is
gone.

I stared at the display for a long time, the glow of it the
only light except for our headlights on the flat straight
ribbon of freeway. We had the moon roof open to enjoy
the canopy of stars undimmed by light pollution. The
crisp desert air poured through, and now it made me
shiver.

'What is it?' George finally asked.

'Let me see the Star.'

'Fran, we're in the middle of nowhere! I can't just pull
over and –'

'Trust me. Get the Star.'

With a huff of annoyance, he slowed and pulled over
on the shoulder. If a cop came along, we'd claim car
troubles.

After we'd left The Venetian, we'd pulled into another
parking garage and shucked our costumes for jeans and
sweatshirts. George rummaged in the back seat and
found his doublet.

'It's right here,' he said, scrunching the fabric to show
the lump in the hidden inner pocket.

A car zoomed by, and ours rocked gently.

'I need to see it,' I said.

'*Fine*,' George snapped. He dug it out, opened the
drawstring bag, and dropped it into his hand. He held it
out to me, and, barely able to breathe, I took it.

It was pretty.

It was very pretty faceted blue glass. Same size and
weight as the Star, but still glass.

The sounds of the night, the rushing of passing cars,
faded away. I felt the blood drain from my face.

'Fuck!' George snatched the stone out of my hand and
flung it out the moon roof. It disappeared into the sand

and scrub somewhere off Interstate 15. He didn't look at me, but I still felt like he knew it was all my fault.

Damn me for an idiot. A horny idiot.

'Joe's' diction had changed as we talked. Still the slight Texas accent – that might even be real – but he'd gone from all 'aw shucks, ma'am' to sounding smoother, better educated, as things got hot and heavy.

Which should have tipped me off that that was his real voice, the one he fell into when his brain wasn't a hundred per cent in gear. But I'd been too busy being seduced.

A month later I was on the road again, this time headed south.

I loved George. Plain and simple, I did. And I loved working with him. But a disaster like the loss of the Lucchese Star could ruin even the most solid working relationship.

The personal relationship unravelled with the same effortlessness. Apparently George lost interest in sex not only when he was planning a heist, but also when he was thwarted in one.

Joe – or whatever his real name was – had texted me again. He'd been impressed, he said, with my creativity, my ability to think on my feet. If I felt like 'upgrading', he was willing to negotiate.

When I answered, he gave me the name of a bar in Tijuana. He'd be there for an hour on a particular night, if I cared to show.

I opened the moon roof, enjoying the wind ruffling my hair. The stars weren't as impressive as a fist-sized sapphire, but they were awfully pretty.

It was important, always, to have a Plan B.

A Whole New City
Nikki Magennis

In ten minutes the office would open. Claire sat ready at her desk, behind the window sprayed with photographs of clouds in blue skies. The name of the agency – *'skylines'* – was etched across the glass in long looping letters. Inside, ranks of shiny brochures leant on the shelves and the grey wool carpet stretched out from the door like a calm sea. Everything was designed to precise specifications, and in the morning everything looked perfect. Including Claire.

She wore a slashed-neck top, showing a sweep of polished skin from her throat to the top of her left breast. It was a considered amount of flesh – enough to suggest her sexuality, but not enough to promise anything. Her breasts had a good firm profile, they smiled up at the customers and Claire knew what useful assets they were. She was an attractive cog in the great machine of life, after all. Well oiled. She crossed a long beautifully sculpted leg over her knee. Her skin was waxed so smooth that her legs slipped against each other.

With her hair sprayed into a solid platinum-blonde knot and her wrists resting lightly on the desk, she waited.

On good days the customers she prayed for breezed into the shop and headed straight for the desk. They wore cashmere and leather, carried monogrammed Louis

Vuitton and had skin tanned the shade of oak. The rich weather elegantly, Claire would think, as she turned to offer them her perfectly clear and undivided attention.

'Tuscany,' a tall man with silvered hair would say, so certain of where he was going and what he wanted. Then Claire would snap into action. Her eyes, as pale as a winter sky, would blink once. Her spine would unroll and her fingers become arrows, French manicured nails pointed straight at the computer screen, searching for flight details and hotels with the requisite handfuls of stars. Inside her fitted suit, her body would thrum with excitement. It was a sensation like flying, a swift and controlled freedom. Like the whole world was there at her fingertips. Airports, runways and gleaming white metal. She'd feel the points of her breasts burning. Her nipples actually jolting with electrical energy. Static, she'd think, as they brushed against the inside of her jacket.

In front of her the customer relaxed into a dream of airhostesses. He would wait patiently as Claire tapped out the codes, playing her part of a beautiful accomplice in his fantasy. Everybody would smile and Claire would squeeze her legs together as she offered the names of cities to her clients: 'Sydney', 'Zurich', 'Jo'burg'. It was the reason why she'd struggled through university, set up the agency and fought her way into the travel industry. For the thought of exotic locations hovering on the horizon and the promise of escape.

The hope for these appointments got her through the day, made the package deals bearable. Claire's flesh crawled when she thought of her usual customers. The vast sweating masses looking for cheap thrills in the sun. They were like cattle, loud and vulgar.

The hunger of those people. If it hadn't been for the fact they paid cash and provided a steady supply of business, she would have refused to serve them. They'd push open the door and clutter up the shop with push-chairs and shopping bags, say 'Ibitsa' and 'Mah-Jorca' like the words were little pieces of gristle they were trying to spit out.

Claire booked them into half-built concrete high rises with dirty pools, wishing them verrucas and cancelled flights as she did so. Spain, Spain, Spain. Did they never imagine anywhere else?

'Coffee?' asked her one employee, Sandy, as she fidgeted with the button on her nylon company-issue blouse. It had tiny pictures of clouds printed all over it, fitted badly and pinched under the arms. Claire nodded, keeping her eyes fixed on the screen. She highlighted several emails. More complaints.

Dear Mr Filkes, she wrote, *I am sorry that the holiday did not meet your expectations.*

It was hardly half-nine and already Claire felt bitterness rising in her throat. Clients like Mr Filkes did not turn her on. He was one of the cheap ones, the cattle clients. They demanded paradise for the price of a week's shopping, and ranted and whined when they didn't get it.

Claire ground her teeth, and her clothes felt suddenly tight and uncomfortable. Something in her longed to just stand up and walk out into the winter sunshine, to lose herself in the traffic and the faceless noise of the city. The clock above the door ticked slowly, forbidding her to leave her desk. Hours, hours till five.

'Got anything planned for the weekend?' Sandy asked.

'Work to do,' Claire muttered, thinking of her flat and its acres of quiet space. Her laptop plugged in and open on the coffee table, files strewn around it.

'I might go and catch a movie. Some good stuff on just now,' Sandy said. 'You're into films, aren't you?'

Claire whipped round to look at Sandy, standing hand on hip at the coffee machine. 'What makes you say that?'

In her mind's eye, Claire saw her living room again: the laptop sitting untouched and next to it the stack of DVDs piled on top of her paperwork. Films with titles like *Pain Slut*. She heard the moans and the wet slap of a hand against flesh. Underneath her make-up, she felt her cheeks burn.

Sandy shrugged. 'No reason. That guy was taking you to see a film last week.'

'That guy' was Don. A month previously he'd come in to the agency, booked his family skiing trip in Switzerland, paid with a platinum Visa card which bore his wife's name next to his, and then asked Claire out to dinner.

She'd gone on a couple of dates with him, expecting the usual extravagance of a married man – gifts, trips, no-strings-attached hotel rooms. But an unexpected development had been his declaration of love.

'This is not the deal, Don,' she'd said on their third date, when he'd let his hands fall open on the table. He'd hinted at the possibility of a quick divorce, his beetle eyebrows lifting up, hopeful. He was practically begging her. Claire had laid down her knife, having only half-buttered a roll. She'd waved the waiter over and asked for her coat.

They'd never gone to see the film.

So tonight, like most nights, she'd be spending alone. She'd take the train home, order a pizza and pull out the hardcore porn. Some of the hard stuff, with sadistic undercurrents which made her pulse race. Claire preferred well-built men, men with shoulders and chests and torsos that rippled. She liked plenty of oil and leather, strong jaws and decisive gestures. In her dreams godlike men pushed her over backwards, tossed her around until her hair came loose and tumbled down her back in a pale-yellow waterfall. They held her down, forced her legs wide open in a beautiful arching V, imposed themselves on her trembling body. Their cocks were huge, made of iron and ruthless. If she fuzzed up her eyes and didn't look at the faces when she watched the films, they almost fitted her fantasies.

Afterwards, she'd turn off the DVD and reach for a tissue to sop herself dry. Her legs would be shaky and she'd feel a little twinge in her stomach, the ache of a fading climax. She'd flick on the TV and channel surf till it was time to pop a diazepam and retire. Eventually sleep would come like a hard black tide, while Claire lay with her back turned to the window and her alarm set, clutching the sheets. She hated those long winter nights.

'Chilly, ain't it?' The words were directed at her – a voice that sounded like a swarm of bees, dark and golden, smoky with a rough sweetness. Claire looked up.

A tall restless figure by the door. Tousled, uncut hair – blond splashed with grey. He could be a down-and-out, she thought suddenly, checking for signs of menace or delusion. Was he drunk?

But his eyes were clear. Green gold, with a gaze fixed firmly on hers. He was staring like a lion watching prey. A tanned face, with high cheekbones and a hooked nose. Weatherbeaten. When he walked towards the desk Claire noticed his limber way of moving, the easy stride of a man who never stays still for long. He was wearing the kind of nondescript clothes that would melt into the background anywhere in the world. His shirt and trousers hung off him in shades of black and grey. They said nothing about him and didn't need to. His face had such an intensity, his body such disturbing grace, that every nerve in Claire's body had sparked immediately to attention.

She noted the silver ring on his right hand and the clean fingernails.

He dropped easily into the chair across from her desk, giving Claire a face full of the pungent aroma which seemed to have drifted in with him. Smoke, sweat and a dark industrial scent, something like road tar – strong smells, but fresh, as though he'd just been labouring on a building site. There was an animal tang about him which Claire recognised as male. She shrank inside her clothes.

'Can I help you?' she asked.

He slouched back in his chair, legs spreading as wide as his smile.

'Well, now I'm not sure if you can.'

'I beg your pardon?' said Claire.

'See, I was just walking down the street, looking at all the grey skies and the miserable faces. And I thought to myself, I need a change. I need some inspiration. Modern world's so damn noisy. Gets you confused and, before you know it, you're halfway to dead and not yet done any of the things you always wanted to do.

'You know how you can lose sight of your dreams, eh? Forget that there's other worlds to explore. You live somewhere, you get complacent. You get stuck in a rut.

'Then, I looked in here, and what did I see?' The guy leant forwards, eyes searching Claire's. She tried hard not to pull back in alarm.

'"We make your dreams come true."' He pointed to the sign that hung on the wall behind Claire, quoting the slogan of the travel agency.

'Only I'm not sure where my dreams might take me. I thought maybe you might have some ideas,' he said, leaning to read her name badge. 'Claire.'

Her name sounded so personal in a stranger's mouth. And his eyes were on the name badge pinned to her breast, like he was eyeing the flash of pale skin there.

He was leaning forwards onto her desk, over the keyboard where Claire's hands rested. His breath, she thought, I can feel his fucking warm breath on me. It crawled up her arm, dancing in the little hairs that were too blond and fine for her to shave. She looked at the coarse stubble peppered all over his jaw. Blond and rough. Like sandpaper.

'I am very busy,' she said, pointedly turning to her computer screen which waited with a patient hiss, cursor blinking.

'The thing is, Claire, I want more than just a holiday.'

'We can offer tailor-made holidays, sir, but –'

'I want adventure,' he cut in. 'I want experiences that get under your skin. I want to go somewhere different, that I've never seen before. '

Claire shook her head, not even pretending to smile any more. This man. He was asking her to provide something that didn't exist.

When the customers came in, hungry for escape, she knew what to offer. She promised paradise. She'd use the word 'heavenly'. She scattered these words in front of the tired hordes, sold them fantasies she knew would never quite be realised. No matter how far they travelled and no matter how much money they threw around, the food would taste odd, the sheets would feel slightly damp and uncomfortable, the foreign language would jar in their ears and they'd find within two days that the person they'd longed to whisk away to a secluded idyll no longer excited them. Claire knew all about the disappointment of travel.

'I thought maybe somewhere like Madagascar,' he said.

'Do you know, they have different words for the wind,

there?' he continued. 'In the morning, there's the warm air that blows off the land. They call it the *"varatraze"*. You wake up to it, coming in the open door. It's like being stroked by a lover, still half asleep and lazy. You know what I mean, right?'

The breath of the man across from her felt like the exotic breeze itself, tickling over her skin.

'Yeah, it makes it kind of hard to get out of bed. A guy could spend all day in there, wrapped up in the arms of his woman, ignoring the paradise he's in. Exploring the other kind of heaven. But then, you have to drag yourself outside. Because, God, it's just so beautiful.'

What was going on? Claire heard the word 'beautiful' and felt a choking embarrassment.

'These huge flowers, everywhere.' He cupped his hands, showing how the petals of the flowers spread wide. 'And all around them, birds. Kingfishers. Love birds.'

'Yes, I get the picture.' Claire knew she'd spoken too abruptly. No matter how rude this man was, she should act with scrupulous detachment. She should be breezily efficient. From the laughter in his jade-green eyes, she knew that he was well aware of her discomfort.

'You don't like Madagascar?' he asked, affecting an innocent surprise.

'Never been,' she managed to growl, closing her lips firmly and clenching her knees together.

'Really? Oh but, Claire, you should come with me.'

Her laugh was a bark, high and ridiculous. This had gone too far. She turned to the computer and rattled away furiously to find a flight, any flight going in the region of Africa. Her eyes raked over flight lists, the coded names for airports in strange cities. The text swam in front of her, numbers and letters spelling out meaningless destinations.

'Nothing. We have nothing, I'm afraid.' Claire was practically certain he was some kind of silver-tongued vagrant, without the money for the bus home let alone a trip to somewhere as exotic as he was describing. She shook her head firmly. 'Sorry.'

'Claire, I don't think that's true.'

'We have *nothing*,' she raised her voice before she could stop herself.

It was late afternoon. She keyed in the security code and pulled down the shutters, closed up for another day. Adjusted her hem and set out with a cool stride towards the station. Since the 'Madagascar' guy had left, the day had turned from shit to worse, with Sandy unbearably overexcited and desperate to make a big deal of the encounter.

'Who the hell was *that*?' she'd asked, eyes like saucers.

'Some time-waster,' Claire had said, trying to brush the matter aside.

'Well, Christ, I wouldn't mind wasting some time with him!' Sandy exclaimed. She was one of the few people who actually did exclaim, with such breathless fervour Claire could practically see the exclamation marks pepper the air above her head. More and more, she regretted hiring the girl.

'Don't you just love that rough-and-ready type?'

Claire had pointedly ignored her, but it didn't seem to work.

'Oh, God, all that stubble and the way he swaggered. Definitely swaggered out of here. Like Robert Redford in denim. Did you see his eyes?'

Of course Claire had seen his eyes. They were burnt into her memory. Like his skinny hips and the way he'd snaked out of the office, his whole demeanour just dripping with don't-give-a-fuck mystique. Behind her desk, she shuddered. He'd disappeared into the anonymous mass of the city, she reminded herself. He was gone.

She nearly tripped over him. Lounging behind a lamp-post, legs crossed, hands shoved in pockets. Just waiting round the corner.

'*Christ*,' she muttered. Was this stalking, or a dreadful coincidence?

'Hey, Claire.'

She felt his voice swarm around her ears again and shook it off. She tried to cross the road, but was thwarted by a sudden rush of traffic.

'Come for a drink?' he asked, making her reach for her hair with a fluttering hand, as though she could brush him off like a stray mosquito.

'No?' he continued. 'A walk?'

It seemed they were already having a walk, whether Claire liked it or not. Trying to ignore him, she was walking briskly down Union Street towards the station. And the guy was keeping pace easily beside her.

'Don't tell me you've got something better to do? Claire? There's a lovely sunset tonight. I could show you some undiscovered corners of our own fair city.'

Claire drew herself up short. They came to a standstill together, Claire gripping her briefcase tightly.

'Leave me alone, or I'm calling the police.'

'Ah, come on. There's no need for any drama. I'm just trying to be friendly.'

She stiffened.

The guy shook his head and laughed. 'Now I'm not going to drag you off and force myself on you. Unless that's what you'd really like, Claire?'

She slapped him as hard as she could, the edge of her hand connecting with his jaw and jolting his head back. Around them, the sea of commuters swerved suddenly, curious eyes hungry to see what was happening but keen to keep their distance at the same time.

Claire watched as a slow strawberry-red stain bloomed on the guy's cheek. They stood facing each other, while Claire's blood froze in her veins. Her hand was stinging. She held it raised still, and it occurred to her suddenly that she was standing there like she was pledging an oath. Ridiculous, overdramatic. She thought she might scream.

'Seems I touched a nerve,' the guy said quietly.

Claire stayed rigid, unmoving, aware that passers-by were staring at her, shocked by her wild-eyed posture and trembling raised hand. She looked like a madwoman.

And then, slowly and very very gently, he took her hand in his. Lowered it to her side. He was holding it with the slightest of touches, so that it felt like she was dipping her fingers into warm water. Not letting go.

'Give yourself a break, Claire. Try something new for a change.'

Her shoulders dropped and Claire took a breath that seemed to fill her lungs like the fresh wind from the sea. It was sweet and sharp and dizzy. The guy's eyes were still on her face, his hand still enveloping hers. Around them the sea of rush-hour commuters swarmed towards the station, making the six o'clock train. Claire looked at the entrance to the station, saw the grim-faced passengers and the silent journey and the dark flat waiting for her and suddenly knew something inside her could not face another long winter night with the computer. Her stack of dirty films.

His hand was warm over hers, warm and strange and promising.

'You want to go for a walk?' she said. Her voice felt strange in her mouth. 'Where to?'

* * *

The river looked different when you stood right by it. Claire usually sailed high overhead on the rail bridge, seated in a train carriage, eyes blank. The Clyde below was just a strip of dirty water, which broke the city in half, easily ignored if you were fixed on your destination.

This evening she stood under the bridge listening to the sound of trains rushing overhead, staring at the choppy brown surface and seeing the sun reflected in a thousand shattered pieces.

The man, who kept close but not too close to her side, was looking downstream at the cranes and warehouses of the shipyards.

'This was where all the ships would come in, bringing their cargoes. Money flowing up the river. Glasgow was built on tobacco. And sugar, of course,' he said.

'Sugar?'

'From the Caribbean, mostly. It's why the native sons are so sweet.'

For the first time in what felt like weeks, Claire smiled.

'You don't believe me? Taste it.'

He came closer, bringing his honey-smoke smell and his stubbled cheek to Claire's face, till she could feel his breath, on her face this time. The distance between them was so slight.

And she kissed him. Put her lips to his smiling mouth, let his tongue dart in between hers, tried to catch the taste of him while she felt the heat of his mouth against hers. His tongue was a wriggling fish in her mouth, and his hand that had held hers so gently was already moving over her ass, feeling the curve of it, squeezing.

Claire pulled away, surfacing. 'You don't even know me.'

'That's true.'

'But you don't understand. I'm not what you think I am.'

'And what would that be?'

Claire struggled to find the words. His knee was pressed in between her legs, and it was confusing her already shell-shocked thoughts.

'I didn't want...' she held her hand up to show him: this body, this face, this hair and these clothes. '...underneath, it's messy. I sleep with married men. I don't ... I don't know how to do this.'

He shrugged. He didn't let go. 'Life is messy.'

'And you don't care?'

'To be honest, babe, right now all I care about is my skin against your skin. You know what I mean?' He reached up to stroke her throat, to feel the pulse there under his hand. His fingers slipped down. They followed the curve of her breast, dragging lightly across her skin, tightening as they met the fabric of her top. Tugging. Pulling the cloth away, exposing her breast to the cold night air. Claire felt her nipple stiffen to a point, and watched mesmerised as the guy bent his head to take it in his mouth.

The feel of him sucking on the tender bud of her breast made her head swim. It was like being plugged into the supply of some dark and strong-running current, as though he were charging her whole body. Claire felt the prickle of his stubble against her and wondered for a moment if she was safe, but before she knew what was happening he had pulled away and left her shaking. Feeling the cold and sudden lack of him was enough to convince her that she wouldn't leave till it was done.

He dropped to his knees, pushing her skirt up around her waist, burrowing in with his head and biting gently at her thighs. Her pussy was at once cooled by the night air and electric with anticipation. His head moved closer till it covered her centre, and his lips met her clit.

He sucked with a strong hot mouth and Claire thought of hummingbirds bent over flowers, licking at the nectar within. Everything was dissolving, sliding away, and the noise of the river carried her voice as she let out a gasp, as his tongue hit the target and slid inside her, opened her.

Claire felt the blind hunger rise in her, the need for a hard cock, the wanting and the ache for him to be inside her. She pulled away and leant back to grip the railings alongside the towpath, hoping the gathering dark would hide them, too frantic to stop now in any case. She spread her legs apart in a mute gesture of need, not caring any more if he stroked her gently or admired her beautiful lines. She wanted to be fucked.

He seemed to understand. As he pulled a little foil packet from his back pocket and bit it open, Claire's knees weakened and she realised that a complete stranger was about to sheath up and take her. His face was a dark gold, clouded with concentration. Claire imagined she could still see the faint stain of her hand on his cheek, a mark of her uncontrolled anger which had transformed now into the ache of desire. He unrolled the rubber over his cock and Claire got a brief glimpse of its dark curving length rearing up before she turned back to face the river and closed her eyes.

When he nudged at her slit with the head of his cock, she felt the shock of unfamiliar flesh entering hers and, at the same time, the sweet recognition of that most natural of sensations – a man slipping inside a woman, moving himself to press as close as two people can get. He sank into her to the hilt, and she pushed back to feel his whole length swelling in her cunt, stretching her open, joining the two of them as though they were fused together.

'That's it. Easy. Nice and slow. Now move against me.' He held himself rigid, arms circling her waist in a tight grip, refusing to fuck her and denying her the rhythm she craved. To feel the delicious push and pull, Claire had to rock her hips against him, thrust and bump and grind herself on his cock. Her body twisted in desperation, fighting him to reach the quickening point that made them both gasp. Beneath them the river seemed to flow faster, darker and rougher as she strained to fuck him harder.

He moved one hand to her face, covering her mouth and pushing his fingers inside so that she sucked and bit, letting him cram three in so that her mouth was as full as her cunt. He had crept inside her, this man, and now he both surrounded and filled her. She could smell the wet reek of the river before her, mixed with his scents of honey and smoke, and feel on her skin the tension of his wiry and supple frame. He was obliterating her careful glamour, smearing her lipstick and pulling her hair loose. Claire had the feeling she was disintegrating, being dragged from her perfectly designed life and thrown into the turbulent currents of a new world.

As she felt his cock tighten inside her and he at last answered her movements with his own, thrusting more urgently and with greater decisiveness, she knew she was on the brink. She would come, violently, with more guttural sounds than she'd ever made before, the scream of an animal being torn from familiar territory and flung high and hard. Her body was loosening, unravelling, fucking itself into the strange cold night with a man she'd never met before. It was like discovering a whole new city, there under the bridge.

She wondered what the world would look like when she opened her eyes.

The Highest Bidder
Sarah J. Husch

'Sold! To the very excited lady in the purple bustier!'

Gemma sat back in the chair, disappointment pouting her lips. She'd wanted him. The extra-cute upstairs neighbour she'd lusted after for the past six months, but had never quite had the nerve to approach. The bachelor auction benefiting the Performing Arts Guild had been the perfect opportunity to stake her claim. But she'd been outbid by Miss Purple Bustier who was even now latching onto that muscled arm and jiggling her pushed-up breasts at him.

'Have another drink,' her friend, Bea, advised. She waved at one of the prowling waiters, and two more flutes of champagne appeared on the table. 'Bid on someone else.'

Gemma sighed, and sipped the bubbly liquid. Already, the auctioneer, Annette Sullivan, the Guild's president, was announcing the next bachelor up for bid. He came out in a tuxedo, dark hair slicked back, a red rose in one hand. He flashed white teeth at the women, not seeming to mind the attention.

'He's cute,' Bea said, leaning forwards a little. 'What about him?'

'Too suave,' Gemma dismissed.

'You are very hard to please,' Bea told her. She tossed back her curly red hair and crossed one miniskirted leg over the other. 'I, on the other hand, haven't had a date in two months, and I'm willing to lower my standards a little.' She eyed the James Bond lookalike on stage. 'Although, I wouldn't have to lower them at all with him.'

Laughter made the champagne bubbles go up her nose, and Gemma coughed. Bea obligingly smacked her between the shoulder blades.

While they'd been talking, the bidding had escalated sharply. The bachelor had taken off his tuxedo jacket and loosened his tie. He slid it from around his neck, and tossed it into the audience. The reaction was intense. Gemma thought two women would come to blows fighting over the scrap of black cloth.

While they were arguing over who'd caught it first, the bidding had continued without them. A demure woman in a tidy business suit walked up to the stage and received the rose from her new acquisition. He jumped down from the stage and joined her at her table.

The evening was turning into a bust, Gemma thought. She finished the glass of champagne, feeling a little light-headed. At least the alcohol was complimentary. The Performing Arts Guild had spared no expense to get the women to loosen their purse strings. And from the looks of Miss Purple Bustier still glued to her prize's side, that wasn't all that was getting loose.

'Stop frowning,' Bea said. 'This is fun. Just bid on someone. It's for a good cause.'

Gemma sighed. It had been for a good cause when she'd been bidding on her neighbour. Now, it was just money to the Arts Guild. 'I'll bid on the next guy,' Gemma promised.

The next guy turned out to be Mr March from the Fire Department's annual calendar, along with a dinner cruise on the river for two. His arrival was heralded by cheers and applause, even a few wolf whistles. Getting into the spirit of the evening, he slowly removed his gear, revealing a white T-shirt which was moulded to very impressive abs.

Gemma raised her card, and Bea's hand slapped it down. 'He's mine,' she whispered. 'I have that calendar and he's the hottest guy on it.'

Never taking her eyes off of the hottie on stage, Bea held up her card and left it there. When it became obvious that she was intent on winning, the bidding slowed to a halt. Chequebook in hand, she went to claim her prize.

Great, just great, Gemma thought, when the two came back to the table. She gets Mr March and I get another glass of champagne.

'Our final bachelor of the evening is Nick Dalton,' Annette announced. She glanced down at the card in her hand. 'Nick is an artist and, in fact, I highly recommend his show at the Blue Moon Gallery. Your date with Nick will include an afternoon of dolphin watching, courtesy of Tidewater Marina, and a romantic picnic for two.'

The heavy burgundy curtains at the back of the stage parted just enough for the bachelor to emerge. He waved at the audience, offering a quick smile before taking his place centre stage.

Oh my, Gemma thought faintly. She was barely aware that she had her card in the air before the auctioneer announced the opening bid.

Nick caught her eye and smiled. He had dimples. His smile was part boy next door, part wicked seduction and it made heat curl low in her stomach. From the top of his tousled brown hair to the tips of his sneakers, he was dressed casually. The faded jeans clung to lean hips and Gemma found herself wondering what it would be like to have her legs wrapped tightly around his waist. The simple black T-shirt under an unbuttoned shirt made her wonder what she'd find when she stripped them off him.

A romantic picnic for two offered a wealth of erotic images for her imagination. Both of them naked against a soft blanket, sunshine warming their skin. The bark of a tree rough against her hands as he took her from behind. She squeezed her thighs together, intensifying the throb of need.

Maybe he could use his artistic talent and decorate her with body paints.

And, best of all, she no longer cared that Miss Purple Bustier had made off with her neighbour.

Gemma wet her bottom lip with her tongue, suddenly realising that the bidding was rapidly climbing out of her range. She did some maths in her head, balancing out the contents of her cheque account, and her rainy-day savings. With a pang of real regret, she dropped out of the bidding.

Maybe she'd console herself by stopping by his gallery and looking at his art.

On the stage, Nick frowned, looking down at her. Her table was close enough that she could see the little crinkles next to his blue eyes. She could imagine looking into those eyes as she climaxed. It was all she could do not to touch herself under the table.

Covering the microphone, Nick leant close to Annette, whispering in her ear. His eyes never left Gemma's. The matron looked at him in surprise, looked down at Gemma, and smiled slyly.

Gemma wondered what was going on. She glanced down at herself. No, she hadn't spilt champagne on her dress. Nothing was hanging out that shouldn't have been. So why the scrutiny?

Annette raised one hand, silencing the crowd. The stage lights danced on the diamonds at her ears. 'We have a rather surprising twist,' she announced. 'Nick himself would like to place a bid. He's assured me that he'll top the highest amount by five hundred dollars if the blonde in the turquoise dress will share the date with him.'

Bea squealed, nudging her in the side.

She wasn't quite able to believe what she'd just heard. Realising her mouth was open, she caught her bottom lip between her teeth. Nick's eyes flared with hunger, and the smile on his mouth was no longer full of boyish charm. Now, it was all about desire, hot, hungry and full of promise.

Realising that the room had fallen silent and she was suddenly the centre of attention, Gemma pressed her hands into her lap. She was so wet, so hot for him, she was sure that everyone knew it. Not looking away, Gemma nodded.

With a final word to Annette, Nick vaulted down from the stage. He was all male grace and confidence as he walked to the table and slipped into the chair next to Gemma.

Beneath the table, his knees bumped hers. The denim brushed the bare skin of her legs, sending a shiver of pleasure through her. Leaning in, Nick brought his lips to her ear.

'Thanks,' he whispered. Warm breath stirred her hair. The spicy scent of his skin teased her. His lips brushed her cheek as he drew back.

'For what?' Gemma asked.

His dimples appeared again, and Gemma had a sudden urge to push back his chair and straddle him right there at the table. Really, the man should be declared illegal.

'For saying yes,' he told her. Belatedly, he held out his hand. 'Nick Dalton.'

The fingers that closed over hers were warm and

strong. What would they feel like pushing into her, moving in and out, driving her higher and higher until . . . ?

'Gemma,' she managed. 'Gemma Carlson.'

'Would you like to get out of here, Gemma?' he asked. 'It's all over except for the networking.'

Nodding, she let him draw her to her feet. She said a quick goodbye to Bea, promising to call tomorrow. Her fingers twined with his, he led her through the tables. His thumb stroked a sensual pattern onto her wrist as they left the building.

The night air wrapped her in sultry warmth. A breeze smelling of the sea stirred the handkerchief hem of her dress, swirling it around her thighs. The theatre was close to the ocean, nestled on a spit of land which jutted into the estuary where the river met the sea.

'Can I buy you coffee?' he asked, leading her into the parking lot. His hip bumped hers as they walked.

'If you tell me why you bid so high to get a date with me,' Gemma said.

Nick drew her to a stop beside a dark SUV. The light from a street lamp threw shadows over his sculpted cheekbones. The sensual curve of his full bottom lip enticed her. Callused fingers slipped under the halter straps of her dress and stroked back and forth. The bold contact shocked her and ratcheted her awareness of him even higher.

'Because I looked at you and wondered what it would be like to peel this off you and lick your nipples until you screamed my name.'

The blatant words should have scared her. She knew absolutely nothing about him. Instead, the hunger that had gripped her the moment she'd seen him surged higher. Her nipples hardened, anticipating.

She was tired of being the wilting lily, the one who

was too shy to speak to her neighbour. Nick made her want to grab onto the possibilities and follow where they led.

She caught her fingers in the belt loops of his jeans and tugged him closer. The metal of the SUV behind her was cool. His body was hot as he pressed close. 'So do it,' she said. She caught his bottom lip between her teeth and teased with her tongue.

Nick groaned. The thrust of his tongue against hers made her dizzy. He caught her hips in his hands, holding her still while he pushed his erection against her. Gemma felt the thick length of his cock through his jeans, and she tipped her hips forwards. It brought a sharp throb of pleasure from her clit.

Oh yes, he should definitely be declared illegal.

'Don't you care if someone sees us?' he asked. He continued to nip at her lips, teasing little bites which had her tipping her head back, wishing he'd do the same to the sensitive skin of her throat.

'Do you?' she challenged.

His lips nuzzled her jaw, teeth catching her ear lobe. 'Not really,' he admitted. His hands smoothed down her arms, and then slowly back up. Over her shoulders, caressing the bare skin.

Gemma felt his fingers at the back of her neck, working at the clasp of her dress. He drew the silky turquoise cloth down over her shoulders, the backs of his fingers teasing her skin lightly. His mouth followed, burning over her throat. His tongue swirled a damp path, sensitising her skin. Breathless, Gemma tugged his T-shirt out of his pants, desperate to touch him. His back was smooth, muscles hard beneath hot skin.

Sensation spiked as he nipped sharply at her collarbone. He'd peeled the top of her dress down to her waist, revealing her breasts to the night air. Leaning back, he gazed at her, at the way the lamplight glowed on her skin.

Gemma glanced down and saw the tight pucker of her nipples, dark against the creamy swell of her breasts. She drew her fingernails teasingly away from his skin and then cupped her breasts in her hands, lifting them in offering. She felt the cock that pressed so enticingly to her crotch twitch and knew he was turned on by her actions.

Made bold by the harshness of his breathing, Gemma brushed her thumbs lightly over the tight buds. Pleasure stabbed straight to her clit and it was her turn to move restlessly against him. His hands rested on either side of her, levering his upper body away so he could watch.

Gemma teased herself, flicking her nails again and again against her nipples. She wet one finger and then rubbed the moisture in slow circles across the aching bud. The breeze blew across her flesh, cooling the moisture, and she shivered from the unexpected pleasure.

She was so turned on, she could barely stand it. She raised one leg and wrapped it around his thigh. It brought the pulsing ache of her clit into contact with the rough cloth of his jeans. She was going to come, and he hadn't even tasted her like he'd promised.

Nick's hands covered hers. He gazed into her eyes as he plumped her breasts. His tongue stroked over her flesh, close, but not where she wanted it to be. Gemma slipped her hands free from his and ran her fingers over the hard planes of his back. Down to his waistband. Cupping his ass, she began to rock against him, each press of her crotch to his sending her a little closer to climax.

The tip of his tongue flicked against her. Her nipple throbbed, followed by her clit. A low moan left her lips as he repeated the action and then sucked her slowly inside his hot mouth. His other hand teased her swollen flesh, alternately rubbing and pinching.

If he kept it up, he would make her scream his name, just like he'd promised.

Laughter drifted their way. Gemma stiffened, suddenly realising that she was nude from the waist up, her breasts puckered from his attentions.

'Nick,' she whispered, the fingers of one hand slipping into the soft brown hair that curled over his collar.

His tongue swirled one last time, and her body reacted with a sudden pulse that told her she was dangerously close to coming. The heavy ache in her womb demanded release and she couldn't help the way her hips bucked.

The soft cotton of his shirt was pure torture against her nipples when he pressed his chest against hers. His mouth teased hers a moment, tongue dancing lightly, before he drew back.

'How badly do you want to come?' he whispered in her ear.

The words drew a desperate moan from her. Heels clicked against pavement, the low murmur of voices right on the other side of the SUV. She couldn't believe how tightly wound her body was. How erotic the thought of coming with people mere steps away.

'Nick, please,' she murmured. She gripped him tightly, partially mortified at the thought of being seen. And totally turned on by this man who had only minutes ago been a complete stranger.

Light fingers drew up her short dress and she caught her breath. They tickled across her hip, following the narrow strip of her bikini panties. He levered his hips away a little and slipped his hand between them. He palmed her through damp silk.

'Do you want to come now?' he asked. His fingers

teased the curls that escaped around the sides of the elastic.

The sound of a car door opening. The murmur of a man's voice. So close. If she cried out, they would hear. If she didn't come, she would go insane.

Nick's fingers slipped under the satin. One finger stroked along her wet lips, stopping just short of her clit. Slowly, he parted her and dipped one finger in. Her pussy clenched around him.

'Tell me yes,' he whispered. His mouth nuzzled her jaw. 'Or tell me no.'

She was so close. Every part of her wound so tightly. The glass and metal behind her was still cool, an erotic contrast to his heat. Still the murmur of voices. Wouldn't they ever go away?

A slow stroke. One finger. Then another. Her hips bucked, a low whimper escaped her. His free hand came up to cover her breast, her swollen nipple caught between his fingers. He pinched slowly.

It was too much.

'Yes,' she cried.

He knuckled her clit, fingers plunging into her wet folds. She came hard, her knees buckling, only the pressure of his body holding her up. Wave after wave rolled through her. She clenched tightly around him, riding the hard thrusts of his fingers. His mouth took hers, swallowing her cries.

Gemma knew though that it was too late. Even as the pleasure eased off, soft little aftershocks rippling through her, she could hear the shocked voices on the other side of the SUV. The quick slam of a car door and the revving of an engine.

'Oh God, Nick,' she breathed. Her face burnt with embarrassment.

He slipped his fingers out of her, even that movement

sending another spiral of pleasure through her body. He painted her bottom lip with her own moisture. She swiped her tongue across his fingertips. She tasted her own musky excitement. She caught his hand with her own and then she slowly licked his fingers.

'Damn, Gemma,' he murmured. His cock was still hard, pressing into her sensitive pussy.

The embarrassment was swiftly giving way to arousal. They hadn't been seen. She'd been heard, her cries only slightly muffled by his kiss. Somehow, the knowledge that she'd had unknown witnesses to her climax served to make her even hotter.

The parking lot was public, the charity auction over but the party still going on. Anyone could come out. Anyone could walk by. They could be seen. Her breasts were exposed, the street light highlighting the damp marks his tongue had left.

And she didn't know him. She could do anything, be anyone. He was a stranger and that made the whole encounter that much more exciting.

Boldly, she cupped his cock through the denim. He growled with approval. She scraped her fingernails over him, circling his balls before squeezing gently. From the feel of him, he was long, hard. He would reach deep inside of her, touching nerve endings which spasmed with the thought.

She wanted him to fuck her. But first, he needed a taste of his own medicine.

The snap of his jeans gave way to her fingers. He hissed as she slowly slid the zipper down. She slipped her hand inside and wrapped her fingers around him.

Completely in control, she made him turn so that his back was against the SUV. She placed her lips against his ear and teased the whorls with her tongue. In response, he thrust into her hand, moaning softly.

'I'm going to take you in my mouth, Nick,' she whispered. 'I'm going to suck you until you scream my name.'

The laugh that escaped him turned into a low growl as she dropped to her knees in front of him. Ignoring the bite of concrete on her bare knees, Gemma flicked her tongue over his tip, tasting the bead of moisture that had collected there. When his cock jumped in her fist, she repeated the motion, then turned it into a long slow slide of her tongue down his length.

The hair of his thighs tickled against her bare breasts. The sensation against her nipples made her moan. Another wave of moisture collected between her thighs. She couldn't wait to feel his cock buried there.

Lapping at his cock, she explored his texture, the soft skin over hard muscle. The scent of his musk made her pussy tighten and she cupped one breast and rubbed her nipple back and forth against his thigh.

She forgot the roughness of the ground beneath her knees. Only the taste and scent of him mattered. Wrapping her lips around the head of his cock, she suckled hard. Controlling the motion of his hips, she let him push into her mouth. Her tongue flicked his length as he bumped the back of her throat.

Drawing back, Gemma breathed over the damp length of his erection, knowing the air would tease his sensitised flesh. She lapped at his balls and tickled the fragile skin at their base with her fingernails.

Nick was panting. The fingers that had curled in her hair urged her to take him deep again. She obliged, but held back when he would have thrust too hard. She wanted to tease him into insanity.

There were more voices suddenly. She laughed around the cock that throbbed in her mouth, knowing the sensation turned him on when he moaned. His fingers released her hair and he was suddenly fumbling for the pocket of his jeans.

Curious, Gemma drew back. He found what he was looking for, keying the remote. The SUV beeped and he pulled open the back door and dragged her inside.

Lying back on the seat, Nick pulled her up his length, then reached down to pull the door shut behind them. Gemma laughed, her legs tangled with his. Her crotch was pressed against the hard ridge of his hip and a little wiggle produced a sharp stab of pleasure.

'Don't like it when you're the one exposed?' she asked shrewdly.

Nick lifted his head off the leather seat. It was dark inside the SUV, but the street light outside provided just enough light for her to see the wicked grin that curved his mouth.

'Apparently not,' he answered. His hands cupped her ass, fingers stroking the cleft.

Gemma wiggled until she could straddle him. The tip of his cock bumped her clit through the silk of her panties. It was like a mini-lightning storm racing through her body, and she shuddered.

Nick bucked his hips up, the contact rubbing him hard against her. Her breath caught in her throat. He was fumbling for something in his back pocket, not quite reaching. Helping him out, she tugged his wallet free.

'Condom,' he gasped, pulling a foil packet from a leather compartment.

It was a toss-up which she wanted first – to get out of her panties or to roll the condom down the length of his cock. He took the decision from her hands when he rolled the latex over himself. Gemma pushed her panties down, trying to manoeuvre over the tangle of their legs.

'Here,' Nick said. Strong fingers wrapped the silk tight and he tugged. The scrap pulled free, disappearing somewhere into the front seat.

Then the broad tip of his cock was bumping against

her entrance. Bracing her hands on his chest, she sank slowly onto him. He stretched her wide and she tossed her hair back at the delicious sensation.

Inch by inch she took him in, not stopping until her curls mingled with his. Rocking back and forth, she felt the caress of his glans against the knot of nerve tissue deep inside.

'Fuck, you're hot,' he said. Questing fingers found her clit and then rubbed as she rode him harder and harder. The added sensations were too much and Gemma felt herself peaking again. The pleasure tore through her and she fell forwards onto his chest, burying her face in his shoulder.

Nick was still hard inside her when the last trembling spasm died down.

'More,' he told her. His hands closed over the sweet globes of her ass, urging her to ride him again. Long fingers probed, seeking her moisture, and he spread it upwards.

She felt the blunt tip of one finger probing at the sensitive bud of her arse. Gemma bit her lip, relaxing her muscles, alternately riding his cock and pushing back against his finger. It popped through the ring of muscle and the sensation of fullness made her whimper.

Gemma closed her eyes tightly, focusing on the cock pushing deep into her pussy and the finger slowly beginning to fuck her arse. It seemed impossible, but she felt the buzz of an impending orgasm deep inside of her. Her nipples scraped against the cotton of his shirt. She realised she was nearly nude, the halter top of her dress around her waist, the skirt pushed up to her hips, while he was still completely clothed except for his cock.

It was erotic as hell.

She lifted her hips high and lingered there a moment, the tip of him nearly pulling free. His fingers, two now, were deep inside of her. She waited until he opened his eyes. The light fell across his face and the look of intensity there made her smile.

She plunged down hard and his cock went deep. The orgasm started in her womb, then crashed outwards in waves of intensity which shook her whole body. She was only vaguely aware that she was still fucking him, fast and furious, her clit rubbing against his length to send even more spasms through her limbs.

Nick's roar of pleasure filled the back of the van. He pounded his hips against hers, his cock throbbing again and again. The fingers in her arse plunged in and out, as if he were rubbing himself deep inside of her.

It was too much. Not nearly enough.

The sounds of cars in the parking lot outside the SUV finally registered. Gemma rubbed her cheek against his shoulder, listening to doors slamming shut, the sound of tyres on concrete.

Nick turned his head, catching her mouth with his. The kiss was sweet, unexpected. It made her smile.

'Just think,' he said. 'We still have our romantic picnic.'

Wet Walls Kristina Lloyd

The bus station was lit up with colour, rain falling in yellow and orange drops, headlights fraying into the drizzle.

I was trying to act natural, standing in the shelter like someone waiting for a bus. My real aim was to talk to the bunch of emo kids next to me, preferably without scaring them. A gang of moody youths with slanted haircuts, they might have intimidated some, but not me. I had them down as pleasant middle-class sixth formers, all dressed up and nowhere to go. Unable to think of a subtle opener, I came straight out with it: 'You know anything about this Michael guy?'

They turned to me with a disconcerting group mentality. Then they glanced at each other, a herd of scarecrow goths, anxious eyes flicking beneath angled fringes. Around us, reflected lights slid across perspex shelters and shimmered in fragments on slick black tarmac.

A skinny kid in drainpipes replied, 'You mean Michael Angelo?'

His tone was eager, and I immediately realised they knew less than I did. Just because they hung out on the streets, didn't mean they knew the streets. Obviously, they didn't think I was the police either. Or if they did, they didn't mind because they'd nothing to hide.

'It's well weird,' said another.

'Publicity stunt,' added a third, lighting a self-conscious cigarette. 'Got to be. How else do you explain it?'

I shrugged, turning away to check an approaching bus. 'Dunno. What's he publicising then?'

'Himself,' continued the third. 'Himself and fuck-all else. Same as everyone.'

There was a bubble of admiring laughter. See? Smart middle-class sixth formers.

A number 25 pulled in, tyres slushing through the wet, and I got on, then got off a stop later. They didn't know anything. There was no point me staying.

On Queen Street, I hurried into the Stationmaster's Arms, a place of seedy theatricality and pickled eggs. Men drank there; a thin crowd of commuters, dealers and pimps, as desperate and shabby as the pub's lost grandeur. Clenched and alone, they stood by the bar or sat at tables, eyes flinching from the deep dim mirrors.

I sipped a glass of red, head in a book, waiting for the shower to pass. I had no plan except to wander the streets in search of Michael Angelo. Or perhaps, given the email I'd received, he'd be out there searching for me. 'I'll find you in the darkest place,' he wrote.

I didn't know where that was, although the Stationmaster's Arms seemed as good a place as any.

I'm a journalist but, strictly speaking, this investigative stuff was way beyond my remit. I'm an agony aunt, writing the problem pages for a local property mag called *On The Up!* Problem pages, TV listings, lifestyle and other articles. That week, for example, I'd been writing a piece entitled 'A Day in the Life of an Estate Agent'. I'd been struggling with it, to be honest, because estate agents don't actually have lives.

But my problem page, oh boy, does that have life. And if it's ever flagging (because even problem pages have problems) then Mike and Aaron in design will offer me material. I never use it but it cheers me up. 'Dear Janie, What's the best way to remove hair from private parts?' or 'Dear Janie, My penis is too big. Please help.'

I wondered what letters the men in the Station-master's Arms might write, scribbling for help in the dark lonely hours. An old guy in a beige raincoat had been watching me, drinking steadily and offering an occasional smashed smile. His lank hair was nicotine yellow. I wondered if he could even write.

I confess I'm not cut out to be an agony aunt. I lack empathy and practicality, two attributes I'd say are fairly fundamental. Take the drunk in the raincoat, for example. Shouldn't I be wondering what damaged him and whether he might benefit from the twelve-step programme and some basic adult education? But, no. Instead I think: Sleazebag, get your eyes off me.

I only got lumbered with the problem page after Moira, our regular columnist, quit. She fell apart when her husband discovered she'd been having it away with his younger brother. 'Haven't I got enough problems of my own?' she used to yell, sobbing in front of her Mac, and I'm sure she'd have chucked letters around the office if all the stuff didn't come by email.

I inherited her desk. It's littered with self-help aphorisms: 'A ship is safest in harbour but that's not why ships are built'. Or 'A strong relationship is made not of two halves, but two wholes'. I crossed out the 'w' on that last word. Sometimes I think I inherited Moira's slump towards disenchantment. 'Haven't I got enough problems of my own?' I want to shout.

My problems, however, aren't as specific as hers. It's more formless stuff that goes on inside me, you know, at my edges and underneath. 'Dear Janie', I might begin, but then I'm pretty much stumped.

There's something I can't reach, a fluttery unsettled part I wish I could tame. Sometimes I feel I have it. It's almost there. For a moment it comes to rest, usually when I'm far from the city, and I'll be struck by, say, the light in a high golden barn or over a white wintry field where mist drapes the stubble. When that happens, I'm fooled by a fleeting sense into thinking everything's all right, now and forever.

But it isn't, is it? It's never all right. The days keep on coming and I can't get out of them. There's nothing I can pin down. There are no sentences such as: 'I've got the blues' or 'My dog died' or 'I wish to God he'd leave me.'

Like I say, I'm not really up to agony-aunting.

Recently though, some of the letters have started to get to me. I'm puzzled and unsettled by them, and I know the usual platitudes I dish out won't suffice.

Dear Janie,
I don't know who else to turn to. I met a man recently and can't stop thinking about him. I know this sounds stupid but it was a one-night stand and he didn't ask for my number. We hardly spoke but I felt as if he truly understood me...

Dear Janie,
I've been going out with my boyfriend for eight months but I cheated on him at the weekend and now I don't know what to do. You see, I've fallen in love with this other guy though I know I'll never see him again...

Dear Janie,
I've been walking the streets at night, looking for a man I once had sex with. I know it's dangerous but I can't stop myself. I need to see his face. I didn't see it the first time and now I'm desperate to know him. It's like an addiction, an obsession, driving me on...

Dear Janie,
A man approached me on Queen Street after I got off the bus and before I knew it, he'd seduced me up against a wall. I thought about going to the authorities but didn't because he means everything to me, even though he's a total stranger...

Idiots! Get a grip, get a hobby, get a life.

I haven't published these letters though I've read them so often I practically know them off by heart. One line haunts me. It's there in every letter, an unvarying refrain: 'With him, I found another side to myself.'

I sipped my wine, aware I was still being ogled by nicotine-hair. Perhaps he thought I was a whore and that gave him the right. But what kind of whore, I wondered, wears knee-length skirts and flat-heeled boots, and sits with a glass of Merlot, reading Barbara Vine? Not one he could afford, that's for sure. It was time I left.

The rain had stopped and I headed up Queen Street. It was early autumn and mild, the kerbs stuck with wet golden leaves. Few people were about. A couple of times I checked over my shoulder but as far as I could tell, I wasn't being followed.

I'll find you in the darkest place.

Was that a threat? Or the first sweet sting of seduction? Either way, as I strode past glass-fronted shops, the thought made me hot and loose. He wanted me and I was scared to imagine the possibilities of his wanting and the state I might be in when he was through.

In a recent half-page article for *On The Up!* I'd written: 'Michael Angelo might think he's an artist, but to many he's just a yob with a spray can. From boarded-up shops to newly painted buildings, no wall is safe from his defacement. The city is his canvas and we, the tax-payers, are footing the bill.'

I didn't actually believe what I'd written. Much of it was paranoia and sensationalism but I'm a hack, unschooled in truth and moderation. Anyway, these days people want a lot more than truth for their buck, especially in a property listings mag.

And the truth is, Michael's graffiti is beautiful. It has an astonishing luminosity, a softness that belies its weird jarring colours, and the first piece I saw of his brought tears to my eyes. ('Undoubtedly, his daubs have merit,' I wrote.) I was walking into work, crossing a dead-end street called Jubilee Gate and, when I glanced right, instead of the usual hoardings concealing the NCP car park, I saw a vista of paradise which briefly stopped my heart.

In a silvery sky, an olive-green sun shone over meadows of purple grass. Unearthly woodland clustered the hills, red-leaved canopies above cobalt-blue trunks. Snaking through the foreground was a river of molten copper, its shimmering bronze tones rippling with pink, and nodding in the breeze were fleshy daffodils of coral, apricot, vanilla and rose.

And yet how could there be a breeze? How could the river ripple? It was a painting, a mural perhaps, although mural is too flat a noun to describe the world I saw. It gleamed as if it were still wet. Perhaps it was. I walked towards it, feeling its dazzle of light on my cheeks. In its presence, I grew radiant, mesmerised by fierce magical colour, convinced I was on the brink of entering an altered, Photoshopped world where normality was oh so slightly out of whack.

There was a smell around me, a half-remembered scent. What was it? The closer I got, the stronger the odour until I felt quite engulfed by it. I inhaled deeply, filling my lungs, and my entire body tingled in response. Ah God, yes! Scents of sweat, skin and warm genitals unfurled in my brain. Sex! This world smelt of sex! I breathed in female arousal, strong and musky, and was embarrassed to think it might be me.

Worried, I glanced back. At the top of the street a man was gawping at the wall just as I was. I could smell cock and hair, so potent there might have been an erection by my lips, a jewel of pre-come quivering on its tip. My body answered, my groin its sudden centre of gravity, thrumming with an deep internal weight.

Ahead of me, paradise glimmered while behind me two people – the man and now a woman – glided towards the wall, equally dumbstruck. The three of us stared, steeped in that maddening air of lust. Did they smell it too? It was inconceivable we might speak, and yet the enchantment was such I could imagine us dropping to the floor and making mad crazy love, all three of us right there on the dead-end street that is Jubilee Gate.

Obviously, I didn't write this in my piece on Michael Angelo.

I stayed staring for several minutes while slowly, imperceptibly, the image and scent began to fade. By the time I walked away, it was just another example of very good graffiti, Michael Angelo's tag in the bottom right-hand corner. Perhaps good graffiti was all it ever had been.

And yet it left me in a state of desire so acute I felt demented. I could barely move. My vulval lips were exquisitely tender, so plump and soft that simply walking roused me further. Pavement to pussy, pavement to pussy; the rhythm drummed in my veins. I was all groin and longing. Each step cranked me higher until, aching for release, I had to nip into the ladies' in Starbucks to have a little wank. Or perhaps, given the locale, I should call it a regular and upgrade my normal fare to a grande.

That didn't go in the article either.

I only wrote the piece in the hope he would respond. 'Perhaps someday,' I declared, 'Michael Angelo will show us all another side to himself.' It was a weak bit of rhetoric and I wasn't happy with the sentence flow either. But I let it pass. The point of it was to try to prove my hunch that the letters and graffiti were connected.

Several days after the article appeared (I guess he's

not a regular reader), I received his email: 'I'll find you in the darkest place.'

I'd trembled at the sight of his name in my inbox.

Michael Angelo.

The man. The mystery. Artist, vandal and demon lover.

I'd brought him closer. He'd come to me. He who did things to women, changing them utterly. The two men were one and the same, I was sure.

Despite my journalistic impulse to try to tempt him into disclosure, I didn't reply.

A couple of weeks later, he got in touch again: 'Won't you come out to play tonight?'

By then, the rumours were really starting to spread. Michael Angelo was no ordinary street artist. His pictures were alive; they breathed; they touched people in unspoken ways. He sprayed his walls in about five minutes flat; his tiny stencils sprayed themselves; those paintings of shadows might not even be his. He was a ghost, an angel, a con artist. He didn't even exist. It was a stunt dreamt up by a record company.

Then there were the rumours about him and women. He preyed on them. They preyed on him. You could feel the pull. Women loved him. Women hated him. He stole their shadows. Six were having his baby. He was actually Jesus Christ come to save us from ourselves.

And he'd asked me to come out to play.

I'd been feeling kind of spacey ever since I'd first seen that wall. It was as if there was a newness in the world, a place of sensual tranquillity waiting to be explored. Desire and hunger spun me around, and I swirled in the midst of it, losing myself in daydreams where I floated among fingers or drowned in a sea of kisses.

Why, of course I'll come out to play.

I started off at Jubilee Gate but there was nothing to

see now except the hoardings of the NCP car park, drab and ugly in the feeble streetlight. I visited other sites, looking out for broad canvases and small botanical stencils. I love his stencils. He sprays pictures of weeds, replacing the real groundsel, ragwort and valerian, removed by the council using deadly colourless sprays, with his own unnatural depictions. His counterfeit weeds grow from cracks in the pavement, and why not? Weeds have as much right to be in cities as they do in the countryside where they're known more prettily as wild flowers.

Michael's bigger pictures, the weird gaudy landscapes, usually vanish within days but the weeds last longer. There are hundreds of them, vibrant splashes of fake flora springing up across the city, ignored by passing feet. I'm not even sure if they're all his any more. It's as if the images are self-seeding.

I'd become something of a Michael Angelo fan, hurrying across town when I heard a new one had been spotted. Though I'd marvelled at the artistry, even getting down on my knees to sniff some weeds, none had affected me as much as the first one. That was the real start of my journey.

I'd been walking for about an hour, eyeing all men suspiciously, when the rain came on. At first, I considered quitting but, after lurking in the bus station, I decided to keep going. My guess was, if he was going to reveal himself, I'd need to be in a place considerably darker than those I'd checked out so far.

Fortified by that glass of red, I walked away from the centre, brain trying to convince gut I should head for the city's edge. It was desolate and lawless on the outskirts, an urban wasteland of burnt-out cars, 60s tower blocks and cold grey concrete, all newly animated by layers of graffiti, a palimpsest of rage and disaffection. The thought of going there scared me, especially since I'd written an article slating Michael Angelo. Perhaps he, or his fans, would want to take revenge.

Thankfully, as I was passing Upper Marlow Street, an area famed for its international cuisine, I had a sudden change of heart. It might have been the sight of people dawdling in front of menus and cosy windows, the smell of garlic or coloured lights on wet pavements. Either way, a buzz of excitement made me linger and, before long, I found myself gazing down Lower Marlow Street, a dark narrow road running behind the restaurants.

It felt like a place he might lurk. It felt right. The back ends of kitchens cluttered one side, a jumble of sloping roofs, bricks, stucco, extractor fans, thick silver pipes and stern, blank fire doors. Wheelie bins and crates lined the wonky pavement and, seeing no one else around, I walked forwards, nervous and alert. A few feet in, the solid hum of ventilation enveloped me, muffling the world. Small windows obscured by grids, grilles or frosted glass glowed softly, and I caught only snatches of kitchen life: a UV fly-zapper, shelves of packaged noodles, a corner of stainless steel; small, still images at odds with the feverish industry of scouring, clanging and sudden sizzles of fat.

It was like being in the cab of a steam train, seeing the furnace that fuels the city. Upper Marlow Street was civilisation; a place where appetites were whetted and quenched amidst tasselled menus, chopsticks, peppermills and candlelight. Here, behind the scenes, was the dark grubby truth of it.

The road was little more than a gap between old rickety buildings, street lamps along its length offering a faint white haze, as muzzy as gas lanterns in Sherlock Holmes' day.

'I'll find you in the darkest place.'

It was here. I could feel it in my bones. And yet,

having arrived, I wasn't sure I could go on. What did he mean by finding me? And did I even want to be found? My heart was hammering and I almost turned back. Not so tough, after all. I could go home, put the telly on, rustle up an Ovaltine. But I was always doing that, wasn't I?

So I continued, walking along the pavement opposite the kitchens and bins, glints of mica on the ground sparkling in the half-light. The steady tap-tap of my footsteps reassured, a noise to pierce the dead murmur of ventilation. I passed walled backyards, doors, gates and alleys, the former tradesmen's entrances to once elegant townhouses. There wasn't a soul around, and I wondered if I'd been mistaken. Maybe this wasn't the place after all.

And then I saw him. Or I saw a man, menacingly still. Several yards ahead, he stood within a doorway, a slim youthful figure, a pale hoodie concealing his face like the cowl of a ghostly monk.

My heart skipped a beat. He didn't move a muscle though he must have heard me. I kept walking, anxiety tightening my throat. Head bowed, hands in his pockets, he stood beyond a pool of lamplight, faceless, hunched and furtive.

Afraid of him, I considered crossing the road but didn't, my main reason being a ridiculously British one: it might appear rude. I wondered how many die from politeness. I wondered too, what his pockets contained. Blood roared in my ears, matching the roar of ventilation as I dared myself to continue. Was I brave enough to walk past him? Stupid enough? And what if he wouldn't let me pass?

He was wearing trainers. His feet were quite large. The laces were tatty. His jeans were frayed. And then the feet moved, off the step, and he was out of the doorway, swaggering ahead, his stride quick and shifty.

I followed without a thought. His footsteps barely sounded while, behind him, mine clipped to keep pace. My mood soared, pulse drumming as I watched him walk, a touch of arrogance in his stride, droopy jeans and a neat little arse. Oh, he could lead me a merry dance around the city and I'd happily focus on that.

Seconds later, he threw a glance over his shoulder then darted into a narrow opening. Gone. In a heartbeat, I was with him, my breath coming in quick shallow gulps. He was there waiting for me. We stood in a shadowed entrance leading to a courtyard cluttered with fire escapes, stucco crumbling from its walls. He kept his head dipped, face concealed by his hooded top, and I simply stared, breathing hard.

Neither of us moved.

Then, 'Michael Angelo,' I pronounced.

Without raising his head, he swayed a fraction before taking a step towards me, shy and gauche. Instinctively, I backed away though something swelled in my heart and cunt. He stepped forwards again to stand perhaps a foot or more in front of me, that gentle pitch and roll in his stance reminding me of a landlubber on deck. I saw hints of a face, pale and angular. His manner was unthreatening, and there was a humbleness in the way he stood, as if he were presenting himself for my approval.

'Who are you?' I whispered.

He wavered a couple of inches closer, and I read it as an offering. Nervously, I reached out, slipped my hands under his top and edged him nearer, my tentative caress sliding over smooth taut skin. Oh, did he feel good beneath my fingers. He didn't respond. He simply stood there, taking it. My hands moved faster, firmer, my confidence rising with his apparent acquiescence. His body felt so healthy and alive, warm resilient skin skimming beneath my touch, muscles shifting as he swayed. His low-slung jeans rested on slender hips and I nudged his loosely belted waistband, palms pressing on the sweet jut of hip bone as my fingers kneaded his flesh.

'You're lovely,' said a soft, stunned voice, and I realised it was me.

I wanted to kiss him. My lips felt lost. But how could I kiss a man who wouldn't show his face? I could have peered into his hood but I resisted, not wanting to scare him. I settled, instead, for letting my hands explore.

It appeared to suit him. He seemed a passive, pleasured creature, allowing me to do what I wished. When I pushed his top high, he didn't object, and I gazed at the beautiful exposure of his body, at his flat honey-tanned stomach, athletic chest and the hair rising from his crotch like a thin line of smoke. His top slid up and down as my hands roamed, my lust snagged between the urge to touch and the hunger to see.

He didn't even squeak, not a grunt, groan or a hint of a gasp. How far might I go before he offered a response, some hint of sentience hidden within the hood? Where was this leading? I was open to all eventualities: he could leave, become aggressive, reveal a face I disliked or even one I knew. For him to be familiar was the most dreaded option. With this strangely docile, rag doll of a man, I felt far and away from anyone I'd ever known.

'Is this OK?' I breathed and, when he didn't reply, I let a cautious hand drift to the great lump of his groin. Still no complaint, especially not from me. Lightly, I stroked the shape of him, so turned on to feel the angle of his cock, its stiff urgency nosing at his jeans. I grew bolder, moulding the soft denim to his shaft, feeling how thick and hard he was. Yes, this was definitely OK. He didn't need words to tell me.

When I delved into his jeans, I discovered he'd gone commando, and the thick meat of his cock jerked to my touch. I curled my fingers around him and, at last, a tiny groan escaped his lips. I melted, bones dissolving in a sudden flood of lust. Within my fist he was vibrant and strong, and I reached deeper for his balls, straining for more sounds as I cupped his sac, toying with his shifting weights. Soon, I heard another faint murmur.

Just that noise, that hint of arousal and vulnerability, had me melting in another surge of wanting.

'Ah, fuck,' I gasped, feeling weak in the knees.

He edged closer, head rocking like someone half in a trance until, when I raked greedy fingernails down his back, his head lolled on a softly hissed breath. His hood slipped a little and, for the first time, I saw his face. Oh, and what a face it was. He had the most beautiful features, the flawless skin and sculpted clarity of someone noble or angelic. Light and shadow shifted within his hood, the gleam of the street casting a sheen on his narrow nose and the upsweep of his cheek. Stubble glittered darkly on his jaw and his eyes were deep set, a small ring glinting in one eyebrow.

Quickly, he looked away, shuffling closer, pushing his body against mine and making me stagger. I freed my hand, needing to balance.

'Careful! Stop it!' I said, but he kept going until I was pinned to the wall, his body pressing into mine, face averted. He clasped my wrists in each hand, then raised them high against the wall. Fear chased my lust, making my heart gallop, my breath quicken, but I didn't struggle, though I was braced in case I needed to.

I couldn't imagine needing to. We seemed to be fading into a world that was weirdly distant and yet somehow the same. While I was lucid enough to understand I ought to be on my guard, I was content to let it all happen. It was as if our here and now existed just centimetres to the left of ordinary. If anyone passed our courtyard alleyway, I imagined they wouldn't even see us. Here, it was all OK. I would wake up before anything bad happened, no problem.

Then, without turning to me, he spoke. His voice was a soft seductive breath. 'Is this what you want?'

I didn't reply. I could barely speak. The question hung in the air and I stood, chest rising and falling, sand-wiched between him and the wall, my arms splayed high in his grasp. Oh yes, I wanted this. I wanted whatever he had to give. I was wide open and reckless, liquefying in his presence. I wanted this, I wanted him, I wanted everything in the world. And soon, very soon, I'd find the words to say that.

'Ah,' I managed.

Still holding me, he leant towards my left hand and, with slow precision, he licked along the inside of my wrist. His tongue moved over delicate veined skin, flat and wet, and a shock of lust darted from my wrist to my groin where it flared to a wild eager pulse. I gazed into the courtyard, scanning small quiet windows. Hints of streetlight shone on black fire escapes and a chained-up bike, and from a washing line dangled an empty bird feeder. I couldn't see anyone peeping but I hardly cared. Michael Angelo had me pinned to the wall and he was licking my other wrist, slow and wet, the wedge of his cock shoving above my hip.

'Yes, I want this,' I whispered, his saliva cooling on my wrists.

'Then turn around,' he replied, releasing his grip.

He stayed close and I had to squirm to face the wall. Immediately he grabbed my hands and held them high again as if he were about to frisk me. I stood with my cheek to the stucco, his body a light pressure behind mine. The wall was rough to touch, the scars of old ivy draped there like giant grey lace.

In my ear, he murmured, 'I paint pictures.' His breath warmed me, then he tongued behind my ear and nibbled my lobe. I could hear the click and snuffle of his closeness, feel fabric brush my neck, and he pressed harder, his cock digging into my buttocks, forcing my pubic bone against the wall.

After a while, I said, 'Yes. I like them.'

He released my hands but I kept them there. 'I know you do,' he whispered, and he scrunched my skirt, bunching it higher until I felt the night air on the back of my bared thighs. He slipped a hand between my legs and rubbed the flesh there. I groaned, a noise like pain, as wetness sluiced through me. His fingers caressed my thighs, and I felt as if my cunt might dissolve down into my legs in search of his touch.

'Please,' I breathed, 'do something. Touch me. Fuck me.'

I leant heavily against the wall, needing its support, arms still raised. He edged my knickers down, firm hands skating over the globes of my arse, and I was so tense with wanting I almost stopped breathing. His fingertips stirred wisps of my pubes and inside I was aching, desperate to take the full fat thrust of him. I stepped out of my underwear, pushing my naked arse back.

'Hard,' I said. 'Do it hard. Please.'

He reached around to the front of me and rolled my erect clit, while his other hand squeezed and nipped my buttocks.

'Please,' I said in a near growl, and he clasped my waist, then jerked my hips back so I was tipped forwards, hands to the wall, hearing the sound of him unbuckle.

'I'm a stranger,' he said, and then the big head of his cock was there at my entrance, easing into my wetness. 'You came looking for me.' With a jolt, his cock slithered straight up me, my flesh rushing open. I was suddenly stuffed with meat, my hole stretched around his thick forceful girth, juices spilling. He shunted into me with slow deep thrusts.

'You walked alone down empty streets,' he said, speaking in quiet huffy breaths. 'And now a man you don't know fucks you against a wall. In the darkness.'

I panted and moaned as he rammed himself faster, keeping me close with that arm around my waist.

'You found this place,' he said, gasping a little. 'Not me. You found it. You're here, getting fucked, liking it, letting it all go. Blank, seedy, anonymous.'

I whimpered, his words making me flush. He was telling me how dangerous and dirty this was. I knew damn well I was at the mercy of how he might use his muscle and, while the prospect frightened me, I couldn't, wouldn't break away. He groped my breasts as we fucked, rummaged under my top, shoved aside my bra, pinched my stiff nipples. I loved the feel of him inside me; loved the furious thrust of him; loved the greed of his hand; and loved, most of all, being scared out of myself and flung into a place of debasement and abandon.

'There's a dark beauty in this, isn't there?' he said. Still thrusting, but slowing the pace, he leant forwards to bite my neck, teeth gently scraping. 'Filthy bitch,' he whispered, and he made the words sound so kind. 'Hot little cunt. Out looking for it. Chasing cock down the street.'

I groaned, an awful plaintive sound, and he dropped his hand to strum my clit. My orgasm began to tighten. My head span with hallucinatory colours, bright, beautiful landscapes and crazy phallic daffodils. I knew I was losing it, falling headlong into a tumble of warping ecstasy.

'You don't know who I am,' he said. 'And I'm fucking you, making you come.'

My body flared with sensation, my cunt dense with cock, heat, nerves and sodden, slippery friction.

'I'm making you come,' he panted as he butted at the

core of me. 'Fucking you. Banging you. My hot little slut. She's coming. I'm making her come.'

His words rippled up my thighs and then I was coming hard, starbursts of colour exploding in my mind as I whimpered and wailed. He slowed, letting my climax grip, my inner walls clenching on him while the rest of me dissolved. Then, as my spasms faded, he shoved fast and rough before whipping himself clear and spurting on the ground. He came with a strained growl that thinned to a yelp. Suddenly I was afraid to turn. What the hell kind of noise was that?

My skirt dropped into position and I leant against the wall, panting. I could see the shape of him moving behind me, feel the brush of his movements, hear the shuffle of his feet. His breath was ragged like mine, and I felt its heat on my skin as he leant to print a kiss behind my ear.

'Goodbye.'

And then he was gone.

'No,' I pleaded.

I didn't see, hear or sense him go.

He simply wasn't there any more.

It was just me, breathless and stunned, violently alone. I stood, tender, sticky and dishevelled, in a grubby alley off a gloomy street.

Confused and a little hurt, I bent to hitch up my knickers. Typical bloody man, I thought, failing to convince myself. Then my heart lurched because the ground by my feet was glowing with bright pearly light. My boots were in a lime-lit mist, a blaze of white smoke illuminating concrete and stone. Afraid, I staggered away, turning to look. Weeds were growing up the wall, actually moving, hyper-real weeds in brash aerosol colours. Their leafy stems wriggled, their garish flowers pulsed, the patch emitting a strange phosphorescence as if a piece of moon had landed.

I clamped my hand to my mouth, edging back to view more of the wall. It was impossible, all of it. Rising from the weeds, dark against the pale scarred stucco, was a life-size silhouette of a woman, legs apart, hands spread in surrender. Me.

I thought of those terrible shadows left on Japanese walls after the hottest flash. And even as I thought that, the image seemed to shift to become something more crystalline, atomised. Was it sprayed? It glimmered wetly but I didn't dare touch it. I could see my skirt bunched around my hips; the shape of my boots; how my hair had got messy; the way my mouth must look in profile when I cry out in ecstasy.

Even now, I struggle to find words for it, and words are my trade. A simple dark shape and yet it felt so intricate. It had a delicate, evanescent quality, despite its solidity.

No, that won't do, that won't do at all. Nothing will fix it. Nothing will describe it.

I felt as if I were in the presence of an extraordinary vision.

I felt as if my life had changed.

I felt scared yet elated and I backed away faster, panic rising.

Was this what they meant by another side? With him . . .

Would it fade? Would it vanish like the walls?

Dear Janie, I thought. Dear Janie . . .

And then I didn't know what to say. Because I didn't know if she would listen.

And even if I screamed, I didn't know if I'd be heard.

Perks of the Job Jan Bolton

What will this one sound like? Will it play an incongruously jolly refrain and set the pet dog off? Will it be the sober Westminster chime or the perfunctory shrill bell? And what will be in the porch? Wellingtons, umbrellas, old newspapers, child's tricycle, recycling boxes, broken tools? What will this garden display – attractive grasses, shingle and shrubs, a magnolia tree? And who will open the door? A busy mum, a petulant teenager, a suspicious pensioner or a self-employed, self-made tradesman? These are the factors I try to predict to keep the boredom at bay, as I conduct my door-to-door survey for the local council.

There's a familiarity to these suburban façades that's comforting, though, as if behind each door lies a sanctuary of reason and calm. It's an area of neat little enclaves where middle-class people who have chosen to eschew living at the heart of the urban sprawl can batten down the hatches and listen to *Gardeners' World* in peace. A zone of relative tranquillity that's proud to be nothing out of the ordinary.

I've been offered a lot of tea on this survey, and I've drunk it too, necessitating polite requests to use suburban bathrooms. I do love getting a nose at the décor. There have been pink shag-pile carpets and perfumed toilet roll cosies; the Body Shop shampoo collections of all-female households and IKEA flat-pack favourites for couples. I have seen tiny pale-blue opaque glass handbasins in the apartments of wealthy singles and child-friendly plastic sea creatures arranged around the bathtubs of family homes. There have been upscale designer wall cabinets into which I've stretched a guilty hand to help myself to Clarins creams – well, you have to have some perks in every job, that's what I say – and miniature perfume collections which have been cheekily dabbed at to freshen myself.

I've asked questions, collected data, handed over information packs and followed up with phone calls. All with a smile and an awareness of my training techniques in customer relations. Even though it's only a survey about energy saving in the home, I believe it is still important to look professional and not let standards slip like some of the other women on the job. I've always thought it is easier to get a better response when you look smart; it doesn't do to look shabby when cold-calling at people's houses. So, glossy hair, a business suit, make-up and some kind of heels are the order of the day. Even though this attire isn't compulsory I prefer to wear it. And I've clocked up more completed surveys than the reps who have worn trainers and sweatpants. The truth is, I actually like wearing outfits that give me authority. Flat shoes and loose-fitting tops do not make the best of my body shape, but fitted suits with jackets that nip in at the waist and pencil-line skirts slit to the knee always get me noticed. And I like that attention. I like walking along the road with a slight swing to my hips as my long hair is ruffled in the breeze. I like feeling my high heavy breasts agitated by my push-up bra, and the attention they receive from the drivers of passing cars. When I wear glossy hold-ups or stockings I always make a point of running a hand 'absent-mindedly' up and down my calves as I sit listening to male customers' experiences of their local recycling facilities – it's always such dull matters that I am obliged to research. And they always get distracted, yet they dare not say why.

And, naughty girl that I am, I like this tension. I like

suburban middle-aged men. I like moistening my lips with my tongue before I answer their questions, playing with my hair and thrusting my chest at them with a coquettish giggle, especially if their wives are present. I like to tease them along to the point where they are overheating, adjusting their trousers, clearing their throats and asking me to repeat that last question, please, as for some reason their concentration wavered. I like their politeness because I know it masks a raging torrent of unrealised desires, or desires that have been trampled on by years of parenthood and conformity. It turns me on.

I don't care that much what he looks like, within reason. He can be overweight, balding, badly dressed or dull. As long as he is clean and presentable and of sound mind he is fair game for my flirtatious sport. And I've been having myself a considerable amount of fun teasing other women's husbands on this job. It can really brighten up the day if I know I can drive some guy to an erotic frenzy – or as frenzied as it gets in Metroland.

The job is actually coming to an end soon. It's lasted three months, and soon the statisticians will take over and I'll be on to my next freelance public-relations contract. Which may be just as well, as last week my little games got out of hand and it's crossed my mind there might be repercussions if my employers at the local authority ever found out. I think things are OK, but one can never be sure.

It was about 3.30 in the afternoon and I'd only been able to find a couple of houses in my designated block for that day with anyone at home. It can be the dead time for door-to-door surveys, as most people are at work or shopping between the rush hours. Anyway, I knew someone was at this semi-detached 1930s property as a

Mozart piano sonata was resounding out of the open window and it did sound so very civilised and soothing. I sensed correctly that a slightly older person would be playing such music when a bloke of about fifty answered the door. As soon as he addressed me with a 'Can I help you?' I clocked that he was public school, maybe Oxbridge educated. His confident posture and tall trim body spoke of a disciplined life, and his dress was very formal for the middle of the afternoon: shirt and tie, pale-blue M&S V-necked jumper and conservative-looking dark-grey suit trousers.

I explained about the survey and its importance for predicting future local needs for waste management and energy consumption. I did this on his doorstep and it was only after a few agonising minutes during which he looked me up and down that I was invited into the hallway. Contrary to all the other domesticated men I had encountered there was a more dominant air about him. I felt for a few moments that I was going to be given a telling-off, which would have been ridiculous as, of course, I'd done nothing wrong but it was made known without anything being said that my presence was an inconvenience to this man. I didn't get a telling-off, but he completely ignored my survey and wasted no time in alluding to what he saw as an irregular situation.

'Do you usually enter the homes of strange men in the afternoon?' he asked. 'I thought there were laws about that sort of thing these days. Hmm?'

He raised his eyes at me and cocked his head to one side as his voice lifted to a questioning tone, which had about it a trace of mockery.

I laughed it off and instead flicked my manicured nails over the leaflets and questionnaires.

'Oh, I'm sure you're not that strange,' I countered,

brandishing the information pack. 'You certainly don't look strange. In fact, you look like one of my old teachers.'

'Is that right?' he said, continuing to peer at me as if I were from some rare species of plant life. A thick lock of grey hair flopped over his face and his wry smile told me that he was finding it very amusing to put me on the spot, as if young female humans were fair game for sport. His eyes flashed with intelligence. He wasn't going to be impressed with my usual flighty act, so I knew I'd have to be every inch the concerned professional if he was going to even look at the survey.

He invited me into the bright and airy living room, which was spotlessly clean and tidy. A piano sat with its lid up and sheet music was open on the stand. A glass bowl of pebbles and a neatly stacked pile of magazines were placed on a long low table and two brown leather sofas of modern design were positioned at right angles to each other. He motioned me to take a seat and I accepted, my eyes casting around the room for some evidence of female occupation. It was difficult to tell; it was a rare man who kept such order in his house, unless of course he was gay, but I doubted he was. His slightly predatory demeanour conveyed his heterosexuality. The air around us crackled with curious electricity.

I launched into my spiel about the new council initiatives for garden waste collection and efficient uses of rainwater but he looked thoroughly bored by the whole thing. Throughout my cheery address he sat opposite, watching me intently, one elbow resting casually on the arm of the sofa and one long leg thrown up onto his left knee.

After a few minutes he sighed. 'My dear, I fail to see the point of all the effort when China is building a coal-fired power station every two days, or whatever it is.'

'Oh, but you can make a difference locally, and that

contributes to a better sense of civic pride,' I returned. 'If we all made an effort to change just one of our habits, it would contribute so much, like turning your TV completely off, rather than leaving it on standby.'

'Is this what excites you? Recycling?' he said, in the most patronising voice I'd heard on the whole job. 'Because to me you look like the kind of girl who gets very excitable about all sorts of things. What we call a sensationalist.'

He hadn't moved, but he had delivered the first probing question that would take the conversation away from the survey and into more personal territory.

I maintained the pretence of not realising his question was so loaded as I answered that I got excited about holidays and going out with my friends, but I felt my face flush and I immediately started playing nervously with my hair and giggling. I knew it was not the answer he wanted. And I began to feel uncomfortably self-aware and warm.

'So, I've got a little giggler in my front room, have I? I can just imagine you creating merry hell with that teacher of yours. You know what excites *me*?'

I knew it. I knew something inappropriate was about to be revealed.

'Let me guess . . . er, classical music?'

'Isn't that a little obvious? Try harder.'

'Your garden?'

'Yes, my garden. And something else.'

My face was burning. I was being brought to book. He'd sussed me out from the moment he answered the door – that I'm used to getting my own way where men are concerned, knowing all the right moves to get them in a state of anxiety. He was cleverly calling my bluff, and I was playing along with it. I began to find the situation extremely exciting. I'd never previously had any kind of sexual communication with an older, intelligent man. It suddenly felt naughty and wrong, being in this man's house, and I felt the atmosphere between us become drenched with erotic energy. I could already feel my sex becoming slippery and, as I looked him in the eyes, I felt a dart of pure lust shoot through my core. It settled as a dull ache that spurred me to carry on the playing, taking the game towards some kind of conclusion. But what exactly? Would I really let this man, who was old enough to be my father, touch me?

'Something to do with ... girls?' I suggested.

'How very delicately put. Yes, something very much to do with girls, especially girls like you.'

'What like me?'

'Spoilt pretty girls who drive men crazy and get away with murder.'

I affected an expression of fake shock and gasped to make some defensive retort but I couldn't muster the words. Instead I sat there with my mouth open, not knowing how I was going to claw the interaction back to a professional level.

'I think girls like that should go over my knee and have their knickers pulled down for a spanking. Don't you?'

Still he didn't move from his insouciant posture and that confidence made him all the more infuriating, and attractive. The salacious image he had created reverberated around my head and brought on a fresh and stronger wave of arousal which attacked me between my legs. I desperately wanted to touch myself, yet could I really let him know how he was making me feel? Supposing I'd misunderstood and this man was really just having a little joke. Or worse, that he was some kind of a lunatic and I was playing with fire. I logically concluded that an educated man with a passion for Mozart would not be the most likely profile for a psychotic and stayed exactly where I was, fiddling with my hands, my eyes darting around the room.

No one had ever mentioned spanking to me before, yet the thought of it was all at once wildly inspiring, enough to make me giddy. It was a eureka moment; a light of realisation was turned on at that thought and, right then, I registered that there was nothing I'd rather experience than to be brought across that man's knees and dealt with – whatever that would entail.

Before I could gather the words that would form a passably coherent sentence he fired another question at me, drawing me ever closer to the moment of shame and reckoning which I so urgently craved.

'Do you think you are a girl like that? A pert little know-it-all who likes to get her way all the time?'

It would be foolish to deny this glaring truth but I knew I had to protest my character, even if I made some exaggeration for effect. It was so very very different from the kind of flirting I had experienced with men of my own age or only slightly older. Yet I felt curiously safe in his company, as if I could confess everything to him and unburden my most private thoughts yet suffer no real judgement. I intuited that I could play 'let's pretend' with him – an adult game infused with a sense of childish glee.

'I'm a girl who is usually right and my way is *always* the best way,' I proclaimed with a theatrical air of superiority.

He got up then and came to stand before me. I froze, wondering what was going to happen. Then, looking me straight in the eye, he took the pamphlets and dropped them onto the glass-topped table so they landed with a slap.

Was this it? Was he going to flip me over onto one of the sofas, push my skirt up and pull down my pants? Was he going to hurt me?

'OK, I'll think about it,' he said casually. 'Come back tomorrow about the same time. I might be in. I might not. If I'm in, I'll let you know if I can be bothered to fill in your little survey.'

My stomach became an empty chasm then. I was mortified to be strung along and then have my playful retort cruelly cut off in mid-air, just as I was beginning to understand the rules. I must have got it all wrong.

'Yes. Yes, of course, sorry, I, er ... about the same time, you say?'

'About the same time, yes.'

It was if I had imagined the whole thing. I had never known such a sense of disappointment and rejection as being ushered out of that man's house, ashamed of my cheeky attitude, my little playing around. As I walked away, towards where my car was parked, I considered that I'd had one of those strange episodes where people drift off into trances and all sorts of bizarre subconscious thoughts float to the surface. But no, he had definitely started the conversation along a flirtatious route. And as I lay in my bed that night unable to relax, was I still experiencing the thrill of hearing him talk about spanking. I knew my intuition was correct. He *was* into it. So why did he not take things any further?

I didn't go to any more houses after his that day but – and this felt really odd, as if I had suddenly turned into some kind of a pervert – I went straight home and looked at spanking sites on the internet. Some pictures showed girls' bottoms glowing red and I wondered how much it hurt. They were dressed in kilts and white knee-high socks or old-fashioned schoolgirl outfits, while other sites that were more downmarket just had girls with their jeans pulled down.

There were women in stockings and flimsy panties being spanked by other women dressed as nurses, strict schoolmistresses and in uniforms. The majority of the photos showed girls being dealt with by older men, though, and it was these pictures that, against my better judgement and beliefs, began to arouse me sexually.

I wanted to go over the knees of some stern patriarch and feel the full force of his attention. Most prominent of the curious psychological aspects of this new-found interest was the feeling that I knew it would turn the man on as much as me. He would pretend to be all cross; and I could hide my arousal behind shouting out in heat and pain, but if and when it happened to me, I knew that I would instantly get so wet. I knew I would have to masturbate or have the man do it for me. Hopefully he would want to do it to me really slowly. It could be a kind of reward. Surely the man – whoever he would be – would be hard in his trousers and ready to fuck me. Wouldn't he? Is that what it would all be about?

I was confused, yet in an exciting way. I so, so wanted the classical music man to act on his flirtatious chat. But if he was just joking, and not really into spanking at all, then I couldn't very well ask him! He could report me to the council, and then what kind of a reputation would I get? I bit my hand when I realised my dilemma. Yet I was so turned on after a couple of hours of looking at websites devoted to erotic punishment, that I slid shamefully into my bed and abused myself in a frenzy, until I came with a violence which propelled me into a new maturity of sexual desire. I had always played the little girl act to no real end but teasing men and feeling smug about being desirable. Now I saw my charms could be used to some other effect; that I could know the pleasure of real adult games, where teasing could lead to sexual chat, could lead to spanking, could lead to ...

* * *

The next day I took even more care about my appearance, although I couldn't be bothered any more with stringing along the usual suburban househusbands that I encountered. It was strange, but I felt I'd moved up a level from ordinary girlish teasing. I wanted something on a more intellectual level. So, instead, I affected a breezy professional tone, whizzing through about ten households and completing as many surveys in record time. I was saving all my creative energy for when I would, once again, present myself on the doorstep of my kinky stranger.

As four o' clock approached I sat in my car, checking my hair and make-up, feeling all the anticipation of first-date nerves. It was ridiculous. I was going to collect a survey from a man in his fifties who was as boring-looking as one of my dad's friends. There was absolutely no need to be fussing so much about my appearance, but still I had dressed for ease of access to my ... oh God, to my bottom, my sex, anywhere else he might want to touch me! I was wearing a wraparound dress in pale blue, which would fall to the floor with the pull of the waist-tie. I had on shiny tan hold-ups, pale-brown peep-toe shoes with enough of a heel to give a sway to my walk and very pretty white knickers with a cherub pattern on them and satin bows at either side. I released my glossy long straight blonde hair from its ponytail and was ready, all bar a slick of transparent lip gloss.

'So, the lady from the council has come back,' was his opening line to me as I stood on the doorstep once more. The cheek! It made me sound terribly dull and old, so I immediately found myself on the defensive.

'I don't work for the council!' I blurted back. 'Gosh, that's far too boring. I'm actually freelancing for a while to get some experience of public relations.' I realised as soon as I was speaking that he was being ironic. Irony is so apt to desert me when I'm anxious or self-conscious.

'Very public indeed, I'd say. Don't you want a nice office of your own?'

'Oh, one day,' I said, flicking my hand in the air to show a spirited devil-may-care attitude, but he was right – I would like my own office for a while. 'I'm planning to go travelling for six months, so I don't want anything too permanent at the moment.'

'You youngsters,' he said. 'You think nothing of flitting off to Australia, South America. You don't know how lucky you are. That would have cost a fortune when I was your age.'

'Well, it may well cost a fortune again, once they put tax on air fuel. It will happen, you know. But anyway, talking of environmental matters, what about the survey? Have you made a decision?'

He stood aside and opened the street door wide to welcome me inside his house once more. Again, we went through into his living room where I could see the neatly filled-out survey sitting on top of the pile of magazines. He picked it up.

'I've done this for you, then,' he said. 'I took a break from music practice and found I'd finished the bloody thing before I knew it. Didn't take long at all. In fact, it's quite interesting. I might even consider having a wormery in the garden.'

'Oh good. You've changed your attitude from the other day I see. But I do appreciate you taking the time –'

I was stopped in my flow by the magazine uppermost on the pile he had revealed. Facing me was something I'd not seen before: a glossy publication devoted to, of course, spanking. His eyes had locked on to mine; he was watching my every move: the nervous moistening of my lips, my increasing respiration rate, my dilated pupils. He took a step closer to me.

'Oh look, I've forgotten to clear away my more private magazines. Does that bother you? You look a little flustered.'

I'd not wanted to, but I immediately went into a flush of embarrassment. I brushed at my hair, put my hand to my mouth, looked at him and I honestly didn't know what to do with myself.

'Yes, I guess I am a little flustered. I've not seen any magazines like that before.'

'That's not surprising. But I must tell you that lots of women are turned on by the subject. Do you think you might be like that?'

Oh, gosh. He was forcing me to admit my new-found shame. I would have to find gargantuan amounts of courage to confess my interest but, as much as I wanted to, I couldn't bring myself to say the words.

'I, er, well, it's certainly different!' I managed, cheerily.

'That's not what I asked you, sweetheart. Shall we try again? I can see you're a little nervous. I do like it when young women get all shy. Why don't you come and sit down next to me on the sofa? We can look at some pictures together. You can whisper to me quietly what you would like.'

I went over to sit down, glad to have something to do, albeit for a few seconds. It dawned on me how useful it was to be given orders. I instantly liked that. I was meek, complicit. I felt I would do anything for him. I was, again, already wet underneath those cherubic panties.

I made myself as comfortable as I could with my arousal levels going off the dial as this tall man with his professorial air plonked himself down next to me, so matter of fact. So close our legs were touching. He could feel me trembling. His large hand went onto my knee and I felt his fingers start to circle the inside of my lower thigh. He then put the magazine in my lap and told me to look through the pages, to tell him which pictures I liked best.

It seemed like an hour passed as I flicked through those pages, so self-conscious was I of him waiting for me to speak. There was one spread that appealed to me: an air hostess in a uniform similar to my dress was being roughed up in the cockpit by the pilot. It wasn't particularly well photographed, but the combination of his uniform and her creamy buttocks, poised for his hand, set me aflame. I managed to croak out a small confession: 'I, er, quite like this one, actually,' I said.

'Like uniforms, eh? You girls are so predictable. But no more so than us men. The female form is such a distraction to us. Is that something you would like? To be spanked by an older man?'

I nodded my head. I couldn't speak. I could barely accept the situation I found myself in, in this stranger's house.

'You are very quiet compared to your first visit. Cat got your tongue?'

'No. It's just that I ... I'd never thought about this stuff before. But I can see you're quite an expert. I don't know anything.'

'My dear, you don't need to. And I think I'd call myself an enthusiast, rather than an expert. But I can't spank you if you sit there all perfect and well behaved, can I? Surely there's something you want to tell me.'

He was right. By being silent I was doing nothing to excite him. The energy had to work both ways. It was time for a confession. So I found the courage to tell him what I'd done the previous day. About looking on the internet, getting aroused and masturbating. It was all that was needed. Within moments his crotch was swollen and my breath was ragged. I'd never told anyone such things before. Not even boyfriends. It was liberating and exciting.

He flicked the folds of my dress apart to reveal my cute knickers, the heat radiating upwards, the scent of me filling our space.

'Show me. Show me how you did it, you dirty little girl.'

I couldn't speak, but it was easy to do as he asked. I slid my right hand down in there and began to make the movements I always used. That never failed me. I closed my eyes and threw my head back as he softly encouraged me, telling me how hard it was making him.

As I gained more confidence and the act didn't seem quite as forbidden as I'd imagined, he must have sensed I was getting closer as he grabbed both my wrists and suddenly hauled me to my feet.

'Oh no you don't. Not that quickly. What do you think this is, a slut's day out? You're going to find out what happens to naughty, badly behaved young ladies who think it's perfectly acceptable to visit a gentleman in the afternoon and start playing with themselves so brazenly.'

My eyes flashed wide open in indignation. 'But you told me to do it!'

Then I realised how easily he could rile me, and I started laughing.

'Come along, giggler,' he said. 'You're coming upstairs. We'll find out who's got the upper hand here.'

So, tingling with excitement, I climbed his immaculately carpeted stairs with his hand on my bottom, up to what I thought would be his bedroom. It felt so right, yet so wrong at the same time. What would happen to me? I hoped I wouldn't start yelling, or be flaky. I'd had no experience of pain on my backside before! I didn't know what to expect. But, anyway, we bypassed the bedroom and he gently pushed me into his study. It was lined with shelves of books about music theory, historical biographies and files probably containing boring papers and sheet music.

I hopped about from foot to foot, finding the cheeky intonation he had been drawn to yesterday.

'Oh dear. Looks like I'm in sir's study,' I said, flicking my hair and affecting the posture of a spoilt teenager.

'How very observant, my dear. Who said young people weren't as intelligent as they used to be? It's their attitude we have to work on – especially that of smarter-than-thou young ladies.'

'You can't do anything to me. You're just jealous.'

'Let's see about that, shall we? You just turn around and face the window and do as you're told. I've warned you about your behaviour before, but you wouldn't listen, would you? You couldn't help yourself, you depraved little slut.'

'What?' I blurted out, feeling the genuine emotions of indignity but quickly realising the role-play aspect to the discourse. For now I would enjoy being that slut. I found my measure and joined in the game. I rammed my fingers once more into my panties and began blatantly masturbating for him. I even soaked my fingers with my juice and then rammed them under his nose. It was the final straw. Suddenly I was spun around, a hand firmly grasped the back of my neck and I was over the desk in a flash.

I felt an assured hand on my rear. If I had been shocked I would have flinched and leapt aside, but it came as no surprise. It came as a longed-for gesture of approval, for the sexual spell I had cast over him, over all of those poor frustrated suburban men. Out of all of them, it was only he who had taken the liberty; only he who was brave enough; only he who was in a position to do so. And I was going to get it.

'That's right, don't move,' he whispered into my ear. 'Just stay calm and quiet.'

His hands began to roam all over my arse, my legs. I could feel his hard-on grazing against me as he moved about behind me. He was speaking obscenities quietly into my ear, his lascivious expression sounding all the more potent for its understatedness.

'You dirty little girls are all the same. Little cock-teasers dying for a superior man to put his hands on you.'

I went to turn around but he held me fast and gently coaxed me to lean forwards.

'You're going to stay right there, that's it, right up against the desk while I take my time with you. You are a silly girl, asking me all those boring questions in your survey about what I do with my old newspapers?' He laughed. 'I've a good mind to whack your backside with an old copy of the *Spectator*!'

I hadn't a clue what that was – some boring older man's periodical, I suppose. I was aching for the treatment he was about to dish out but, of course, I made some protest. 'No! You wouldn't dare,' I countered. 'You wouldn't do that to a council official.'

'I'd especially like to do that to a council official, but I'm not going to waste time. I'm going to give it to you the old-fashioned way – my hand on your backside, you dirty girl.'

And with that he stole a hand under my skirt and agonisingly slowly pulled down my cherubic knickers. Up came the dress, right up over my waist and neatly flattened over my back, to reveal my bare bottom and stocking-clad legs. It was time.

And then the blows came, tingling at first, then in

rapid succession so hard it took my breath out of me. I squeaked and squalled but the protests were all in vain. My backside was warming up like a radiator.

'That's what you get for being cheeky to your elders and betters,' he said. 'And if you think that's all you're getting, you're in for a surprise. Stay right there, facing the window. Don't move.'

I did as I was told, but I was laughing uncontrollably. The spanking seemed to have unlocked some new gleeful part of me. I felt him busying about behind me, and then a blindfold was tied around my head.

'I don't need this,' I protested. 'I want to see.'

'It's to heighten your sensation. Remember, you are in the hands of an expert.'

I acquiesced. In one way, it actually made me feel even more liberated. He'd put on some concerto or other. It was the first time I'd had my knickers taken off to a classical score. Then I felt his hand on the small of my back and the sense that something else was about to happen. Then it landed. Like molten fire on the cheeks of my arse. I yelled.

'This is the strop – a nice thick band of leather, especially suited to the meaty buttocks of well-built girls. I could beat a symphony out of you, but you'll be pleased to know this room is sound-proofed.'

I groaned and cried out and shouted my protest as the hot lashes rained down on my poor virgin arse. It was too much. I was feeling weaker by the minute, all my spirited playfulness being literally beaten out of me. Yet, with this curious weakening feeling came a flush of something else – it must have been the endorphin rush I'd read about on the spanking websites. The heat of my flesh spread around my middle and then further inflamed my sex. I was literally desperate to be touched. It was torture to not have the attention where I needed it most. And he must have wanted to touch me, surely.

At last he put the strop aside and finally, finally, I was rewarded with the sensation of his musician's fingers against my cunt.

'It's what I've dreamt of too,' he said. 'You do know you are in the hands of a very skilled enthusiast, don't you?'

'Yes. But please, please, make me come. Please do it to me,' I begged.

'I'm teaching you patience, my dear,' he said. 'Something you have been missing, I'll bet.'

He was right. I'd been so used to getting my own way for so many years. Being pretty and blonde made life so much easier. Now I was being taught a lesson in humility, as I was begging a man old enough to be my father to bring me off with his hand. Oh, the shame!

But he worked me so skilfully. My nails raked along the sides of the desk. I began grinding my hips into the wood, uncaring that I was chafing myself, that I was displaying everything to him.

His cock rubbed against my legs and I visualised it from the confines of my blindfold. I yearned to touch his velvet hardness. I yearned to have it inside me. All I could do was groan. My stomach ached with the prolonged arousal I'd suffered – yes, suffered – at this man's behest.

He was truly skilled. He knew exactly when I was about to come because he made me ask him if I could.

'Please, sir, please may I have my orgasm now?'

It was as much as I could do to hold back those few more seconds. And then, when it hit me, it was so powerful, so extreme that I saw stars. Fireworks went off behind my eyes and I flew to the outer reaches of my universe, crying out my beautiful dirty ecstasy. And, while I was enjoying the waves that juiced my sex even more, I felt the enormity of him. He had finally entered me.

The thrusts came deep and slow. He was huge! I flopped over the desk, wanting to relax completely after my body-wracking orgasm. Surely he wouldn't take long. I couldn't believe he was that hard, that big. I laughed uncontrollably, with a sense of fun, disbelief and good humour. His hands gripped onto my sides and he pounded for a few exquisite minutes until he stopped, withdrew and leant up against my ear to say, 'I think we'll have you on the floor now.'

Still blindfolded I sank to my knees, grateful to have a new position to stretch my back and arms. Once more he pushed that amazing cock into me and I settled into the rhythm of it, egging him on with praise and thanks and dirty encouragement, completely happy now in my role as a dirty girl. Except I wasn't play-acting; I was wholeheartedly engaged in the activity.

But I slowly became aware of something near my face. Something musky and familiar – the movement of a man masturbating.

'Oh God, you dirty little girl, you know what you're going to make me do, don't you?'

It was his voice, but it was coming from in front of me. In my woozy state from the intensity of my orgasm I was disoriented. And then, before I could work out what was going on, the blindfold was whipped from my head and my friendly stranger was in front of me, pumping his huge cock in the final strokes.

'Oh yes, yes, you're going to get it all over you, sweetheart,' he said. And as a fountain of come erupted from his cock I swivelled my head around to see exactly what or who was still filling me so handsomely from behind.

She was beautiful. Mid forties, blonde hair falling around her shoulders, a strap-on harness around her hips. She said nothing but smiled sweetly and stroked my back.

I flung my head back to him as he was just coming out of his own moment of ultimate pleasure.

'Sorry, darling,' he said, somewhat breathless. 'I didn't get the time to introduce you to the wife.'

Reflections Maddie Mackeown

Water slides past as she slices through the blue-white underworld, hair streaming out behind, waving like fronds of seaweed. Following the lines that run along the bottom of the pool, her body is sinuous with minimal movement that nevertheless propels her forwards. Legs and bodies hover out of reach in the disturbed depths, wavering strangely as if in a hall of mirrors. She's nearly made it to the wall and begins to let out bubbles of captured breath. Jack-knifing, she pushes strongly against the floor, shoots upwards and breaks through the surface in a froth of agitated bubbles.

She treads water, which is good for the thighs, and takes greedy gulps of humid air, then lies on her back to enjoy the floaty sensation of weightlessness. Sunlight streams down through glass panels in the ceiling and she drifts gently out of its touch and into a pool of shadow. With thirty lengths behind her, only the final bit submerged, it's time to get out and get on with the day.

The dressing rooms are warm, too warm for such a hot day. She allows cool water to flow freely in the shower, closing her eyes and giving in to the luxury, a moment of calm to set her up for what promises to be an exhausting day. Mmm. Maybe she should have left it at twenty lengths today. Oh well. Too late now. She's allotted this single slot of time to sort the double problem of a tired wardrobe combined with an imminent wedding – not hers, not yet – and there's the library to visit and an appointment with the dental hygienist.

It's quite an empty changing room because she came at an hour late enough to avoid the early-bird brigade but early enough to beat the organised classes. She isn't kindly disposed towards frenetic female chatter and prefers a people-free zone as often as possible. Especially on a rare day off.

Water trickles across her skin for longer than is necessary, an act of pure indulgence to set her up for the tasks ahead. At last she emerges, loosely wrapped in a draping towel. She sits on the bench and rummages in her bag for a pen and piece of paper.

OK. Let's be organised about this. Plan of action: 1. Library 2. Post Office 3. Dentist 4. Dress 5. Underwear (be prepared for any eventuality. You never know what might happen when romance is let loose. If it hits you smack in the face, something may have to be done about it right there and then) 6. Card (must remember to look at the wedding present list).

She reads through the list, crosses out number 2 and adds 7. Candles – scented. Jasmine. (For me.)

A drop drips onto the paper, causing 'Candles' to melt into an artistic blob. She lifts the corner of the towel to pat her hair, turning the paper this way and that, tilting her head this way and that, wondering what the smudge could be – a Christmas tree? a teddy? – when she is checked by soft sounds. She looks up, listening. Yes, there it is again: some sort of rustling, almost squeaky, and muffled voices. Not the usual noise of a changing room. It's coming from the locker area.

Wondering what's going on but not wanting to be caught spying, she steps quietly, which is easy in bare feet, and is about to peep around the corner when her eye is drawn to a mirror in the opposite direction. A shock streaks through her and she grasps the towel close to her body. A slight sweat has sprung up all over her skin. There's no need to look around the corner for she can see what it is in the alternative world of reflection.

There are two women together. One leans back on the bench, knees raised, while the other kneels between her legs. One is naked and the other is not and still in wet bathing costume. Both women are totally involved with each other and oblivious to her surreptitious approach.

Fascinated, she continues to watch but after a few moments realises that she's been seen by the woman on the bench. Their eyes lock briefly. She immediately jumps back into hiding out of mirror range, frozen into stillness while warm air presses against her. The sounds carry on around the corner.

She is shocked not simply by what is happening but by her own sudden arousal. She's aware of a pressure between her legs and a dampness that wasn't there before. She closes her eyes and, like a screen capture, sees a female hand caressing a breast and fingers buried in damp curls. Opening her eyes, she blinks at the empty air, seeing a head move between open thighs; blinks again and sees a wet costume clinging to bottom cheeks with drops of water trickling down the backs of legs. Blink, and there's a face contorted in the pleasure of these grabbed moments.

She presses her back against the wall, feeling its coldness. In her imagination she can smell the musky scent of female fluid mingled with chlorine. Her nipples are tingling as they harden against the towel. She touches where she has secured it, for some reason now doubting its effectiveness. She's tempted to peep again but resists this urge to spy on a private act. Then she thinks, hold on, this is a very public place. Discovery is their risk. Her head tilts back against the wall. Maybe that's it, the risk of being seen. Maybe the thrill of being watched is an objective.

She's intrigued. Blink. She sees a hand reaching high to the hooks above, fingers gripping. Her own fingers grasp the knotted towel. A blink, and she sees the erect nipple on a beautifully formed breast. Should she make her presence more obvious and see what transpires? No. She decides to pull away from this. Other women are not her style.

Annoyed that she's been faced by this without seeking it out, she goes to the hairdrier and flicks it on to high speed, effectively drowning out any pleasure sounds. How dare they!

A little while later the two women emerge and head for the showers. She notices through a veil of blown hair but ignores them. They notice her and blatantly look as they pass. She resolutely concentrates on drying her hair, refusing eye contact. Only when they've gone does she lift her head, glancing after them but they've disappeared round another corner into a nebulous, steamy world. She switches off the drier. This is ridiculous. Why should I feel embarrassed? Yet she can't let it go and imagines them now soaping each other.

She takes a deep breath and begins to dress, wondering why the scene has aroused her so. Surprise obviously has played its part as has the fleeting role of secret voyeur. A yearning to be involved in such a pursuit is also possible, well, probable. Although not with another woman. Not her thing.

She glances at the soggy list – could be India – then crumples the paper into her bag and continues to dress, putting on sensible cotton knickers and bra in deference to the hot weather. The linen of the blouse is cool, albeit now as crumpled as the discarded list. She slips on the skirt which neatly outlines her natural shape and slips feet into comfortable shoes for walking.

The place is now abuzz with the hyped-up chatter of

children. They only just got away with it in time, she thinks. The audacity of it!

On the way out she pauses at the mirror for a final check. A movement behind catches her eye, coming into view at a distance. The two women hurry past, hair still wet, grinning at her, drawing her into a conspiracy. Her eyes slide from theirs and she pretends not to have spotted them. After a few moments to allow for them to be gone, she makes her way down to the exit.

Outside, it doesn't take long to wipe out what little coolness remains from the swim. Getting into the car, trapped heat hits like a mini sauna. What a day to traipse around town! Maybe she could put it off until another time? Maybe just go home and sit in the garden with a magazine, cold fruit juice and sunblock? Tempting, but she's left it too late. She's already missed one dental appointment and the wedding is looming. It'll have to be today. 'Library' also gets mentally crossed off the 'To Do' list. At least most places now have air conditioning. And with that comforting thought she leaves the car park and heads for the mall, driving slowly to conserve some aspect of composure.

Red lights, but she refuses to be riled. No point in wasting energy. A man walks past, too briskly for the heat, she thinks, noticing the spread of sweat between his shoulder blades. She watches his neat, receding butt in the side mirror as he diminishes into the reflected world. He passes a young woman who saunters along towards her, overtaking the car at a leisurely pace. She watches the progress and her eyes are drawn to the swaying outline of breasts in tight T-shirt. No bra. Blink.

A small beep from behind tells her that the lights have changed. She revs up and takes off speedily.

Nearly there. She stops at the crossing. A hunk on legs swaggers across, cool in his tight jeans and shades.

A woman crosses in the opposite direction, bottom wobbling as she walks. Does mine do that? She checks the outline and wonders if people see her knicker-line. She clenches her bum cheeks. Jazz! she admonishes herself. Get a grip, girl. Concentrate.

The car park is nearly full. She has trouble finding a space, which is bad news for it suggests crowds. Oh well. She can but hope that her search will be quickly successful and then she can go home. Come on, girl. Go for it.

She's feeling smugly pleased. It's mid-afternoon and she has beautifully smiling teeth. Candles, jasmine scented, a card, cute, and underwear, peach, have already been bought and she's seen a dress that she likes. A break is now required. Time for a coffee, or maybe chilled juice, and then try the dress. At this rate, hopefully, she could be finished by four.

The store has a café. It's a little expensive but the convenience is worth the extra. Actually, it's very expensive. It's one of those places where a subdued hush reigns instead of incessant music, where everything is nicely spaced out and the assistants hover discreetly in the background.

She sips the juice and indulges in a slice of homemade carrot cake. Home-made? Yeah, right. But it does melt deliciously on the tongue.

There are designer clothes aplenty hanging on gym-fit bodies that are beautifully toned, sitting nearby in the hushed surroundings. A flash of memory reminds her of the explicit duo at the swimming pool. Cheeky! And she smiles a radiantly white smile at no one in particular.

The people around her are mainly female in a decidedly moneyed-class bracket that fails to faze her. Recently groomed shiny heads of hair tilt towards others in the gentle art of gossip as well-manicured nails shine at the handles of afternoon tea cups. Bags with store names and logos perch at well-shod feet and bulge unobtrusively with purchases which she reckons are probably needed to spruce up wardrobes that are at least half a season out of date.

She rummages for her mobile and selects 'Write message'. 'Hi Ricky Baby. Just had hugely calorific carrot cake. Oops! Naughty me. Hope 2 b home by 5. I'm knackered. See U later. Jazz xxx.'

OK. She stands ready for the final furlong, slipping cooled feet back into her shoes and picking up her tote bag. Fingers crossed, the dress will be all that is desired and then she can go home, put up her feet and chill with a glass of white wine from the fridge. Sounds great.

She steps between the rails of dresses. Where was the one I liked? An assistant smiles but doesn't approach. Jazz likes that. She'd prefer to flounder rather than have to deal with an in-your-face oh-so-helpful saleswoman.

She goes down the next rail and yes! There it is. Checking the sizes and holding one in front of her, it drapes fluidly from tiny shoulder straps, reaching to about mid-calf. She likes the mix of muted colours and the floaty quality of the silk, which will suit her, even though the price does not. Maybe she can get away without the expense of new shoes and bag because the dress seems perfect for the occasion and could be used for all those smart events she thinks she should attend and must remind Rick to arrange.

Feeling satisfied and confident that the day is nearly at an end – and actually has been fairly enjoyable – she approaches an oh-so-helpful but oh-so-discreet assistant. 'Excuse me. Where are the changing rooms?'

'Around the corner, madam, just to the left.'

'Thanks.'

Her mobile buzzes. She opens the message: 'Jazzi Babe. Carrot cake! Naughty girl! I must put you across my knee and ... Randy Ricky xx.'

She giggles at the thought and feels a ripple of interest between her thighs. Later, baby, later. Things to do first.

In the cubicle, which is more like a small room Jazz closes the door, puts down her things and hangs the dress on one of a range of hooks. There is a small shelf on which stand hand lotion, dusting powder and a water spray. The containers are still quite full, telling of the trustworthiness of the clientele. A mirror dominates the area without being overdone. It's all very tasteful in rose-tinged cream, which won't detract from or challenge the garments that are to be tried.

Beginning to undress, she appreciates the air conditioning, which is as cool as dawn on a morning in spring with the promise of heat to come. She throws discarded clothes onto the chair that stands alone in the corner. The ever-present hubbub is relegated to a satisfying distance that allows a quiet piece of space and lack of interruption in which to make careful consideration.

She decides to give a light dusting of powder to her skin. Might as well use what's on offer. Anyway, it's probably been bought out of the profit from the oh-so-delicious home-made cake. It feels decidedly fresh and smooth. It smells decidedly bland. Mustn't clash with all those expensive perfumes that waft through this little haven of space.

The silk feels wonderful as the dress slips over her head. It slithers around her body with a touch like trickling water. She looks at the image in the mirror, pleased. But not pleased enough for the price tag.

Shit! I don't want to start searching again. She studies her reflection. OK. Colour's good, contrasting with the darkness of her skin without being too pastel or too bright. She sways and twists from side to side and the fabric moves softly with a slight swish. It'll look better without the bra straps of course. She wriggles them from her shoulders and arms and tucks them into the bodice. Mm. Better. Strappy heeled sandals will help. The cream ones from last year will do. She stands on tiptoe. Yes. Better still. She performs a slow swivel while keeping her eyes on the reflection. Not bad but something's still not quite right. It's the size. A little too big. Wow! I've gone down a size! The reflection grins at her. Must be all the swimming and toned muscle.

She opens the door and peers out to see if there's an oh-so-helpful assistant within reach. Bingo! A woman is just leaving another cubicle, looking very purposeful and carrying a skirt on a hanger. She is middle-aged and dressed in the smart black skirt with white blouse uniform of a saleswoman.

'Excuse me.'

The woman glances at Jazz and hesitates mid walk. 'Yes?'

'I wonder if you could help me with this dress.'

The woman is silent for a moment. A slight frown is swiftly followed by a friendly smile, with teeth not so white and sparkly. 'Certainly, madam. What's the problem?'

'I think I'd like to try a smaller size.'

The woman comes over to Jazz's door. Jazz steps back. The woman steps in and closes the door.

'What do you think?' says Jazz, looking in the mirror.

'The colour is perfect for you. Just a minute. Let's see.' She hangs the skirt on a hook and stands behind Jazz. With knowing hands, she takes hold of the high waistband and pulls it in. Immediately the dress moulds to Jazz's body, suggesting the curves beneath but not clinging.

'That's it! So much better!' Jazz is quite excited that

the search could be over after all and also, well, she looks really good. Just wait till Rick sees me in this. He won't be able to keep his hands off.

'Let me fetch a size twelve for you, madam.'

'How did you know?'

'It's my job.' The woman smiles again and unzips the dress. Cool fingers slip the straps from her shoulders, holding the dress so that it slithers down without falling into a little heap on the floor. Jazz steps out of it and stands there in her sensible knickers and bra. The assistant takes the dress and the skirt and leaves, closing the door behind her.

Jazz takes out her mobile: 'Hi Rick. Nearly done. Wait till you see me! Super Slinki Jazzi Baby xxx.' She is just sending the text when the door opens. The woman enters discreetly, pushes the door shut and checks that it's properly closed. Pure efficiency. A dress rests across her arm and Jazz touches it, smoothing the silk. The woman hangs it up.

'Excuse me, madam, but a different bra will make the dress hang better.'

'Oh, yes. Actually, I've already bought one.' Jazz opens a bag and takes out the new bra.

'Might I suggest that you try wearing it this time?'

Jazz laughs. 'Good idea,' she says and is about to undo what she is wearing but stops, suddenly feeling embarrassed. She blinks and images fill her mind.

The woman steps behind her. 'Let me help.' She unclasps it at once with a no-nonsense approach and the bra disappears. Jazz turns to the mirror and, as she lifts the new bra into place, notices the woman's eyes on her, only for an instant before she's covered again in pretty pastel peach which shapes in a smooth curve.

She stands very still as the clasp is done for her. In the mirror she sees the swell of her breasts, which are pushed upwards as they rest in lace that is strap free.

The woman touches at the edge and runs her finger along its line, trailing across each soft curve, as if to check the fit. Jazz watches the rise and fall of her breathing as the fingertip traces its undulating path. It's a strange sensation, non sexual but stimulating in its delicateness. She is captivated by it and curious of her own response. The path ends and the touch too.

There is movement behind her and the dress is lifted over her head. It swishes down, clinging to her body in a gossamer hold. It fits perfectly. The woman stands back. 'Beautiful,' she says and Jazz doesn't know if she's referring to her or the dress. Their eyes meet in the mirror and something passes between them but it's too subtle and fleeting to grasp. Jazz licks her lips and moisture settles there. She feels beads of sweat settle on her brow. In the mirror, the woman's eyes shift.

The hush seems to deepen to silence. Footsteps tread quietly outside the closed door. They pass, accompanied by a fading murmur of voice.

'Are you hot, madam?' The woman's voice is soft.

'I am a little.'

Jazz turns this way and that into different poses which show off the dress from many angles. She sways and the skirt sweeps loosely around her thighs, hanging from the hips where the fabric clings, revealing the curves beneath. It tickles at her knees because the silk is so light and fluid. The thin straps accentuate her shoulders, asking to be slipped down, which is what the woman does.

'See how the fit here is secure. The dress won't slip.' The bodice is close fitting but not taut and lies on her body like a second skin, showing off the breasts which swell out from the merging colours. 'And the fit here is very good.' A pause. 'Maybe you should wear a thong.' Hands slide firmly across her hips, resting on her bottom for a touch longer than is necessary. 'The colour really suits you. It's good against your skin, pale against your darkness.'

The woman's fingers rest on her arms, light as a feather which drifts on the breeze. Jazz feels the touch as a tremble through her body and stands motionless. 'You are still very warm, my dear.' The fingers slide up into the heaviness of her hair and lift it away from her neck so Jazz feels a creep of cool air. The fingers run through like a comb, pulling firmly. Jazz closes her eyes. There are muted sounds outside the cubicle but she doesn't want to go to them. In a minute maybe. But not yet. She lets her head tilt back and feels the strong fingers twist her hair into a knot.

'Are you still hot, my dear?'

Jazz opens her eyes. Indeed, there is a film of sweat on her chest. She can see it. 'Yes.' Her voice comes as a whisper.

Without saying anything else the woman lets the hair fall, unzips the dress and peels it off. Jazz lifts her arms automatically. She stands in her new lacy bra and sensible cotton knickers, looking in the mirror at the mismatch which somehow seems appropriate.

The woman puts the dress carefully back on the hanger, onto the hook, and picks up something from the shelf. Jazz watches her in the mirror. Standing in front of her, the woman delivers a fine spray of water from the bottle. It hovers in the air between them and settles as a mist onto skin. 'There, that's better, my dear, isn't it?' She moves around Jazz spraying as she goes and it's deliciously cool on the warmth of her skin.

There is a pressure at her back and the bra is undone. Jazz takes hold of it and throws it behind her to the chair, where it misses and falls unnoticed to the floor. There is a moment when they both wait. Their eyes find each other in the mirror. Jazz can feel a blush steadily rising to her face.

The woman moves in front of her and sprays deliberately onto her breasts. Jazz lifts her hands and smoothes the dampness into her skin, watching the woman who watches her fingers. She touches her neck, tips back her head and shakes her hair loose, running her fingers through to lift it from her forehead. Another spray and she feels female fingers on her breasts. Her hand stops, buried in her hair, while she watches in the mirror from beneath half-closed eyelids. But the woman blocks the view as her breasts are stroked and lifted, pressed and squeezed. There is a slight intake of breath and the woman moves behind her.

Jazz blinks, then watches as female hands slide over her ribs, reaching to cup her breasts. Thumbs circle around both nipples which have sprung to hardness. A hand slides down over her belly and stops at the top of her knickers.

Both pairs of eyes flick and meet in the reflection. The blush builds on her cheeks and Jazz gives the merest hint of a nod. She feels an ache between her legs as the woman begins to pull down her knickers. She bites the inside of her lip. What if someone walks in? Should she stop this?

Too late. The fingers have gradually slipped the knickers to halfway down her thighs. They move into the thatch of hair at the top of her legs. It needs a trim, she thinks, absent-mindedly, as she is gently pulled open to view. It is like looking at someone else in the mirror.

She is almost aloof, at one remove, while these things are done to her body. The woman steps back and Jazz can see her looking greedily at her bottom. Fingers squeeze the ample softness, then spread her open. Kneeling behind her, the woman leans forwards and is hidden from view. There is wet warmth as she feels a tongue push between the spread cheeks and slide along, up and down, lingering each time.

Jazz listens as footsteps and muffled voices pass outside. The probing tongue halts its exploration. Her heart misses a beat. But the steps walk on without pause. No. It's OK. Saliva dribbles onto her in a cool slick. She reaches round and helps to keep her bum spread for the tongue is pressing in an interesting place.

Her knickers are pulled down to her knees. Casually, she parts her legs a little further. It's far too warm to hurry. So, what next?

The woman stands up and drags the chair closer to the mirror, sideways on. Clothes tip onto the floor. 'Bend over, dear.'

A thrill explodes within Jazz. She bends over, lying across the seat and opening her legs. Looking over her shoulder to see the image in the mirror, she is a voyeur to herself. Her heart is pounding in the excitement of seeing her own body thus exposed, thus handled. What if someone were to come in now? There is a rush of moisture between her legs. Am I about to be spanked? But that isn't the intention.

The woman sprays water liberally over her bum. Jazz can see the droplets as they settle on her skin and begin to trickle, can feel the wetness and coolness. She watches as the woman leans over her and smears hand lotion into the wetness, slicking smoothly and widening her further, hands sliding firmly, pale against her darker skin. Jazz watches as one finger is pushed inside, just the tip, but she presses back against the intrusion and it slides more deeply into her. She feels moisture trickle slowly down her thigh.

The woman finds her eyes in the reflection. 'You like that?'

'Yes,' Jazz says.

'Would you like two fingers in you?'

Jazz's eyes open wide. Her lips part and the tip of her tongue licks at the corner of her mouth. She nods, and watches as the finger withdraws and pushes in again with another. She turns her head away, averting her eyes as the fingers begin to move insistently inside her. She finds herself rocking in time with the probing fingers, her bum lifting and falling as she lies across the chair. She looks round again to see. It is so exciting. It is so naughty. She sees as if from a distance, involved but remote at one and the same time. She blinks then shuts her eyes.

The fingers are withdrawn and in the darkness there is a touch between her legs.

'Open wider, my dear.' The voice is confidential, matter of fact.

She spreads her knees as far as the knickers will allow and is explored anew. Jazz gives in to the sensation. Where will this end? Although highly turned on, she doesn't feel a climax coming, but as foreplay it's exquisite.

Opening her eyes to the mirror Jazz sees a finger insert. Is that really me? The woman pulls the knickers down to her ankles and tells her to kneel on the floor. Do I let this go on or finish it now? But it feels so good, looks so good ... Maybe in a minute.

She scrambles down, shoving the chair aside for she wants to be within range of the mirror. She leans on her elbows so that, as she pushes her bum up into the air, she can see each finger that slips into her. One, two, then three. The woman is leaning over her and watching where her hand moves. It is glistening. Jazz is panting. A knuckle is rubbing on another very interesting place, as the fingers twist inside her. The pleasure is building fast. They must stop. But, maybe just another few moments. It feels so good, looks so – and just when she's thinking that she really should finish this now, her body takes over as an orgasm rips through her, taking her by surprise because she really was going to stop. Wasn't she? She cries out, immediately snatching her hand to her mouth to stifle the sound, her bottom bouncing as the relentless intrusion continues.

'That's a good girl,' comes the quiet efficient voice.

Jazz wipes away the sweat that trickles into her eyes then turns, reaching behind and –

There is a tap at the door. The woman jerks away. Jazz jumps up, yanking at her knickers. She hides behind the door as it's opened but the woman prevents it from opening too far. Jazz presses her naked back to the wall. It is cold against her skin. She holds her breath and hears the woman say that they've just about finished. Another moment or two, please.

The door closes. The woman has left and Jazz is alone, frozen to inaction. She hears her shallow breathing in the hush, feels the dampness on her knickers, feels the heat between her thighs where a pulse still throbs.

Then she moves. She grabs her clothes from the floor and pulls them on. Ready to leave, bags and dress in hand, she glances in the mirror, taking one deep calming breath. And blinks. The reflection smiles back at her.

Beyond the cubicle Jazz feels rather bemused because everything is carrying on as normal. She lingers behind the first rail that she comes to, finger-combs her hair and breathes deeply ten times, hoping that her high colour is fading fast. Glancing around, she peeps from behind the hanging clothes but the woman is nowhere to be seen. Probably seeing to another lucky customer, being oh so attentive. What excellent service this store provides! Does everyone get such treatment? Jazz wonders.

'Dear Rick: I'm on my way. Be ready 4 me. I'm hot hot hot! Yours expectantly, Jazz xx.'

The clock on her mobile tells her that it is only seventeen minutes since she last sent a message. Is that all! She is surprised for it had seemed much longer.

At the pay point as she stands behind another customer, she is caught in a beguiling waft of something floral with musk undertones. Or is that me? she wonders. The assistant is smoothly efficient and looking very smart in blue blouse and black skirt. Jazz waits, patiently detached, and then blinks twice. She does a double take. Blue? Name badge? Her eyes flit to another assistant. Then another. Both are in the same blue-bloused uniform. It's not white at all. And both wear name badges. So the woman wasn't –

'Can I help you, madam?'

Jazz returns from her startled thoughts and lays the dress on the counter. The oh-so-polite assistant takes it and adds, 'Oh, by the way, your friend thought that you might like these to go with the dress.'

On the dress she lays some earrings that perfectly reflect the deeper tones of the fabric. They are a triple of suspended chains, dropping to differing lengths with shimmering glass beads that catch the sunlight. 'Your friend had to rush off.'

Jazz looks at the earrings. They are beautiful and cannot be resisted.

'What do you think, madam?'

Jazz considers for a moment, picking up one of the earrings and holding it in a sunbeam. She blinks, smiles and nods. What do I think? You really wouldn't want to know.

Stag Hunt Elizabeth Coldwell

When an unexpected present is left on my doorstep, it's usually a dead bird one of the neighbourhood cats has caught or a jar of home-made chutney from Minnie in the cottage down the lane, not a naked man. Not that I actually notice he is naked at first. I'm too busy looking at the golf umbrella he is holding. Blue-and-white striped and bearing the logo of a financial services company, I assume it was what he used to rattle my letterbox and get my attention. Anyone else would have used the door knocker, of course, but in his predicament I guess that wasn't an option he had available.

As I finally realise the extent of the state he is in, I have to stifle the temptation to laugh. He is half-crouching beneath the umbrella in a cramped, uncomfortable-looking position, which I eventually twig is due to the fact that not only have his wrists been fastened together with parcel tape, his cupped hands have also been secured around his cock and the crook handle of the umbrella – presumably to preserve what remains of his modesty. He is wearing nothing but a pair of green wellies, an 'L' sign is hanging round his neck and he looks completely wretched. If I were to close the door on him in shock and disgust, which I am sure a couple of the neighbours would have done, I think he would burst into tears.

Instead, trying to act as though I am confronted by this kind of thing every time I open my front door, I say, 'Can I help you?'

'I – er – I don't suppose I could use your phone, could I?' he asks.

I grab the walking stick I keep in the hallway and walk out on to the doorstep, brandishing it with menace. As I look up and down the road, an ear cocked for any suspicious rustling in the hedgerow, the stranger stares at me, baffled.

'What are you doing?'

'Just checking you haven't got an accomplice with you,' I tell him. 'We've had a couple of burglaries round here recently, and for all I know you could be standing here distracting me while your mate's up in my bedroom rifling through my knicker drawer.'

'I haven't got a mate with me, and if I was going to distract you I'd have at least kept some clothes on to do it. It's freezing out here.' He shivers slightly as he speaks. 'I'm not a burglar, I'm an investment banker in the City of London and my name's Ivor Curtis. Normally, I'd be able to show you some identification to prove it, but . . .'

He could be spinning me a line, but I am beginning to doubt it. And I haven't heard anything to suggest there is someone taking advantage of the situation, creeping around in the cottage while we stand out here. 'OK, I believe you. And I'm Alex, by the way. You can come in, but we're going to have to take that umbrella down before you come inside. It's bad luck to have one open in the house, you know.'

I am teasing him now, and we both know it, but I can't resist. 'You'll have to give me a hand,' he says sheepishly.

'Of course.' I take hold of his wrists, searching for the loose end of the tape that binds them. Finding it, I pick at it with my fingernail and pull until it begins to come away. All the time, I can't help but be aware of how close my hands are to his cock; I can't actually see it, but once or twice as I unwrap this unorthodox parcel, my fingers brush unavoidably against the soft skin of his balls.

'I warn you, this might hurt a bit,' I say, and yank the rest of the tape away. Some of the hairs on his wrists come away with it, as do some of the longer and curlier ones from his groin. He bites his lip hard and drops the umbrella, but he doesn't cry out. I am impressed.

Leaving the umbrella where it has fallen, he follows me into the house. 'There's a phone in my office,' I tell him. 'It's the second room down the hall. I'll get you a towel and make you some hot sweet tea. You look like you could do with it.'

'Thanks, Alex,' he says. 'I really appreciate it. Oh, and before you go, you couldn't give me some idea of where I actually am, could you?'

His eyes, brown and soulful, meet mine and I suddenly realise this stranger is actually rather attractive in a rough kind of way. He's somewhere in his late twenties, with a strong-jawed face, slightly overlong dark-brown hair and a growth of beard on his chin which gives him the air of a pirate, rather than a banker. I suspect he has to be pretty damn good at his job to get away with looking quite that scruffy on a daily basis. And then I consider his body. Now standing at his full height, he is well over six feet tall, with long taut thighs and a stomach which, while nicely flat, isn't an over-defined six-pack. Sporty, I reckon, rather than obsessed with spending hours in the gym. Unsportingly, though, he is keeping his hands firmly in front of his cock. As I think about just what he might be covering up, I feel something tighten in my pussy and rush off to find that towel before it becomes too obvious I am having filthy thoughts about him.

When I come back downstairs, I not only have a towel with me but the only item of male clothing I keep in the cottage – a dressing gown which normally hangs on the back of my bedroom door and used to belong to Mike, my ex. It's one of the few things he left behind when he walked out on me, and somehow I have never quite got round to throwing it out. I hand it to Ivor and he turns his back on me as he shrugs it on. I can't resist taking the opportunity that offers to admire the small neat cheeks of his arse before they disappear under the white towelling.

'How did you get on with the phone?' I ask.

'Not great,' he replies. 'I tried my mates, but they're either not answering or they've got their mobiles switched off. I've left a couple of messages, so I suppose I've just got to wait till one of them comes and gets me. I mean, even if I had the number for a taxi firm, I can't exactly see them giving me a lift anywhere with no money and dressed like this.' He looks ruefully down the length of his body. He is taller than Mike and the dressing gown finishes higher up his thighs, which I don't exactly have a problem with. And he has ditched the 'L' plate and the wellies somewhere on the way from the hall, leaving his feet bare against the 200-year-old floorboards.

'So tell me the story,' I say, as he follows me into the kitchen, bending his head to avoid cracking it against the low lintel. That's something I've never had to contend with, but this cottage wasn't constructed for a man of Ivor's height. 'How does a nice boy like you end up naked on my doorstep?'

He smiles. There is something of the rogue in his smile, something that makes me think again of pirates, and of men who might want to see a woman bound and helpless before them, to do with as they wish. 'If only I knew. I was – am – on my stag weekend. My best mate, Jonny, arranged it all. Half a dozen of us had gone down to Bournemouth for what he was calling my "Last Days Of Freedom Tour" – he'd had the T-shirts made up with that printed on the front and everything. The plan was to get a bit of surfing in during the day and then go clubbing at night.'

Surfing. So that explains the body; you have to be strong and supple if you're a surfer, not all bulked up and heavy. I can just see him in a skintight wetsuit, whooping with exhilaration as he rides the waves down by Bournemouth Pier, his wet hair plastered to the nape of his neck. It's an appealing image, an arousing image, and I busy myself with the kettle and the teapot so he won't notice the way I am studying him again.

'OK, so where did it all go hideously wrong?' I ask, handing him his tea.

He blows on it, then takes a sip before continuing. 'I wish I knew. We ended up in this table-dancing club – they call it something like Cleopatra's Palace, from what I remember.' I know the place, down in the part of town they call the Triangle, just over the road from the restaurant where Mike and I had one of our first ever dates. It's no more than half an hour's drive from there to here; he's been dropped closer to civilisation than he knows. 'Anyway, Jonny gave it the chat, blagged our way into the VIP area even though they had a private party going on in there. It must have been about midnight by then. So there we were, drinking champagne, with this absolutely gorgeous pair of twins dancing for us in nothing but matching silver G-strings. One minute I had these two girls writhing on my lap with their big bare boobs rubbing in my face, then I start to feel a bit woozy and the next thing I know it's morning and I'm waking up in the middle of nowhere with nothing on but those lousy wellingtons, parcel-taped to an umbrella. I assume my so-called friends spiked my drink, bundled me in the back of Jonny's Jeep and drove me out here. I suppose it could have been worse. They could have left me tied up naked on the promenade for a policeman to find me.'

'Yes, but Bournemouth's crawling with stag parties at weekends, and I bet the police are used to things like that. For us country bumpkins, it's a bit of a shock.'

'You don't strike me as the bumpkin type.'

'I'm not. I inherited this place from a distant relative on my mother's side. I'm a writer and I moved here because I thought the peace and quiet would be good for my work.'

That, of course, had been when Mike was still with me and the commissions were coming in so fast I was actually having to turn some of them down. When he left, it seems that he took my inspiration with him and now I have a half-finished novel sitting on my PC, peopled with characters I'm not even sure I like any more and with absolutely no idea of how the plot should progress. If ever I am blocked like this, I always seem to look for distractions and I tell myself that's the reason I find Ivor so fascinating. But then, I had a man round to read my electricity meter the previous week and I didn't start fantasising about him bending me over the kitchen table and giving my bare bottom a good spanking before slipping his cock into me from behind.

'So what are you going to do now?' I ask him.

He shrugs. 'I suppose all I can do is wait and try ringing them again later. They obviously want me to stew for a while.' He sits down heavily on one of the high-backed chairs that ring the table, his legs just wide enough apart as he straddles it to give me a glimpse of the shadow of his pubes through the gap in the dressing gown. I tell myself he isn't aware of what he is doing – he is too preoccupied with getting back to his friends and his personal possessions and his wedding preparations to notice that he is practically giving me an uninterrupted show. 'I know it's silly, but the one thing I regret most about this is that I never got to properly enjoy that lap dance. I mean, *twins*.'

Don't ask me why I say what I do. Maybe it's the thought of another long morning sitting in front of my PC, wondering where the next paragraph is coming from, or maybe I am just hornier than I have been in a long time and see the sudden chance to indulge myself with this sexy stranger. Whatever, the words are tumbling out of my mouth before I've really thought about them. 'Maybe there's a way you could still have your dance.' He looks at me, tea mug frozen halfway to his lips as I continue, 'I'm sorry, I don't have an identical sister tucked away upstairs, but I do have a full-length mirror in my bedroom. All it'll take is a bit of imagination. What do you say?'

For a moment he hesitates, and I start to think I've blown it. Then he nods. 'Yeah, let's have some fun. Let's show Jonny I don't care about his puerile little stunt.'

I lead him up the stairs to my bedroom, which isn't quite as tidy as it could have been, but then I haven't been expecting to show it off to anyone else. Not that it would have the ambience of an upmarket gentlemen's club even without my discarded clothes from the day before and the magazine I was reading before I fell asleep strewn across the floor. I kick everything in the general direction of the laundry basket then, feeling a little silly but undeniably turned on, haul the mirror into the centre of the room. In the absence of a suitable chair, Ivor positions himself at the bottom of the bed, legs spread in that inviting way again, and I twist the mirror until he has the best view of my reflection.

Next comes the music. I hunt through the CDs in a rack by my bedside cabinet and pull out one of those compilations of dance music where each track segues endlessly into the next. I used to enjoy having it on in the background when I was working, back in the days when I could lose all track of time as my fingers pounded away on the keyboard. I set it playing at a low volume, encouraging Ivor to relax as I wonder what I'm going to do about my outfit. I am dressed in an olive-coloured T-shirt and a long grey gypsy-style skirt, comfortable to wear while sitting at a PC, but not exactly appropriate for writhing about on a man's lap. I pick up a pair of high-heeled strappy sandals and disappear briefly into the bathroom. When I emerge, I am in my underwear – a black bra with just enough frothy trim on the cups to turn it from functional to decorative and a matching pair of little lacy shorts. I think I look the part, and Ivor's expression is certainly appreciative, but it only serves to stoke the nervous fluttering in my belly. I've never done anything like this, not even for Mike, who was on the receiving end of most of my kinkiest exploits, but it's too late to back out now.

The heels push my bum backwards, my chest out, giving me a slutty little wiggle as I cross the bedroom floor and begin to dance in front of the mirror. It's hard not to feel self-conscious at first, but it's obvious that my audience of one is getting into what I'm doing, and it gives me the confidence to run my hands gently, teasingly over my breasts as I sway to the music. I glance into the mirror, make eye contact with my own reflection and blow myself a little kiss. Getting bolder, squatting on my haunches and opening my thighs, copying moves I've seen in any number of music videos, I begin to realise why this kind of dancing gets offered as an exercise class. I can feel muscles I haven't used in ages, in or out of bed, groaning back to life, reminding me of how good it feels to move and stretch. Not only that, but offering up my body to this man in such a blatant way is getting me wetter than I've been in a long time. There's an itch between my legs that won't go away and only one way to scratch it.

I strut over to the bed and straddle Ivor's thighs with my own. I can't help but notice as I do that his cock is beginning to rear up out of the folds of the dressing gown, as though it can sense the heat of my sex, so tantalisingly close. I put my hands on his shoulders so my cleavage is only inches from his nose. He glances down at my breasts, then up to my face, and I know I've got him exactly where I want him.

'Just like the twins, eh?' I smile.

'Not quite,' he says, swallowing hard. 'When they were on my lap, they were topless.'

'All in good time,' I tell him, and I sink down so that his cock is just touching my pussy through my soaking wet shorts. Part of me wants to pull them to one side and take him inside me, but this is his dance, his stag treat, and I can't be greedy. He tries to grab me by the hips and pull me down harder onto him, just as impatient as I am, but I catch his hands and wrap them round my neck instead. We're both laughing, both turned on by the tease and the game, and our faces are almost touching. He raises his head towards mine, straining to make our lips meet, and I just shake my head and drop a kiss on the end of his nose. It feels good to know that he wants me and to have the power to make things happen at my pace.

Though it's time to step that pace up a bit. Taking a deep breath, I reach behind me, searching for the fastening of my bra. I pop it open, freeing my breasts, and let it drop to the floor. I am all over him now, my smooth bare thighs pressed against his hairy ones, my soaking crotch rubbing against his cock, my tits dangling invitingly in his face. When Ivor rises up and catches one of my nipples between his lips, I don't pull away. I can't. The electric thrill that goes through me as he sucks on my flesh is making me dizzy with desire.

Should I be doing this with a man I met less than an hour ago? Probably not. Should he be doing this when he's days away from getting married? Almost certainly not. But I don't think either of us cares. We're lost in the moment, only aware of our need for each other, a need that's getting stronger by the minute. Fate dumped him on my doorstep and maybe this was meant to happen. After all, it's not as though we're ever going to see each other again.

His hands are on my breasts now, squeezing them together so he can lick my nipples in turn. The feel of his mouth is exquisite, but it's still a shock to realise that the woman who is moaning and begging him to suck harder is actually me. What happened to being the one in control? I try to assert myself again, unfastening the dressing gown and pushing it off his broad shoulders so I can get at his body, but he's doing something to my nipples with his thumbs now and his teeth are nipping at a spot on my neck that seems to be connected directly to my cunt, because I can feel the sensation down there, too, and I just want him to go ahead and fuck me.

His fingers push their way down the front of my shorts, homing in on my clit. Again, he teases me, not touching with quite enough pressure to help me on the way to my climax. The pad of his thumb brushes against my rosebud, threatening to sink into the tight little hole. I whimper in frustration, wriggling against his fingers, wanting to be filled. And then he's pulling my shorts down and off, and grabbing handfuls of my bum so he can lift me up and onto his cock. He's so hot, so hard inside me, and I rock to and fro, quickly finding a rhythm that suits us both. I stare into his eyes, not quite believing how good this is, how right. How can two people who don't know each other at all make this happen so perfectly, when others try for years and never reach the heights we're reaching now? And then I can't try to puzzle it out any more, because the pleasure is peaking and peaking and his cock is pulsing inside me. As he comes, he calls my name.

We roll together on the bed, my head on his chest, his arms wrapped round me. He's asleep within moments, which doesn't honestly surprise me after everything he's been through. As I begin to drift off myself, I don't regret what I've done, only the fact that it won't ever happen again. Whoever the future Mrs Curtis may be, I just hope she appreciates what she has.

When the knocking on the door wakes me, I feel disorientated. I have no idea what time it is or why I'm still in bed, until the sight of the naked man lying beside me reminds me of what's happened. I shrug on some clothes, as Ivor sits up and runs a hand through his messy hair, and tell him I'll be back in a moment.

There's a Jeep parked in the road outside the cottage and a lanky blond standing on my doorstep who, even out of a suit and tie, looks every inch the City boy. My second stranger of the day, but I'd know it was Jonny even if his T-shirt didn't have the words 'Last Days Of Freedom Tour' emblazoned on the front. I'm pleased to see he seems more than a little worried.

'Hi.' He's holding a pair of sunglasses, even though it's January, and he twiddles them compulsively between his fingers. 'I'm looking for a friend of mine. I – er – dropped him off here last night and he left me a message to say that you were taking care of him for me.'

Funny how he neglects to mention the umbrella, the parcel tape and the complete lack of clothes. 'I'm not sure, maybe you ought to call the police,' I say, wanting to laugh at the look of panic that streaks across his face. 'Or maybe you just ought to come inside for a minute.' I call up the stairs, 'Ivor, I think there's someone come to apologise.'

He appears at the top of the stairs, wearing Mike's

dressing gown, and comes trotting down when he realises it's Jonny.

'You OK, mate?' he asks nonchalantly.

Jonny's expression is thunderous. '"Come and get me," you said. "I'm in a thatched cottage with ivy round the door," you said. Do you know just how many cottages round here look like that? It was like driving through the picture on a fucking chocolate box ... But it's still good to see you.'

The two men envelop each other in an awkward blokey hug and, to his credit, Jonny does actually say sorry for what he's done.

'You're lucky, you know,' I tell Jonny. 'There are people round here who wouldn't have treated Ivor quite as well as I did.'

Jonny looks from me to his friend. It can't be hard for him to work out what's happened, given that both Ivor and I are radiating the aura of satisfaction which follows spectacular sex, but he doesn't say anything. He's brought a carrier bag full of clothes from the Jeep with him, and he hands them over to Ivor, who slips his boxers on before removing the dressing gown. When he's dressed, in baggy combats and stag-tour T-shirt, he takes me in his arms and kisses me goodbye. The kiss goes on for so long that by the end Jonny is shifting from foot to foot uncomfortably, anxious to be off. Tough, I think; the whole point of leaving Ivor out here was to embarrass him and now you're the one who's embarrassed. I don't even think I'll become some dirty little secret to be picked over in the best man's speech; I sense it will leave Jonny with far too much explaining to do if the story ever comes out, too much guilt about how it could have all turned nasty. Best to leave it as it is: a one-off as delicious as it was unexpected.

Ivor finally breaks the embrace, and he and Jonny

make their way out to the Jeep. I wave them off as they head for Bournemouth and normality – or as normal as a stag weekend ever gets. Another mug of tea, I think, as I shut the door behind me, and then straight back to the PC. Inspiration has returned and a new character is forcing his way into my novel. He's a tall sexy stranger with great thighs and a roguish grin and, for some reason, I picture him as a surfer.

Vacation A. D. R. Forte

'A few extra days won't hurt.'

'But . . .'

'Whsst! No buts. Jas, you need it.'

Jasalina Milford looked up from her computer and frowned at her boss and best friend, Dani Thompson.

'I don't *need* a holiday. I *need* you to stop pestering me about it.' She stuck her tongue out at Dani and turned back to the screen where her hotel reservation blinked patiently and waited for her to confirm dates and enter a credit card.

Dani sat down on the opposite side of the executive office desk and stretched out her turquoise-beringed hands in appeal.

'Just two days after the conference. Get some sunshine, some sand, some waves. Get a man for God's sake!'

Dani put one hand to her eyes in tragic despair and Jas burst out laughing.

'You make me sound as pathetic as you, you old hag.'

Jas swirled the mouse pointer around the screen, but didn't click the 'OK' button to take her to next page. She sat tapping her fingers on the side of the mouse and frowning at the screen instead.

Dani pounced on that fragment of hesitation. 'You see? You do want to stay. At least when I was your age, I got some action. Well . . . a lot of action.'

'Woodstock princess, right?' Jas said, looking up at Dani from under her eyebrows with a smile.

'Bet your sweet ass! Oh, those were the days. Music,

love...' Dani swayed to the invisible strains of some long-gone acoustic guitar. Then she stopped abruptly and turned to Jas. 'But you! Look at you.' She pointed, jabbing palms upwards, summing Jas up in exasperated disapproval.

Jas shifted in her chair; released the mouse. She leant back, biting one short, already-jagged nail. 'What about me?'

Dani's eyes took in what Jas was already painfully aware of. Pressed business pants suit over a crisp T-shirt. Sensible loafers. Quality socks. Clean, short, sensible hair.

No dangles, no sparkles, no glitter. None of the whisper of feminine allure that women like Dani carried with them even when they weren't dressed up. Nope. Jas Milford was sensible. And clean. Clean was a bonus, at least.

Dani didn't have to say anything; she simply clucked her tongue and shook her head. 'And these nails!' She reached across the desk again and grabbed Jas's hands, staring at the blunt well-chewed surfaces before her in despair. 'Short of Louisiana hot sauce I don't know how to keep them out of your mouth, but I *know* I pay you more than enough to get a manicure.'

Jas shrugged and pulled her hands away. 'Don't have time.'

'You know, anybody would swear I chained you to that desk and beat you with a stick.'

'You don't?' Jas grinned at the older woman. 'Look, Dani, darling. I know you're trying to help, but I'm just not –' she waved her hands in the air in an exaggerated approximation of Dani's own flamboyant gestures '– frilly. Girly. And OK maybe I work too hard but it's not like I have anything else to do.'

'Whose fault is that?'

Giving in, Jas sighed. 'Mine. Mine, mine, mine. But I'm fine. I'm OK. I –'

'You got bags under your eyes, honey.'

Sigh. 'I'll stay. Two days.'

Dani clapped her hands and started to talk but Jas cut her off with a slicing gesture. 'No. No new clothes, no manicure. No men. Or women. I'm just taking a short holiday.'

Dani's face fell again, but she knew when to cut her losses and move on. 'Did you book an ocean-view suite?'

'Yes, ma'am.' Jas turned back to the screen, tapped in her credit card and confirmed the reservation. Then she swivelled the monitor for Dani's perusal. 'OK?'

'OK. But next time . . .'

'Next time.' Jas waved her towards the door. 'Now get out, you're making me lose productivity.'

With a laugh Dani left the office and Jas sighed again. Two whole days at a beachfront resort. What the hell was she going to do?

Admittedly, the resort was gorgeous. South Florida in May, before the tourists flooded it in messy, loud droves was a beautiful, beautiful place. And best of all, there was no line at the check-in. Just one lone traveller in faded blue jeans and a white T-shirt.

A white T-shirt that was rather tight across a muscular back and jeans that hugged a very toned ass. South Beach diet and hours on the treadmill no doubt. Nice to look at, but not much more. Dani didn't get it: those worth a second look weren't worth the time and vice versa. This was why she worked and watched movies; it was time far better spent.

She walked up to the counter, credit card and ID at the ready. And her phone rang. She reached for it, mistimed her grab and her conference name-tag spun to the floor. The phone followed it because her fingers had gone all thumbs suddenly. A happenstance she was sure had nothing to do with Blue Jeans having turned and knelt to retrieve her name-tag. Nor the fact that he was still on one knee and looking up at her, all Viking ice-blond hair and green eyes and features that could cut cold butter.

She held her breath as he handed the phone back to her and then the name-tag. He glanced down at the card as she took it and he stood.

'Jasalina? Is that right?' A voice like war drums rolling across northern seas. And he had the pronunciation perfect, rolling her name off as easily as if he'd said it a thousand times.

'Erm, yes. But I go by Jas. Usually.'

'It's pretty. Tyrell.'

'Nice to meet you. And thanks.'

'My pleasure.'

She extended a professional hand and he took it, her tiny palm swallowed in his, her skin pale as moonlight against his tan. The grasp lasted no longer than it should, and he smiled, shouldered his bag and left. But the sound of his voice still rumbled in her ears. Confusing her. Jas Milford, who was never confused. And the desk clerk had to ask her name twice before she could find herself again.

When Dani called to check on her, she lied. Nothing of interest. Just got here, checked in, ordered salmon for dinner.

'No cute guys?' Dani asked.

'Not a one.'

After she hung up, she lay staring at the ceiling. Why hadn't she said anything? Dani would have been thrilled.

Because there was nothing to tell. This was a hundred-plus-room hotel and she was never, ever going to see him again. And what were the chances he was there for the same conference she was anyway?

Exactly none. Just as she'd predicted.

She looked over the faces at breakfast and in the meeting rooms simply because it was natural to seek out familiarity. And beauty. But it wasn't disappointment she felt in not finding the face she sought. It was vindication. Because she'd been right.

And she continued to be right, up until lunchtime the next day when she sat beside the bronze mermaid fountain, ostensibly reading the ten or fifteen 'Steps to Effective Negotiation and Communication'. Fussy tourists and harassed business travellers were proving more interesting than the fourth step, however, and she was busy people-watching from under her lashes. Which explained why she didn't know she had company until *that* voice tore through all her safety nets, and proved her wrong.

'Hi. Can I join you?'

She looked up and forgot the fourth step, the tourists and pretty much everything else. In jeans and T-shirt he had been rugged, dashing, attractive. In shirt and tie, hair slicked back from his face to reveal all of its knife-edge beauty, he was beyond words.

'Yes. Yes, certainly.'

She shifted to create unneeded room on the bench. Better to put as much distance as possible between herself and that powerful body. In those powerful, treacherous clothes that made her think of taking them off. Slowly.

It was a good thing, a very good thing, she didn't blush easily.

'Thanks,' he said. He dropped his laptop bag on the ground and dug out an energy snack bar, opened the soda bottle he carried. Jas only watched. No, she stared; she couldn't help it. She had to say something.

'Busy day?'

He smiled. Oh God, he smiled.

'Yes. Client meetings all day. Then wouldn't you know I leave a contract for my afternoon meeting in my room this morning. And the softcopy won't open.'

She nodded eagerly, vigorously. Glad for common ground, something safe she could talk about without thoughts of captured Viking warriors and stone towers and whether that pin-straight hair would soften in the steam from a scorching hot bath.

'Been there,' she agreed. 'Many times. And it's always the presentation for the most anal-retentive v.p. that decides not to work.'

He nodded, munching on his power bar. He swallowed, took a drink of soda and raised his eyebrows. 'But all *you'd* have to do was smile and nobody would care.'

Act stupid. Act as if she didn't get the implication. That was safe. 'I only wish. Smiling and nodding only works when you're *not* over budget.'

She looked away at the two church ladies chatting nearby.

Don't look at him. Pretend he's not looking; divert his attention.

It worked until a sharp jolt of pain shot through her hand, making her hiss and jump. She'd bitten clear through her nail to the quick and it was bleeding. Damn.

'Are you OK?'

'Yeah, I'm fine I just … oh.'

A warm hand was over her wrist and another was wrapping a half-folded sheet of paper over her thumb.

'Sorry, I don't even have a napkin. But might as well put this contract to good use.'

Horrified, she stared at him, ignoring the painful throb in her finger. 'That's your contract?'

He shrugged, flashed her a wicked smile. 'Only the part that details our liability. They don't need that in there.'

'But. Your meeting's this afternoon!'

'Jas, it is Jas right? I can have my assistant fax them a copy tomorrow. It's fine. You're hurt *now.*'

Forget her thumb. It was her mind she couldn't hold on to.

Somehow she mumbled, 'Thanks.' Putting a hand over her makeshift bandage, and thereby dislodging his grasp, she risked a glance upwards. 'I should just learn not to bite my nails.'

He laughed and rubbed a forgiving hand along her arm. 'You should. Took me years to break the habit myself. Sometimes I still slip up when I'm really worried.'

She looked down at his hands. Warrior's hands. Broad, powerful. Long fingers with rough cut but even nails. Impossible to imagine they'd ever been bitten.

'You know, like when I forget important contracts.'

She looked at him, guilt and desire and all kinds of uncomfortable, inconvenient things conspiring to make her heart pound and her finger hurt even more. 'I'm sorry, Tyrell. Thank you, yet again. That's twice now.'

He stood and reached down for his bag. To watch him move was an indulgence in itself. A sweet lazy one. Like expensive chocolate.

'Good thing I'm around at the right times. But I have to run. Maybe I'll see you later?'

This was going too far now. Clutching her thumb, she frowned. A small polite frown tempered with an even politer, keep-your-distance smile. 'Maybe. Good luck this afternoon.'

His smile faded and he nodded as if waiting for her

to say something more. 'Thanks. You have a good after-noon too.'

He nodded goodbye, turned away. For half a heart-beat, one insane moment, she drew breath to call him back. But she didn't. Safer that way.

She ate dinner alone, early, skipping the post-conference happy hour. In the half-empty restaurant dining room, she got a seat at a window table where the sunset did its best to seduce her with vivid reds and burnt oranges. She promised herself a walk later when the sky had cooled to deep purple and the sand would be soft pow-der under her toes.

But the way things were going, she probably would run into him. The last thing she wanted.

She called Dani.

'How was the conference?'

'Good! Absolutely worth it. Now I get to waste two days doing jack.'

'Honey, if you *were* doing Jack or Jim or even Point-dexter it would be time well spent.'

Jas laughed. Thought of who she *could* be doing.

Good God, what a thought! Sleeping with a man she'd met in the hotel lobby. He could be a serial killer or a paedophile or ... far more likely, simply lazy and self-absorbed in bed and prone to making her feel like a bumbling idiot the entire time. Just like every other guy she'd ever dated.

'And stop giving me that look through the phone!'

'I'm not!' Jas sighed and rubbed a finger along the bruised surface of her thumb. 'I'm too tired to be doing anybody.'

'I know baby, I know,' Dani relented. 'So just relax then. Sleep late. Eat too much.'

'That I can do! How's everything at the office?'

'Fabulous. We don't miss you, don't hurry back. I . . . Damnit! Got to go. Grandchildren fighting.'

'Run along then. I'll talk to you later.'

She hung up, frowning. She couldn't explain to Dani anyway. That she wanted him so badly; wanted him to be different. Just for one night. Not a lifetime, not a get married and live happily ever after. Not even a fling. Just one night to make her feel sexy and beautiful and amazing. Just one.

She made her way back to the mermaid bench. Criminal returning to the scene of the crime. She kicked off her shoes and dug her feet into the dewy grass, not caring that her socks were getting wet. Closing her eyes, she imagined what she would do if suddenly he came striding through the dark and stood over her, tall and strong and icy beautiful. Wanting her.

This was pointless. She should have brought her laptop. At least she could have read the news online. Pathetic, but so what?

The sound of footsteps made her open her eyes and, as she waited for her vision to adjust to the night-shadows, she heard the footsteps pause.

'Hi.'

Oh for crying out loud! Criminals, scene of crime. Maybe fate was trying to tell her something after all.

'I'm not following you, I promise,' she said with a half-laugh. Not intentionally.

'Oh?' He sat and leant back. Noticing her shoes were off he grinned and leant forwards to unlace his. 'Well, even if you weren't this is still a good thing right?'

She closed her eyes again, shrugged. 'Right.'

For a few heartbeats he didn't say anything. Then, 'You know I was just sitting at the bar wishing I'd brought my laptop. And I thought, 'How lame is that?

But I was on my way to get it anyway. And now I'm glad I was.'

She laughed. She laughed and laughed and he stared at her in pleased surprise until she confessed her own moment of weakness. And when she did, he smiled that dazzling, dizzying smile at her and said, 'So there.'

As if that proved everything. And maybe it did.

'Meet me for lunch tomorrow. Please?' he said, sometime long after they'd lost count of the hours they had spent talking.

'I . . .' she faltered. Even now, there was still a line that hadn't been crossed. What if she said 'OK' and then her illusion came toppling down after all?

He reached out, a warm, reassuring hand on her arm in the dark. 'Look, just think about it and leave a message for me at the reception desk. Tyrell Andriessen. I should be back here around twelve thirty, maybe one. If you decide not to that's OK.'

She twisted her arm from under his, wrapped her fingers around his hand before he could withdraw it.

'I don't need to think about it.' She smiled.

He was silent a moment, just smiling. And then he squeezed her fingers, brought her hand to his lips. 'Tomorrow then. At the pool? I know you brought a swimsuit.'

'I didn't. But I'll . . . I'll improvise.' Had she really said that? Where had *that* come from?

But it worked. He looked at her for a long aching moment, shoes in hand, as they stood in socked feet beside the fountain. Before they said goodnight and turned to go their own ways.

But that look, it made her absolutely giddy. Made her head hurt with impatience. Lunchtime couldn't come soon enough.

* * *

The hours between dawn and noon, however, didn't care a fig for her nerves. They crawled by at their own snail's pace, and post-breakfast found her at the hotel boutiques where she stared at the racks of skimpy Lycra and mesh netting laid out in glitzy display.

'Can I help with anything?'

Jas turned to the smiling shop attendant and shook her head. 'Erm. Just looking. Forgot my swimsuit so I'm looking for a replacement.'

Undaunted, the attendant looked Jas over twice and nodded.

'You can get away with most anything. But I'd go with a two-piece.' She plucked a strappy cocktail of pale yellow and lemon shades from the rack and held it up to Jas. 'This.'

Jas looked down at the so-called bikini and burst out laughing. 'Not a chance in years. Not me.'

She would never buy it, never wear it. But the attendant was holding the hanger out and nodding with perfect conviction. And just to see ... Jas took hold of one end of the hanger.

'Just for the sake of argument,' she said.

And it was just the sake of argument that she stood before the mirror of her own room later, wondering what she'd been thinking. Might as well go naked. But, if she just forgot for a minute who the woman in the glass *was*. If she could pretend that she saw through the eyes of a stranger: a hotel guest, a traveller.

She swallowed and turned away. Heart beating, avoiding the glances of strangers, she left the safety of her room and headed for the pool deck. There, heat and ocean breeze touched her skin. Her very bare skin. And as she stepped under the icy pool-shower, she thought for a blushing panicked moment of the lack of padding or lining in the bikini top.

But she'd known that when she bought it, this thing that two days ago she would never, ever have worn. And in two days never would again.

Just one night, she reminded herself.

She had this bikini, and she could have anything she wanted.

The sunken bar at the end of the pool was deserted. She didn't know if she was relieved or disappointed as she waded around to the side of the bar bordered by the pool deck and hopped up on a stool. The bartender walked over and smiled, wiping his hands on a towel. 'Hi, what can I get ya?'

She followed his gaze and knew that he didn't see sensible Jas at all, and once again she felt that prickle of impatience.

She started to reply, but a flicker of motion caught the edge of her vision and interrupted her. Splash and movement of a swimmer along the open stretch of the pool. A strong swimmer, closing the distance to the deck with powerful rapid strokes.

She forgot how to form words. Forgot the bartender.

And then like a surfacing river god he was beside her, water streaming silver from his hair. Water shining like ice on his bare chest. Except that the heat between their bodies should have dried it.

'Hi. I . . .' She swallowed. She was still Jas inside. No matter what she saw in his face as he looked at her. How was she going to pull this off?

Don't look at his eyes. Don't think of the male attention focused on this stranger's body: from the bartender, from him. Just talk. Like this was her office and she was in her plain, ordinary, boring suit.

'I was just about to order a drink. What are you having?'

He swallowed. 'Whatever you're having,' he said.

That made it easy. She ordered: some fruity rummy concoction. She watched the bartender give her a last appraisal and walk away. And then it was just *him*.

'I thought I would beat you here. Things wrapped up earlier than I thought.'

She couldn't look at his eyes. She'd lose her nerve, her mind, everything. Barrel chest, ice-blond hair so wet against his tanned skin, waterproof watch on one broad wrist. James Bond as Viking.

'Everything go OK?'

'Yes. Like clockwork.'

'Despite not having half of your contract?'

Strong fingers under her chin turned her eyes to his anyway.

'Despite that.'

She stared up at him, not daring to move. The corners of his mouth curved upwards, but she couldn't remember how to smile back.

'I know what it is with you,' he said, as if answering some question he'd asked himself.

'What?'

'You. You're much.' He took a step back. 'Too.' He reached for her arms and she only had time for a token yelp of protest because it was too late already. 'Serious.'

He yanked and with a splash she went under, spluttering. And came up in his arms. He was laughing as he helped her to get her balance again, and before she could regain enough composure to think of resistance he pulled her inwards. To his chest. And kissed her. Soft kisses. Tugging her at her lips, licking water from her chin and the corners of her mouth. Turning up the heat in her to a blaze.

His hand on her back pressed her into him and her body responded, wanting to move towards his. His cock was hard between them and this stranger Jas, soaking wet in her lemon-yellow bikini, being kissed in full view of the public without shame, squeezed herself against it.

Shocking herself and him in the process.

With a catch to his voice, breathing hard from the kiss or from her daring, he gave a low chuckle and whispered into her ear. 'See? When you stop thinking about being serious, it's much, much better.'

She laughed and pulled away, scrambling back to the stool. Their drinks had arrived and she made a relieved grab for her glass.

He joined her with a sideways glance and a smile, reaching for his own glass. He sipped his drink and then, ever so casually, he slid the cold glass along the side of her bare torso. She gasped and flinched. And like a waiting hunter he took advantage of her parted lips. Bending down to kiss her hard this time, the glass still burning icy fire against her skin while he sucked on her tongue, her lips. Draining her of all power to resist.

He put the drink down and, unsteadily, she followed suit. He was pulling her to the edge of the stool and she grabbed his waist for balance. No doubt that was exactly what he'd intended, but she didn't care. Not now. She didn't care when he smoothed one hand against her breast. When he pinched one aching nipple and then the other, while he kissed her neck and her shoulder.

She was his plaything. And for just once in her life, for one day, she could be a plaything. For him.

For today she could enjoy the sweet sensations he was kindling in her without wondering what would happen tomorrow or wondering what he thought of her. Because it was obvious with this man what he thought; it was in his eyes and his touch. He wanted her and that was enough.

She closed her eyes, floating in pleasure. Little waves washed over the top of the stool, nudging her ass and thighs like so many thousands of gentle touches all flowing together at once. And his fingers were moving in, following the curve of her thigh. Moving over the tiny patch of yellow spandex, which was all that lay between her and indecent exposure.

She opened her eyes, clenched her fingers on his back. 'Tyrell!' It was a half-whispered question. Or a reprimand, or plea. She didn't know which.

'Hmm?' was the only reply.

He pushed aside the bikini crotch and she thought that he'd probably done it a million times before, the movement was so expert. So knowing. A man who'd had countless women, who could have countless more. And yet, he wanted *her*.

After that, she couldn't think any more. Because his fingers were sliding into her. Out and in, and in and in. She dug her own fingers into his back as he used those incredible hands on her. As he rubbed her clit in tiny circles before sliding back into her pussy. Found the places that made her gasp and shift, and concentrated his grinding, tickling caresses there. Almost lifted her off the stool with his efforts.

And she was trying so hard not to make a sound, to not draw any attention. Although, God knew, the bartender knew and so did the middle-aged guy he was talking to at the other end of the bar. And they were both watching her get a hand job, watching her enjoy it. And Jas felt the flame that was burning all through her body rush into her face.

She was blushing. Blushing and squirming on Tyrell's attentive fingers, about to come. Unable to fight the intensity in her pussy and her thighs or Tyrell's voice at her ear commanding her to come for him as his fingers moved inside her, faster and rougher. And so she gave up, gave in, wrapped her legs around his calves, threw her head back and silently screamed the most intense orgasm of her life.

But it wasn't over, far from over. He kissed her cheek and, with a smile, brazenly sucked his fingers off before taking a sip of his forgotten drink. Flaunting it for the other men. Showing them how much he had enjoyed pleasuring her. And all she could do was blush and pant for breath and try to calculate whether his room was closer or hers. Because right now, those were the only places she wanted to be.

He must have read her mind. Or her body. He grinned and turned away to scribble his room number and signature on the tab.

'I, umm . . .' She was still out of breath. 'I'll pay you back,' she said and then bit her tongue when he looked at her and lifted an eyebrow. Even her words were conspiring to drive her beyond all safe boundaries, making dirty promises where she had meant none.

'Will you?'

Might as well follow through now. So she lifted her eyebrows in return and smiled. 'Whose room is closer?' she said.

It turned out to be his. She walked in and halted, uncertain where to go and what to do. She was suddenly all thumbs and left legs and a glimpse in the mirror at her tangled, flushed, shameless reflection only made it worse. Turning away, she made it to the window and put her palms on the glass, staring out at the ocean beyond. Willing herself to calm down. To be confident and sexy. Not skittish, foolish Jas.

She didn't want to run away, but she didn't know what to do now that she was here. He came to stand behind her and rested his chin on her shoulder. His hands wrapped around her stomach, pulled her into his hard body, and she sighed. Wanting more than she could put into coherent thought.

'Jas,' he mumbled into her wet hair, nibbling her ear,

her neck. 'Serious, pretty Jas.' His hands moved up her torso and his wrists pressed the curves of her breasts. She looked down to see his hands held together in a gesture of supplication at her chest. She stared, knowing on the innermost level what he was about to ask of her and wondering how she ever would.

Knowing she would anyway.

'Tie me up,' he said, voice like a winter storm over the ocean. 'Use me.'

She turned then, digging her fingers into the back of his neck as she kissed him. Before she could think about it and stop herself, she dragged his swim trunks off. Then she stood up slowly, looking him over, filling her gaze with his naked, gorgeous body.

'Are you sure?' she asked, still afraid. Still some part of her demanded she be sensible.

But he shook his head. 'Don't ask me if I'm sure, Jas. Just take me.'

She didn't know she had this in her. When she made him kneel and tied his hands behind his back with his own silk tie, biting her tongue to keep from asking if it was OK to use it, she wondered at herself. She wondered when she undid the straps of the bikini, slid it off her arms and over his mouth. When she stuffed the fabric into his mouth and retied the straps behind his head, before leaning back to study her handiwork.

All along he silently followed her movements with his eyes and, when she was done, his gaze travelled over her half-naked body. Moving where his touch could not.

But she could touch.

She looked down at her hands and smiled, grateful for her short blunt nails. They would be perfect.

On her knees, she moved behind him, ran her arms up his arms to his shoulders and kissed the back of his neck. Her breasts pressed hot against his smooth back, his ass hot against her stomach and, leaning her head on the back of his, she traced the knobs of his spine. A lover's embrace. How she wanted to give him the kind of desperate ecstasy she'd known at the pool.

So, to calm her fear and doubt, she used words. Silken nets of words that had waited inside her to find a voice for so long.

'I fantasised about you as my captive Viking warrior. Did you know that?'

He shook his head.

'But you must have.' Her fingers moved down his back with purpose. She cupped the curve of his ass, squeezed gently. Then harder. Harder. Harder, the flesh turning white from the pressure of her fingers.

He clenched his muscles, resisting, but she didn't relent.

'You must have known how beautiful I found you. Do you deny it?'

She twisted and kneaded flesh until he shook his head, his breath coming rough and harsh. And at that she released him, felt the relief sag through his body.

'So you knew. And you pursued me. You wanted to be captured.'

Nod.

She moved back a little, putting space between their bodies and smoothing both hands down his back this time. So hard and strong and so vulnerable. She spread his cheeks, widening the delightful dark crevice between. Wider. And wider.

'And now you *are* captive. Do you regret it?'

Shake.

'Are you certain?'

With her knees she shoved his legs further apart and stumblingly he spread them for her. Wider. He grunted softly; she was digging her thumbs into the inner curves of his cheeks, forcing him open.

'Even when I hurt you like this.'

Nod. Nod and nod.

She stared at his exposed asshole, feeling her heart pound, her pussy getting wetter. Good God. Don't think. Just do.

She stretched one thumb out and stroked his tender bud and he jerked forwards with a half-strangled gasp. Twisting away. And she saw him close his eyes.

Oh God. This was as new to him as it was to her. Not being dominated, but *this*. Oh dear God. But it was too late, far too late to go back now.

He was breathing hard but he was relaxing again, moving back into her touch. Pressing his virgin ass to her hand.

Jas bit her lip, but her voice was steady. 'Good. Just like that.'

She worked her thumb into his entrance, bit by bit, caressing. Exploring his ass and her own desire with slow careful movements. And she thought that for this, for both of them, it was a good thing she had sensible Jas along.

Further and further she pressed – halting when he tensed, resuming when he breathed again – until she had to withdraw. She drew her thumb out, massaged the reddened flesh around his hole while she squeezed and released his cheeks, and smiled as his cock bobbed before him helplessly. His breaths were harsh rasps, but he was ready.

She worked her way in again, easier this time. Deeper. And she was fucking him. *Fucking him*. His ass was open to her now, and she licked her fingers one by one. Slid each one, wet with saliva into him and fucked him, and held him to her while she did. Rubbed her naked breasts on his sweating back and refused to think about what she was doing. Just gave herself to the hunger.

He groaned, moving with her rhythm, clenching

around her fingers and she laughed. Laughed because this just couldn't, didn't happen. And yet she was here. Inside him. In sweet violation.

She circled his cock with her other hand and began to stroke him. A stroke for every thrust, trapping him between sharp points of pleasure. Her captive. She was paying him back everything she owed and tenfold besides. But she couldn't talk any more; she could only give him her invading fingers and her kisses on his neck and her pumping fist.

And he took her, all of her. He writhed and thrust his hips into her punishment, twisting his head from side to side, ice-blond hair streaking the window with moisture. Groaning so beautifully into his gag when his come flooded over her fingers, snowy drops on the carpet, the window, his thighs. Splattered and stained, her icy river god imprisoned and branded by her desire.

He was shaking still, shuddering, when she lifted wet fingers to pull away his gag and cover his mouth with her own. She fumbled with the knots of the tie and got them loose enough that he could drag his hands free. So he could pin her to the floor and rip the bikini panties away, the material welting her skin as it tore.

'Witch. Pretty little witch, what have you done?' he demanded. 'And now I can't even punish you.'

She caressed his shoulders and looked down at his soft cock as he knelt over her. A drop of come fell onto her belly, lay there like a single gem adorning her skin. She looked up into those eyes blazing green fire at her and she smiled.

'Then I'll wait until you can. All night.' And she pulled his mouth to hers again.

In the dark of morning, made darker than night by the blackout shades over the window, she left.

She wore one of his shirts and a pair of his shorts. He

had wrapped her in them when he discovered her shivering after her shower. Insisted she put them on and snuggle between the folds of blanket before he would even order dinner from room service. Then he'd wrapped his arms around her, smelling of crisp soap and dewy skin from his own shower, and buried his nose in her hair.

She closed the door and leant her head on it. The hotel corridor was empty and quiet, holding its breath and waiting for the morning rush. Somewhere far away a vacuum hummed. She was swimming in these clothes, drowning in them, but she was going back to her room to pack so that she could check out one day early. She had promised herself just one night. And that night was over.

'Standby passenger Jas Milford, please come to the ticket counter.'

Here it was: the last chance to turn back. She closed her eyes and gripped her carry-on bag, ignored the throb between her sore thighs as she stood. No and no. She wasn't going to think of the way he'd fucked her: hour after sweet hour until they fell asleep from sheer exhaustion. She was going home.

She stood and walked to the ticket counter.

She didn't notice until the plane was halfway to its cruising altitude that she'd bitten through to the quick of her thumb and spattered the paper boarding pass with red. She stared down at it, feeling her throat tighten. But it was futile. Too late, Jas. Really too late. He goes back to his life and you to yours.

But he had a name. And she had a name. And if it mattered, if it was fated and she was to be proved wrong once again, then that was more than enough.

Fish Stella Black

The thing about Stephen Moore was that he was fabulous looking. He was in very good shape from the swimming, dark in a Mediterranean way and six foot two. His eyes were flecked by long black lashes from under which dark-blue eyes would look at women in much the same way that women sometimes look at men – with a smile of appreciation and subtle messages of gentle encouragement. Stephen liked to look and, like most voyeurs, he was able to listen – a very unusual characteristic in any man who does not work as a psychiatrist.

Women were attracted to Stephen and he was admired. Some went after him, plighting the various advantages they had been born with. They were all disappointed. He did not reject them exactly, he was always polite and friendly, but he did not wish to make love with them. So they gathered in gastropubs and told each other that he was gay. Well. He must be. It was all very well moisturising and wearing nice suits (they told each other) but he was in his thirties and he was displaying none of the procreative impulses that propel heterosexual men to appreciate visual evidence of fecundity.

Stephen Moore was not gay. He loved women. He was passionate about them. But his tastes were very particular and did not conform to the conventional stimuli whereby the hypothalamus co-ordinates the nervous and hormonal systems through the pituitary gland and stimulates the adrenals and testes to engage in the wonderful transcendence that is arousal.

His 'chemistry of love' operated outside the normal conventions of hip-to-waist ratios and glossy evidence of health.

He liked women to be plump, hirsute and underwater.

He was excited by the sight of women swimming underwater and he always had been; ever since he could remember being aroused by anything, he had enjoyed watching the flesh and hair of female bodies floating and rippling in translucent waves. And the more flesh and hair there was, the more excited he became.

This taste had inevitably lead to a personal life whose recreations were largely aquatic. He was a member of Club Sportif, the most expensive health club in London and the one known to offer three fine clean and enormous swimming pools. One was for teaching, one was outside (open in the summer) and one, inside, was crystal clear, blue and heated to the right temperature for maximum enjoyment.

It was lucky for Stephen that he swam extremely well. At a grammar school in Manchester he had been in the important swimming teams, being the master of a competitive crawl whose speed had earned more than one coveted cup. As a teenager he had considered taking the sport up competitively, but maturity and reflection had told him that the person who is able to swim very fast is not necessarily the person who has time to float and watch, and watching was the pleasure rather than the triumph of victory. He did not want to turn a hobby into a profession that forced him to flash past the sights that he appreciated – sights that he could not have ignored even if he had wanted to.

So he became a senior development manager for a transnational mobile phone company (which earned him an executive salary of £80,000 a year) and spent his spare evenings in the Club Sportif.

The health centre was, of course, frequented by young hairless women whose lives were devoted to obeying the dictates of contemporary aesthetics and who concentrated on manipulating their shapes to conform to those advertised on billboards. They were proud to 'keep in shape' and asked no questions about the boardroom decisions that created that shape. But there were also women who were losing the battle, whose genetic birthright defied personal management and whose emotional lives had lead to the comfort of eating.

They were told by well meaning 'friends' that men did not like fat women and by doctors that if they did not lose a stone they risked high blood pressure and heart disease. Fear, then, propelled these ladies towards the Club Sportif, and fear propelled them up and down the slow lane of the swimming pool, doggy-paddling frantically to save themselves from the prophecies.

Stephen always swam in the slow lane. He had developed a swimming style that allowed him to hide the fact that, if necessary, he could probably swim to the Isle of Wight and back. Prowess was not the point. The front crawl and the butterfly stroke were not the styles of the slow lane; a friendly bobbing breaststroke, slow but sure, this was the style that served his purpose. This and a pair of goggles.

So he would follow behind the women swimming in the slow lane and enjoy the vision of rump and chubby thighs. As these thighs opened to propel the body through the water so they revealed the latex-covered shapes of mons and buttock; she was only her flesh, fluid and vulnerable.

If he was lucky he would find himself behind a woman who was not only plump, but also negligent in her personal grooming. That is, the hair of the pubis would escape from underneath the gusset of her swimsuit, or it could be seen under her arms, bushy and generous. The combination of a plump white arm, a cheeky frond, rippling buttocks, rippling thighs – everything moving, the body struggling, these were the visual experiences that inspired Stephen with a passion so intense he was occasionally actually frightened by it.

Sometimes his desires felt like strong cocktails; sometimes they were overwhelming; often they seemed like love. As he watched these glittering female forms move through ferments of bubbles, he was possessed by a desire not only to possess them, to have and own them, but to join with them, to protect them, to take them away somewhere and live alone together where there was only silence and sex. And water.

The swimming pool of the Club Sportif was disappointing in one aspect. Though there were no actual rules about swimwear, women chose to protect their hair with hideous Zoggs latex swimming caps. Stephen disliked these intensely. They were an unforgivable eyesore whose only purpose seemed to be to intentionally detract from the beauty of the wearer and which confined the hair of the head to a boring pate when it should have been floating in the water, free and soft, so that every filament could be seen and appreciated.

At this stage you might ask, did Stephen ever manage to engage in intercourse and, if so, was it on dry land?

The answer is that this depended on the vagaries of luck and the practicability of location.

He liked to make love in the water, but, if necessity and the law required, he would make out in other places.

He liked the pudenda to be wet and the hairs of the pubis to be widespread and damp; he liked to press his palms down on the pudenda, feel the wiry fuzz and the soft lips underneath, then caress the brush which spread from the thighs and around to the back of the buttocks. He liked to nuzzle the forest under the arms and he loved the different smells exuded by wet hair.

He would kiss cold lips while pushing his fingers through the mesh of hairs, manipulating gently or not, depending on the messages received by his instincts. These were uncannily accurate and meant that he was a good lover. He knew the secrets of submission and he knew how to play them for maximum enjoyment. He knew which women liked to be dominated with mouth and fingers and strength and who needed the gentle kindness of soft intimacy.

When he heard their arousal and felt their clammy flesh and the tickle of bristle, when he was allowed to look deep into the dark hairs around their cunt and anus, sniffing and licking and stroking, then the blood would pump, his dick would fill. Hardened and dizzy with need, disorientated by those seconds of desperation for satisfaction that must precede love-making, he would spread them on their back, lift their unshaven legs over his shoulders and push himself in, big and hard and slow, until they moaned and screamed and lost themselves. As he was swept away, so there was gratitude and affection, the emotions that are the satisfaction of fantasies fulfilled.

His early experiences, the adventures of his twenties, had been spent discovering how best to meet his needs. Accessing esoteric portals on the internet, his experiments had taken him to some unusual places. He had enjoyed many marvellous hairy encounters.

His adventures had been aided by his membership to the Hairy Mary Club of Great Britain, a network of fellow enthusiasts who shared his interests. The Hairy Mary services (known, collectively, as 'Fringe Benefits') included a gallery displaying pictures of 'Bushy Pussy' and a forum, entitled 'Muff Meetings', which was designed to encourage personal encounters. There was also a well-produced newsletter, with a centrespread showing 'Minge of the Month', and a lively letters page where debates tended to focus on the questions initiated by a society whose male majority liked the body of women to be smooth, but their hair to be long.

Through these useful networks of information and mutually satisfying exchange, Stephen soon found a professional Hairy Diva or HD as they were known in the personal columns of the Hairy Mary website.

She – Margerita – was Portuguese. She had a child, no qualifications and no husband. She needed money and was grateful to be paid to remain unshaved when the alternative would have been to spend a fortune in depilation. Having sex with Stephen was certainly preferable to getting up at 5.30 a.m. in order to clean offices.

Margerita complied with Stephen's wishes. She had a round brown body, large orbular buttocks, smooth fleshy thighs, plump arms, large breasts. The hair on her head was long and shiny and black and reached halfway down her back; the hair of her armpits bristled as a brown froth; her pubis was a black bush which displayed itself over her stomach, between her thighs and curled as a shade between her buttocks.

Margerita preferred to work at home as it saved on childcare expenses. Stephen would relish her naked body lying in the bath, lit by candles so that she became a delicious form of where malleable flesh met with textured crevice and textured crevice sprouted floating filament. He would gaze entranced and then fuck her while she was still wet, lying on a towel on top of her candlewick counterpane.

Her tiny room was uncharming – with yellow walls, plastic furniture and a view over a railway track – but once she was in it the place was fantastic with body and fur and hair and sexual possibility. She had a yellow bedcover and the tones of her brown skin were offset by it, giving them a sheen that highlighted her own particular beauty.

He familiarised himself with the luxury of her tex-tures, the bristles of her hair and her soft skin. She allowed him to photograph her, close up, the red flesh of her vaginal lips spread at the centre of the massive fur of her pudenda. Her anus, the inner thighs, all hairy, all recorded on his digital camera so that they could be enjoyed again on his Mac when he was alone. She was a beautiful screensaver.

Then he bought her a one-piece swimming costume from the La Senza collection in Harvey Nichols. He ensured that at a size 14 it was a size too small. As she tried it on in front of her mirror, he realised he was right. The cut and colour were perfect for her: the neon orange magnified the dark tones of her skin and the blue streaks of her dark hair; the high cut of the legs revealed the full bush. Her breasts, constrained, moved provocatively within the neoprene. All parts of her fab-ulous figure strained to break out.

She agreed to accompany him as a guest to the Club Sportif and happily swam up and down the shallow end in a way that confirmed an urban existence where life had started on a housing estate in Stockwell and gradu-ated to her father's tapas bar on the South Lambeth Road.

Margerita could not swim well and struggled up and down the blue lanes in a charming disorder of legs and arms, struggling and splashing, her head out of the water, but her long hair flowing behind, round her shoulders and back, floating beautifully in the clear blue.

Stephen swam behind her, revelling in the sight of her buttocks, encased in the tight orange, wobbling in front of him, her pubes wild and, because she was his, he knew he could draw up behind her and finger her provocatively, feeling between her legs, exciting her and himself. Afterwards she gave him blow jobs in the car park. They were always mind-blowing.

But the time came when the process of aging arrived with unwelcome intimations. He knew he still looked great – the moisturising and skin care had been worth it, as had the sensible eating and responsible drinking, the swimming and bench presses. His muscle tone was fine, his biceps were respectable; he had more money than he could spend. He had friends but they were all beginning to marry each other.

Loneliness began to claw. Margerita was fine but he wanted more than a bovine supplicant to whom he could not really talk. He wanted a relationship with a woman who could enjoy his needs but who was also fun to be with, who he could love in a meaningful way, with whom he could discuss the future.

He began to feel slightly depressed. Work began to be a chore; the business trips a bore; the senior management operational strategy meetings worse. His concentration started to go; his enthusiasms dwindled; he slept badly.

Unaccustomed to misery, he repaired briefly to a 'psychosexual relationship counsellor' who advertised herself in the back of *Time Out*. He did not think that he had sexual problems, exactly, but he felt confused and he did not want to talk to his friends about his innermost anxieties.

The therapist expressed no surprise when they discussed his proclivities. One of her clients, after all, could only achieve an erection whilst lying underneath a Jaguar XJS.

She lead Stephen to his early experiences and they uncovered the memory of his goldfish, Elvis, who had died without receiving an adequate burial. He had stared into the tank for some days, immersed in a deep misery which he had not felt either before or since. The therapist said that at that key moment he had learnt to cut off his feeling, his subconscious had taken over and he had started to sublimate.

'You are afraid of your emotions,' she said. 'And you have intimacy issues.'

Stephen didn't really believe her. And he was still depressed. Not as depressed as the day that Elvis had died. But miserable. Especially when he got the bill.

'You're tired,' his mother told him on the phone from Manchester. 'You need a holiday.'

'She's right,' he said to himself. 'I should have paid her the five hundred quid.'

So he packed his Paul Smith swimming trunks, bought some Clarins sunblock and departed for the Greek island of Thassos.

The Hotel Herakles, named after the white beach over which it looked, offered 'spectacular views', 'mini-bars', 'air conditioning', 'syrtaki classes' and 'all mod cons'.

These were not the reasons for his choice. The Hotel Herakles had 'magnificent' pools. One, split-level, was photographed in the midst of landscaped gardens and tasteful sun terraces with blue-and-white striped parasols. One, a curvaceous lagoon, wound through Japanese-style wooden bridges and had a 'wet bar'. The third, inside, was of 'Olympian dimensions' and covered by a plexiglass dome designed by Terence Van Rausing, the architect known to have designed modernist water features for the gardens of one of the wives of the sultan of Brunei.

Stephen's first three days were bliss. The sun shone hot and dry. He lounged on loungers, read his books, ate salads and felt the aches of a sedentary job leave his body. His dark glasses enabled him to watch people without being offensive and he began to observe the subtle differences of the pool-side scenes.

He was disappointed to note the abundance of thin women with bony hips and ungenerous bosoms who smoothed themselves out on the loungers, iPods in their ears, magazines and water bottles by their side. They rarely swam. They were too weak from hunger.

On the fourth day he pottered about in the lagoon pool. A group of beauty therapists from Stratford-upon-Avon began to stare at him. They had arrived the night before and were slathered in block 25. Stephen knew that, seen underwater, their bodies would be disappointing, involved as they were in a profession whose primary skills involved waxing and electrolysis and many other techniques unfriendly to the conservation of nature's growth.

He swam slowly to the wet bar. This was in the middle of the lagoon pool. The roof was made out of bamboo and palm leaves. Nico, always stationed underneath it, served a range of wines, cocktails and cold beers. Stephen was pleased to see a generously proportioned Indian woman sitting on one of the stools. She had a gin and tonic in one hand and a Marlboro Lite in the other. Her hair, loose, was a shining raven black, while her red swimsuit offset both the brown tones of her flawless skin and the gold jewellery that she wore on her fingers, wrists, ears and around her neck. She was exotic and gorgeous and, as it turned out, garrulous.

'I'm Sabina,' she said. 'I'm spending my alimony.'

'Well done.' He smiled. 'Can I buy you a drink?'

'I'm OK thanks,' she said, shaking her cocktail so that the gold bracelets tinkled against the glass and a spectrum of tiny lights refracted from the ice.

'I'm Stephen.'

'Are you here alone?' she inquired.

'Yes,' he said. 'I have a stressful job and needed a rest. What about you?'

'No, I'm here with my friend Andrea. Cheering her up actually. I'm afraid she lost her son last year – heroin overdose at seventeen – awful thing – she hasn't got over it, probably never will. The husband, Joe, well, he drank and then he left with a barmaid from Rayners Lane – they live in a caravan in Torquay apparently – anyway he took the shed and that was that.'

'Poor woman,' said Stephen.

'Well,' said Sabina, 'life is full of surprises and most of them are unpleasant.'

'Do you ever go to the beach?' he inquired, wishing to ascertain her relationship with water and, in particular, whether she enjoyed swimming in it.

'I'm not a sandy person,' she replied, 'and I don't really swim. I mean I can, but I don't want to. It makes the hair frizzy, let alone the effect on the skin. I don't believe in exercise really or all that chat about health they go on about. I mean! Carrots should stay in the ground if you ask me. They are roots after all. And all that water you're supposed to drink! I had a friend in Cheltenham, Veejay, drank a load of water and had to be taken to hospital – he exploded – literally exploded.'

She stubbed out her Marlboro Lite, drained her gin and tonic, and said, 'We'll be around tomorrow – perhaps we will see you then.'

She walked slowly out of the pool holding her handbag over her head. Stephen stared after her with a sense of disappointment. She would have looked magnificent submerged in translucent blue, that beautiful black hair floating in it. He allowed himself to fantasise about her, how she looked in her bedroom, how she would appear unshaved . . .

The next day Sabina hallooed him from underneath a parasol. She was wearing a white floppy hat and pair of vast dark glasses. The nail polish on her fingers and toe nails was crimson. Her feet were in high black mules and decorated with gold toe rings.

By the side of her, whiter and quieter, was a vision of adipose loveliness stretched out as a mass of thigh, stomach and white bikini. This two-piece structure was built to support, contain and confine. The bra was under-wired to provide a balcony for the FF cup. The high-waisted white pants were cut at the leg in such as way as to allow brown fronds to poke through in the crevices of the inner thigh.

These crevices are ever present in places of leisure and Stephen had long enjoyed them from the safety of his self-containment. Female holidaymakers, relaxed by heat and drink, little realise the porno positions they allow themselves to fall into while lazing in the sun. Having lost their self-awareness their bodies become a permissive display of spread legs and half-covered geni-talia whose mirror reflection would mortify them or gratify them depending on their age and ambition.

The two women had commandeered a low table to support their needs. Sabina's side was a mess of plastic tumblers, glossy fashion magazines and expensive sun lotions. Andrea's side had an economy-sized Boots sun-block, a Danielle Steel novel and a box of chocolates whose lid described them as Arpeggio – 'a creamy selec-tion of champagne *ganache* sandwiches'.

A spasm of lust gripped Stephen for three or four fleeting seconds, taking him by surprise and momen-tarily risking his dignity. Recomposing himself with subtle effort, he gazed at Andrea with an expression of overt admiration which she failed to interpret as she had never seen it before, especially on a handsome man who was ten years younger than her. Joe, her ex-hus-band, never looked at her unless he was waiting for his tea and that was if he was there for tea. On most evenings, well, the evenings after ... that day ... Those evenings he would stagger in from the pub, crawl up the stairs on all fours, and either pass out on the landing or grope around until he found something that he assumed was his wife, though on one occasion it had been the dog.

Andrea dismissed the vision of her husband's bleeding leg after it had been bitten by their German shepherd and realised that this dark youth had removed his sunglasses and was actually smiling at her. She looked around to see if there was anyone behind her – and turned back. His mouth was full of expensively whitened teeth. A blush seeped down her neck and crept into her cleavage, which further excited Stephen. Mortification was not his primary trigger, but he did like it, it signified vulnerability and stimulated his need to protect. And this, inevitably, made him very very hard.

She was perfect.

He studied her hair. It had received a home bleach and black roots were beginning to reveal themselves as a dark streak. In some positions her face had two chins. Her stomach was huge, her arms fat, her buttocks wide and without muscle tone. He loved them immediately and he knew that they would be awe inspiring when viewed underwater.

Andrea couldn't believe what was happening to her. This handsome young man actually appeared to be checking her out, flirting with her even. She suspected a hidden television camera and determined to be very very careful. It could easily be a joke, or a bet, or worse. Maybe drugs ... so that he could violate her like on *CSI Miami*. If there was one thing Andrea wanted to avoid it was drugs. The death of Seany had put paid to that. She hadn't taken an aspirin since that day, though the doctor had tried to make her have some diazepam or something to help her sleep. She did not want drugs, she had told him, they had caused enough trouble. If she wanted to sleep she would have a nice cup of hot chocolate with whipped cream and a packet of Penguin biscuits.

That night, to Sabina's amazement, Stephen and Andrea dined alone on the Sundowner Palazzo Terrace.

Stephen did not pursue the male practice of speaking entirely about himself for a period lasting three courses. He was blessed with some femininity, after all, and this was one of the reasons why he was so attractive. He could commune on emotional levels without losing his male appeal. He complimented her on her apparel – a low-backed lilac chiffon evening dress from Debenhams. This allowed her arms and shoulders to be beautifully exposed and it exhibited the full panorama of her décolleté. Round breasts were immersed in a magnificent cleavage, which was slightly flushed from the sun, and bejewelled with small round plastic beads bought also in Debenhams especially for the holiday.

He noticed the white band where her wedding ring had been but did not know that she had pulled it off her finger an hour earlier for the first time in twenty years.

'Do you swim, Andrea?' he asked.

'Not too bad,' she said. 'We used to go to the seaside when we were children.'

They drank a lot of retsina.

After dinner he lead her, tipsy and giggling, to the indoor pool which he knew, from prior investigations, would be both lit and empty after 10 p.m. They would be able to enjoy themselves away from prying eyes.

'I've not got m'bathers here,' she said.

'Nobody will mind, you can go in your underwear, or naked!'

Andrea had obtained a little confidence from the wine, but, through the heady jollity of this adventure an unwelcome picture presented herself. She knew she was overweight; she wasn't blind, after all, and, even if she had been, she would have felt her heart beating when she went upstairs. Furthermore she was wearing her Marks and Spencer bra and pants, far from new and far from attractive. These undergarments stimulated serious reservation about the wisdom of undressing in front of a man, who, for unfathomable reasons, had taken it upon himself to take an interest in her.

God she hoped he didn't feel sorry for her. She had had enough of that. For God's sake. She had once run her own lawnmower business.

'I'm not sure,' she said.

Stephen dropped his chinos, retained his white Calvin Klein boxers and dived in to the luminescent blue water with the grace of a seal. Then he swam quickly under-water and popped his handsome head up in front of where she was standing, vulnerable and anxious and still fully clothed. The water glittered in front of her.

'Come on, darling,' he said softly. 'The water is won-derful and I want to kiss you.'

Andrea realised that she had to surrender. She had to do what was called feeling the fear and doing it anyway. She had read about it in *Best* magazine. Moments like this were rare and to waste them would be insulting to the God in whom she no longer believed. She allowed herself to enter the present, to let go of the past misery and drudgery and vast hurts, to forget that she was too fat and her neck was tense and her ankles often swelled.

She pulled down the zip in the side of the dress, smoothed it down over the curves of her round hips and, after a second of standing in her white bra and pants, she walked down the steps that led into the shallow end and launched herself into the warm water.

He caught her and kissed her. She laughed. When had

she last laughed? She laughed and swam slowly and with some finesse towards the deep end. Her body moved as a glittering green and white palette of fluid flesh, her buttocks and legs shape-shifted in the water as Stephen followed behind, eyes open, seeing her in the clear blue, seeing everything.

Her hair now looked almost black in the water and swirled as a mist around her head. Her round white arms moved to allow the growth under her pits to poke shyly through. Her buttocks were the sexiest he had ever seen, the white orbs straining to escape from the underwear, full and fat and mobile. He resisted an impulse to place his hand between her legs to feel for himself the full bush whose bristles emerged from either side of the leg of her pants.

He followed her to the end, so hard now he thought he would sink, wanting to fuck her more than he had ever wanted to fuck any woman in his life. He knew that he was almost losing control. If she rejected him he would explode under the emotional and physical pressure of unmet needs.

Slowly she turned around at the deep end and slowly she swam back towards the shallow end.

'I want you,' he said, kissing her wet face. 'Swim back to the steps.'

Andrea, now, was twenty years younger. The essences of youth and femininity were touching her as the memories of the sweet brief fleeting moment when she had turned heads. The blokes had come after her then, there was no denying that. She had had her pick. Her friends had been jealous. Joe had been the one that everyone wanted. A plumber for a start, and they were rich, plumbers. Joe had fallen for her. Hook and line.

Suddenly she was lovely again.

She swam towards the steps in a mental turmoil of

happiness and desire, aware that he was swimming behind her, that he was in control and that he would take control at the other end of that Olympian length.

She was lying on the steps as he swam up. He walked out of the pool and lay on top of her, kissing her passionately, his tongue far into her mouth, holding her face, stroking her neck, feeling her wet hair in his fingers.

Then with a strong and expert stroke he pulled down her pants and threw himself face down into the cold wet bristles of her pussy and, underneath the cool wet bush, the warm wet stickiness of passion. She thrust her pelvis up and he buried himself in the rolls of cold wet flesh and tongued her clit until she could have cried.

Silently he hurled his groin into hers and filled her up, filled her up in a way that she had not known was possible. And he, immersed in cold damp ripples of female flesh, plunged again and again into her, losing himself, but sensing her, knowing her needs, fucking her hard, but not coming, not coming until he heard her final surrender, felt the internal twitching that signified release, and allowed himself to go. The cries of their passion resounded around the silent pool as echoes.

They lay side by side on the steps, chests heaving, bodies in the lukewarm water. Andrea, silent, like most women, began to feel the reality of her emotions.

But she was calm, so calm, calm and warmed by the sensation that she knew was love.

She wanted to say so many things, reveal so much, tell all. But she knew she must not. She knew that she would probably never see him again, that she would have to address the ignominy that was the fleeting lust of a stranger. Her psyche started to prepare for defence, while her body? Her body wanted more.

She wanted to splay her legs out for him, allow him

to do anything, take her anywhere. Fuck her hard again and again.

Stephen was silent too, but he knew something and he said it first.

'I love you.'

WICKED WORDS ANTHOLOGIES –

THE BEST IN WOMEN'S EROTIC WRITING FROM THE UK AND USA

Really do live up to their title of 'wicked' – Forum

Deliciously sexy and explicitly erotic, *Wicked Words* collections are guaranteed to excite. This immensely popular series is perfect for those who enjoy lust-filled, wildly indulgent sexy stories. The series is a showcase of writing by women at the cutting edge of the genre, pushing the boundaries of unashamed, explicit writing.

The first ten *Wicked Words* collections are now available in eye-catching illustrative covers and, since 2005, we have been publishing themed collections beginning with *Sex in the Office*. If you never got the chance to buy all the books when they were first published, you can now complete your collection and be the envy of your friends! Look out for the colourful covers – guaranteed to stand out from everything else on the erotica shelves – or alternatively order from us direct on our website at www.black-lace-books.com

Full of action and attitude, humour and hedonism, they are a wonderful contribution to any erotic book collection. Each book contains 15–20 stories. Here's a sampler of what's on offer:

More Wicked Words

ISBN 978 0 352 33487 9
£6.99

- Tasha's in lust with a celebrity chef – it's his temper that drives her wild.
- Reverend Billy Washburn needs salvation from Sister Julie – a teenage temptress who's set him on fire.
- Pearl doesn't want to get married; she just wants sex and blueberry smoothies on her LA poolside patio.

Wicked Words 3

ISBN 978 0 352 33522 7
£6.99

- The seductive dentist – Nick's encounter with sexy Dr May turns into a pretty unorthodox check-up.
- The gender-playing journalist – Kat lusts after male strangers whilst cruising as a gay man.
- The submissive PA – Mandy's new job fulfils her fantasies and reveals her boss's fetish for all things leather.

Wicked Words 4

ISBN 978 0 352 33603 3
£6.99

- Alexia has always fantasised about being Marilyn Monroe. One day a surprise package arrives with a sexy courier.
- Bridget is tired of being a chef. Maybe a little experimentation with a colleague is all she needs to get back her love of food.
- A mysterious woman prowls the back streets of New York, seeking pleasure from the sleaziest corners of the city.

Wicked Words 5

ISBN 978 0 352 33642 2
£6.99

- Connor the tax auditor gets a shocking surprise when he investigates a client's expenses claim for strap-on sex toys.
- Kate the sexy museum curator allows a buff young graduate to make a thorough excavation of her hidden treasures.
- Melanie the interior designer and porn fan swaps blokes with her best mate and gets up to nasty fun with the builders.

Wicked Words 6

ISBN 978 0 352 33690 3
£6.99

- Maxine gets turned on selling exquisite lingerie to gentlemen customers.
- Jules is stripped naked and covered in cream when she becomes the birthday cake for her brother's best mate's thirtieth.
- Elle wears handcuffs for an indecent liaison with a stranger in a motel room.

Wicked Words 7

ISBN 978 0 352 33743 6
£6.99

- An artist's model wants to be more than just painted, and things get pretty steamy in the studio.
- A bride-to-be pays a clandestine visit to the bathroom with her future father-in-law, and gets much more than she bargained for.
- An uptight MP has his mind (and something else!) blown by a charming young woman of devious intentions.

Wicked Words 8

ISBN 978 0 352 33787 0
£6.99

- Adam the young supermarket assistant cannot believe his luck when a saucy female customer needs his help.
- Lauren's first night at a fetish club brings out the sexy show-off in her when she is required to wear an outrageously daring rubber outfit.
- Cat's fantasies about hunky construction workers come true when they start work opposite her Santa Monica beach house.

Wicked Words 9

ISBN 978 0 352 33860 0

- Sarah gets a surprise when she and her husband go dogging in the local car park.
- The Wytchfinder interrogates a pagan wild woman and finds himself aroused to bursting point.
- Miss Charmond's charm school relies on old-fashioned discipline to keep wayward girls in line.

Wicked Words 10 – The Best of Wicked Words

ISBN 978 0 352 33893 8

- An editor's choice of the best, most original stories of the past five years.

Sex in the Office

ISBN 978 0 352 33944 7

- A lady boss with a foot fetish
- A security guard who's a CCTV voyeur
- An office cleaner with a crush on the MD

Explores the forbidden – and sometimes blatant – lusts that abound in the workplace where characters get up to something they shouldn't, with someone they shouldn't – someone who works in the office.

Sex on Holiday

ISBN 978 0 352 33961 4

- Spanking in Prague
- Domination in Switzerland
- Sexy salsa in Cuba

Holidays always bring a certain frisson. There's a naughty holiday fling to suit every taste in this X-rated collection. With a rich sensuality and an eye on the exotic, this makes the perfect beach read!

Sex at the Sports Club

ISBN 978 0 352 33991 8

- A young cricketer is seduced by his mate's mum
- A couple swap partners on the golf course
- An athletic female polo player sorts out the opposition

Everyone loves a good sport – especially if he has fantastic thighs and a great bod! Whether in the showers after a rugby match, or proving his all at the tennis court, there's something about a man working his body to the limit that really gets a girl going. In this latest themed collection we explore the sexual tensions that go on at various sports clubs.

Sex in Uniform

ISBN 978 0 352 34002 3

- A tourist meets a mysterious usherette in a Parisian cinema
- A nun seduces an unusual confirmation from a priest
- A chauffeur sees it all via the rear-view mirror

Once again, our writers new and old have risen to the challenge and produced so many steamy and memorable stories for fans of men and women in uniform. Polished buttons and peaked caps will never look the same again.

Sex in the Kitchen

ISBN 978 0 352 34018 4

- Dusty's got a sweet tooth and the pastry chef is making her mouth water
- Honey's crazy enough about Jamie to be prepared and served as his main course
- Milly is a wine buyer who gets a big surprise in a French cellar

Whether it's a fiery chef cooking up a storm in a Michelin-starred restaurant or the minimal calm of sushi for two, there's nothing like the promise of fine feasting to get in the mood for love. From lavish banquets to a packed lunch at a motorway service station, this Wicked Words collection guarantees to serve up a good portion!

Sex on the Move

ISBN 978 0 352 34034 4

- Nadia Kasparova sees the earth move from a space station while investigating sex at zero gravity
- Candy likes leather pants, big powerful bikes, miles of open road and the men who ride them
- Penny and Clair run a limousine business guaranteed to STRETCH the expectations of anyone lucky enough to sit in the back

Being on the move can be an escape from convention, the eyes of those we know, and from ourselves. There are few experiences as liberating as travelling. So whether it's planes, trains and automobiles, ships or even a space station, you can count on the Wicked Words authors to capture the exhilaration, freedom and passion of modern women on the move. Original tales of lust and abandon guaranteed to surprise and thrill!

Sex and Music

ISBN 978 0 352 34061 0

- Tess sings in key with the pianist-masseur who can play such beautiful music, up and down her body
- Alison will go to any length to be taught violin with a maestro, and the discipline is all part of the pleasure
- Chrissy's a fast disco girl who wants to try it slow and easy with the blues

From the primal sexual scream of heavy metal to the delicate brush of a maestro's fingers on the pale neck of his pupil, the latest themed collection from Wicked Words plays on ten and delivers at full volume. Whether it's in the front row of a stadium, or during intimate lessons in a private study, the passion is as much about the performance as the performer. And you can trust Black Lace's authors to produce the most thrilling scenarios and kinks to expose this electric connection between sex and music.

Sex and Shopping

ISBN 978 0 352 34076 4

- Francesca exchanges the man in her life after an encounter in the men's changing rooms
- Juliet gets a ladder in her stockings, but meeting the mysterious stranger who replaces them hits a few snags
- Adele creates an internet shopping experience with a twist: her new online business launches with only one item for sale: herself

Who says shopping is a sex-substitute? Wicked Words discovers it's just about the best time to make all kinds of deals and special purchases. Transactions of the sensual variety that keep the tills and senses ringing long after the stores have closed. Whether you're shopping for shoes, jeans, a corset, or the guy that delivers it to your door, *Sex and Shopping* is a must-have item.

Sex in Public

ISBN 978 0 352 34089 4

Sex in the great outdoors – there's nothing quite like it! Whether taking a few leisurely hours in the countryside or a frantic five minutes on a city street, *Sex in Public* explores the height of female misbehaviour in public. Impetuous passion, frenzied intensity, reckless daring, unlikely settings, the thrill of almost getting caught to the thrill of deliberately getting caught, this is edge-of-the-seat reading. There are no end to the varieties, the locations, the positions and the limits of *Sex in Public*!

Black Lace has never been naughtier. Our short stories are kinkier and more daring than ever before; this new collection of fantasy fiction will make you blush, flush, squirm and dream.